JAMES PATTERSON

VIRGIN

BANTAM BOOKS
TORONTO · NEW YORK · LONDON · SYDNEY

VIRGIN

*A Bantam Book / published by arrangement with
McGraw-Hill Book Company*

PRINTING HISTORY
McGraw-Hill Book edition published June 1980
A Literary Guild Alternate Selection September 1980
A Preferred Choice Bookplan Alternate Selection November 1980
A Doubleday Book Club Alternate Selection January 1981
Bantam edition / August 1981

ISBN 0-553-14652-1

Published simultaneously in the United States and Canada

PRINTED IN THE UNITED STATES OF AMERICA

0 9 8 7 6 5 4 3 2 1

ACKNOWLEDGMENTS

I would like to thank the following people who helped so much in making the background information and worldwide locales of this book more authentic and interesting:

Lea Guyer Gordon—New York City
Ms. Joan Ennis—Irish Tourist Board
Dr. Marjorie Pollack, Robert Alden—Federal Center for Disease Control, Atlanta, Georgia
Dr. Donald Gray, John Wilcox—Manhattan College
Mrs. Ann Natanson—Time-Life News Service, Rome
Father Kenneth Jadoss—Catholic Archdiocese of New York
Dr. Jean Packtor—New York City Department of Health
James Mahoney—St. Joseph's Seminary

Mrs. Constance Stringer
Mrs. Puspha Gupta—Consulate General of India
Father John Lynch—St. Mary's-by-the-Sea (translator par
   excellence)
And most of all, Jane.

PROLOGUE

Tell me the old, old story
Of unseen things above ...

— *hymn by* KATHERINE HANKEY

THE MIRACLE CHILDREN
The hill country of Portugal; October 13, 1917.

One hundred ten thousand witnesses came from all
white downpour, waiting for the three small children.

The torrent had been mercilessly flooding the desolate sheep pasture since before dawn. Thousands upon
thousands of umbrellas shrouded the crowd against the

1

chill, numbing rain. The smells of gamy, half-cooked lamb, petrol, and onions were thick in the air.

At five past one in the afternoon, the children appeared wide-eyed and trembling inside a tight procession of severe-looking nuns and priests. Behind them came more priests in dripping soutanes, holding flickering red torches and golden crosses.

What happened during the next twelve minutes fully deserved the description *miracle*.

The children—Francisco, Jacinta, and Lucia—suddenly began to point up toward the whipping, black skies.

Ten-year-old Lucia dos Santos cried out, almost like a child possessed:

"Put down your umbrellas! *Put down your umbrellas and She will stop the rain!*"

The little peasant girl's urgent command was passed back through the swelling crowd.

"Please, madame, your parasol . . ."

"Señhor, your umbrella, please."

At that moment, at 1:18 P.M., October 13, 1917, the black thunderclouds which had cloaked the sky since dawn suddenly began to shred and fall away.

The sprawling festival of people, Christians and skeptics alike, stared upward with open mouths and widening eyes.

A burnished gold glow fanned out at the cloud edges. The sun then suddenly appeared with blinding brilliance.

"The rain? . . . The sun has come out!"

"Our Lady is here!"

Thousands began to kneel in the sloshing mud.

The strange afternoon sun began to quiver and oscillate, then to rotate on its axis, spinning at a terrifying speed. The drama of the moment was matchless.

The sun shot forth splinters of bright red and violet light. Brilliant-hued light rained down on the awed, transfixed crowd.

The reporter for *The New York Times* wrote:

> To the astonished minds and eyes of this baffled
> and terrified crowd—whose attitude goes back to

Biblical times, who, pale with fear, with bared heads, dared to look up at the sky—the sun clearly trembled violently. The sun made abrupt "lateral" and "diving" movements never seen before. Outside of all possible cosmic laws. The sun did a macabre dance across the sky today.

"Please pray to Our Lady," begged little Lucia dos Santos. "She says the war will end soon! She says the Devil will be stopped this one time as a sign!"

"Nossa Senhora! Nossa Senhora!" Prayers flew up all over the faded yellow hillside.

"Miracle!"

"Santa Maria! Rogai por nos pecadores!"

A horde of men and women surrounding the three children spontaneously pounded their breasts and began to scream full voice. A young socialite from Lisbon fell to her knees and cried like a baby:

"Mai de Jesus, *I see Her! . . . She is so beautiful! . . . The Mother of Christ has come back to earth here at Fatima! . . . Our Lady is speaking to the little children!"*

BOOK I

Have you ever believed? Do you
*   remember the feeling?*
What is it that you believe in now?
In yourself?
In nothing at all?
What do you really believe in right
*   at this very moment?*

—from THE SIGNS OF THE VIRGIN

ONE

EDUARDO ROSETTI
Rome, July 30, 1987.

Eduardo Rosetti had the kind of striking appearance that could cause a priest difficulty and embarrassment. His was a workman's build that insinuated years of hard labor and outdoor life. His smile was warm, disarming, self-assured.

As Father Rosetti walked, he found himself staring up at the familiar, shimmering gold domes, the two-thousand-pound crosses and needle spires of St. Peter's Basilica.

How he loved the Vatican and Rome. There was so much incredible history and grand ceremony here, so much inspiring tradition.

In a way, Rosetti was like the towering stone archi-
tecture all around him: rugged, secure enough to with-
stand the attacks of the ages—of this troublesome age in
particular. In truth, the young priest was one of the most
important figures in the Vatican. On this day Father
Rosetti was perhaps the most important of all.

His already brisk pace toward the Basilica accelerated noticeably. His stiff black shoes snapped and clacked
against the uneven sidewalk cobblestones. There was a
definite quickening of his heartbeat; a glint in his dark
eyes. Father Rosetti began to pray out loud on the Vatican street. *He thought that he had never been this frightened in his entire life.*

As he waded across Bernini's majestic piazza—the
great swarming Square of Saint Peter's—the young priest
found that he could still hear the recent words of His
Holiness, Pope Pius XIII, ringing above the din of the
Roman streets.

"Father Rosetti . . . Eduardo," Pius had said to him.
*"You are the Chief Investigator for the Congregation of
Rites. You are the Investigator of miracles and would-be
miracles all over the world. . . . Father, I want you to
investigate a miracle for me. A private investigation. A
papal investigation."*

Father Rosetti strode quickly past the four magnificent candelabra built at the base of the Egyptian obelisk
which had once towered center-ring in Nero's Circus.

*"Father, seventy years ago a controversial message
was left at Fatima, Portugal, by Our Blessed Lady. To
this day, the great secret of Fatima has never been revealed to the world.*

*"Father Rosetti, circumstances dictate that I must
now reveal the extraordinary message left by Our Lady at
Fatima. . . .*

"I must tell you the secret, my holy Investigator!"

Father Rosetti was surprised to see that he had
already come to the Gate of Santa Anna. He was now
about to leave the one-hundred-nine-acre private state
called Vatican City.

As he turned down the ancient, crumbling Via di
Porta Angelico, the priest felt a surge of sudden dizziness.

Vertigolike. Accompanied by shooting pains around the heart. *"Oh dear God,"* he whispered out loud.

Clutching, grabbing hard onto a lamp post, Father Rosetti felt searing hot flashes. He thought he was going to be sick. Then came a sharp stab that pierced deep into his broad chest.

Dear Lord, Please . . .

His black Roman hat fell, spinning down the cobblestone gutter. Then Father Rosetti toppled over, crumpling to the sidewalk. A *Foyer Unitas* tour, a Sister of Charity walking a Vespa while she shopped, Vatican priests, looked up from their chores and sightseeing. "A priest is sick!" someone shouted in Italian.

Rosetti gasped hoarsely. An excruciating pain was lancing down his left arm, entering his leg like a long needle. He was desperately aware of increasing dyspnea: dramatic shortness of breath. His lips were the color of plums.

The thirty-six-year-old Jesuit understood that he must be having a heart attack or stroke. How, though? He had been in excellent health just days before. Hours before! . . . He had jogged near the Tiber that morning!

Looking up, helpless, he saw faint blurred faces. Strangers. Swimming, fading colors. He writhed on the cold stones. Another ice-pick stab exploded in his chest. He gasped. *Please help me.* He had no voice.

Once again he could hear Pope Pius XIII. *I must tell you the secret. . . .*

The incredible revelation just moments before inside the gold-domed Apostolic Palace, in the papal apartment itself.

Rosetti's sacred mission.

"Father Rosetti, Our Lady of Fatima has promised the world a divine child in our age.

"The time of the Last Judgment will be at hand.

"You must find the true Virgin, my Investigator! The Church must find the mother of the divine child!"

Everything before Father Eduardo Rosetti's eyes suddenly turned blazing fire-red. Then receding, blinding white. Then a pinwheel of light went spinning into an opening of pure blackness. . . .

TWO

ANNE FEENEY
Holts Corners, New Hampshire, September 18, 1987.

Dressed in a black wool turtleneck and jeans faded almost bone-white in places, with her hair in a loosely bound ponytail, Sister Anne Feeney was busily preparing two ten-egg omelets, a regiment of crisp bacon strips, homemade honey buns twice the size of store-bought ones, rich, delicious coffee.

Anne liked making breakfast at Hope Cottage. She felt so very comfortable and relaxed in the woodsy, make-shift kitchen, especially when she was alone there with the mountains just waking up.

As she ladled out healthy servings of pears, Sister

11

Anne listened to the mouth-watering sounds of bubbling eggs, bacon grease, perking coffee,

the insistent hum of a fourteen-year-old vacuum down the corridor in the living room,

a crazed Boston dj babbling about his year as a crazed, babbling dj in Baton Rouge, Louisiana,

a work song (a terrible parody of the lyrics to the marine corps recruiting song) coming from three of the Hope Cottage girls:

> *Who's that Sister break our ass?*
> *Sister Anne, she really bad!*
> *Sound off—one, two!*
> *Sound off—three, four!*

Anne Feeney found herself starting to break into the day's first smile. Sort of. Half a smile anyway.

What a loony bin I've come to. Anne shook her head. *How nice it is most of the time.*

Just seven months earlier, Sister Anne Feeney had arrived at the St. Anthony's School for Homeless Girls (St. Tony's in the Mountains). She'd come to St. Anthony's straight from an important job at the archdiocese office in Boston. Before then, Sister Anne hadn't cursed; she had enjoyed reading nonfiction books and the more serious novels; she'd had a more-or-less orderly view of the Universe.

In a very short six weeks' time, however, the nineteen girls in Hope Cottage had changed her speech patterns, her lifestyle, to some extent her moral outlook on the world. Which was probably why her Mother Superior had assigned Anne to St. Anthony's in the first place.

Faintly above the din and clatter a doorbell rang.

"Will one of you poor deaf monkeys please answer the door?" she called out.

The marine work song was moving toward the rumpus room.

"Breakfast is served!" Anne's high-pitched voice rose a half-decibel above the clattering noise of Hope Cottage on a school morning. "Will someone please get the door?"

A tiny black girl named Reggie Hudson peeked a large brown eye around the nickered door jamb into the kitchen.

"I got my evil eye on you, Sister Anne," Reggie smiled.

"Good morning, Regine. I have my benevolent eye on you. Would you get the front door, please? Thank you, Reggie. You are a godsend."

Reggie Hudson gracefully danced through the kitchen, tasting syrupy pear juice with her finger, opening the fridge and peering in at milk cartons and gaily colored relish and jam bottles.

It wasn't that the girls ignored Anne; it was just that they were too ingrained in the habit of not listening—not listening to *anybody*.

Anne finally ran for the front door herself.

She flung open the warped oak door and saw Monsignor John Maher, the principal and chief administrator at St. Anthony's.

"Is it the usual madhouse here, Sister Anne?"

Anne ushered the red-faced priest inside Hope Cottage.

"It happens to be pretty calm this morning. No catfights. No knife threats. No one on room suspension. . . . Come, Monsignor. Have some breakfast with the girls."

"Sister, I would love just the smallest sip of coffee," the florid-faced priest said, "and perhaps a quiet room to drink it in, and have a word with you."

Anne went and got two cups of black coffee, then she and Monsignor Maher climbed rickety stairs to the girls' library and schoolroom.

Anne switched off a rock-blaring portable radio and the two settled comfortably into the sudden silence.

Monsignor glanced out the small dormer window at waving elm leaves and beautiful patches of china-blue sky.

"So, Monsignor. It's nice to see you," Anne said.

Monsignor Maher stopped to clear his throat. "I wish I were here on a social visit, Anne." He stared at Sister Anne for a moment. His thought was that Anne was the most terrific young woman the Archdiocese had sent to St. Anthony's in years.

"I was speaking to a dear friend of yours already this morning," Monsignor finally said. "Cardinal Rooney called me at five. Just before he offered Mass in his private chapel. His Eminence said he was going to offer a few prayers for you and me."

"Hopefully he'll offer a few for my girls here, too."

For an oddly uncomfortable moment Monsignor seemed to have nothing to say. His visit was becoming more and more strange.

Anne finally realized that something must be wrong.

"I don't know how smoothly or very nicely to lead into this." Monsignor John Maher sighed heavily. He set down his coffee mug and clasped his hands.

"I was thinking about it on my walk over here from Coughlin House. I simply don't have a good way to say this. Please forgive me, Anne."

Anne felt a chill climbing, pushing up her spine; she felt frightened inside. Her stomach rumbled.

"I'm afraid that you have to leave St. Anthony's." Monsignor suddenly blurted the news to her.

Anne couldn't believe what he'd said.

"Oh, Monsignor, no. Oh no, Monsignor Maher. I can't leave these girls."

"I'm so sorry about this. I can't begin to tell you how sorry. You've been so good for the girls. For all of us."

Anne wanted to run out of the room. Her eyes were starting to fill and she didn't want Monsignor to see her cry. *Oh why, why, why?* There was nothing she could do as a Dominican that would be more valuable work; she had realized that months before. She had never done better work than at St. Anthony's. Anne was certain she hadn't.

Finally she had to put her hands over her face, she felt so intensely ashamed. She wanted to be out of the room and Monsignor's presence more than anything else in the world.

"Let me try to explain this to you," she heard

Monsignor say gently. Then, continuing more firmly, "Believe me, Sister Anne, it is absolutely necessary that you leave St. Anthony's. You wouldn't be asked if it wasn't important. Please listen to what I was told by His Eminence early this morning. The reason for his urgent call. It will take all of your faith to believe what I have to tell you. . . ."

By eleven-thirty that morning, Anne Feeney had taken care of all her goodbyes. Her two black suitcases were packed and ready to go. All her earthly possessions dangled from her arms like the kit and caboodle of a Yankee peddler.

Monsignor had supplied her with one of the school's station wagons for the important trip. The shining family car seemed incongruous parked in front of the stark clapboard house called Hope Cottage.

Fifteen girls, mostly black and Hispanic, were milling around on the rolling lawns. Some of them were clearly sulking. A few were crying.

Anne had tried to explain the situation to them.

She had told them everything she possibly could.

Everything except the incredible truth about where she was going now, what she was expected to do.

Laura Harding and Gwinnie Johnson finally made their appearance, swaggering out of the cottage, both of them smoking cigarettes.

Laura and Gwinnie were the worst troublemakers at Hope Cottage, no doubt about it. But they were also Anne's absolute favorite people at the school. They were the two girls who represented everything good Anne had been able to do at St. Anthony's.

Neither of them would come anywhere near her now.

They stood in the gray-yellow shadows of the porch, looking at her like a complete stranger. It was the same look they'd had the first day Anne had come there.

One of the girls finally started to scream at her.

"You leavin' now, huh! Just like the other big-shit sisters before you. You never loved us, Sister Anne!"

Anne had to lean back against the station wagon. They were all staring at her like enemies and she could barely breathe.

"I love you all so much." Anne finally began to cry.

The girls suddenly came running to her. They fell on her like pathetically hungry birds: they reached out for Anne; they begged her to please stay; they said they loved her, and held her, and kissed her.

The tall, willowy nun finally climbed into the big station wagon. There was the solid thunk of the car door.

Their faces crowded in every window space. Anne flipped the automatic gearshift. She took off the brake and waved at them without really seeing.

Then Sister Anne Feeney let the station wagon slowly roll down the long hill trailing away from St. Anthony's.

She was on her way to witness a miracle.

THE VIRGIN COLLEEN

A burnished gold light was shimmering down across Father Eduardo Rosetti's pale, deeply lined face.

The light originated in one of a half-hundred green reading lamps hanging in Dublin's Trinity College Library. Father Rosetti had been very ill, mysteriously, deathly ill for several days in Rome. But the attacks, the shooting pains and fever had left him as quickly and miraculously as they had appeared. He was still weak, drawn and peaked, but able to work, to travel.

This final night before he journeyed to the village of Maam Cross, Father Rosetti found himself making obsessive written notes, elaborately detailing his findings thus far, organizing and compulsively recording the evidence from his depositions and interviews.

Three times before this, Rosetti had been called upon in investigations when no other priest in the Church would do. Three times he had succeeded; at least he had survived when no one seemed to expect success.

The first time was northeast of Sevilla in Spain. The painful three-month investigation of a holy nun whom the local bishop was promoting as a saint. The unauthorized cultus of this Sister Maria Avila explored by Father Rosetti. The sister's "miracles" examined . . . Rosetti had finally, rigidly, judged that Sister Maria was indeed a holy woman, a proper model for all Christians. But not a holy saint. No, for Rosetti could see *no evidence anywhere that there had been supernatural intervention.*

A second investigation came at the Mahurdi Mission in the African Cameroons. This time, a deadly confrontation with the Beast: *Damballa.* Eduardo Rosetti had nearly lost his life during his three weeks living among the Tiv tribesmen. In the end he had rescued an African cardinal's immortal soul away from the Evil One.

Finally, most recently, there had been a mission to Egypt. Here Father Rosetti was said to have triumphed. His triumph had firmly established his reputation all through the Curia. He had become the Chief Investigator for the powerful Congregation of Rites. It was whispered in Vatican corridors that Father Eduardo Rosetti had actually bested the Evil One among the sempiternal ruins in Egypt. That he had come up to the very portal of the Gates of Hell. . . . Only Eduardo Rosetti knew the terrifying truth about that rumor. *No man or woman, no priest or Holy Father, had ever defeated the Beast. Not once. Not since the beginning of time. . . .*

As he worked very mechanically in the flooding yellow light—"A technician of the spirit," he sometimes thought during the more dispassionate investigations of the supernatural—Father Rosetti's red-rimmed eyes kept sliding over to one particular packet of notes. Notes which Rosetti had taken when Pope Pius XIII had permitted him to view the actual parchment letters of Fatima to learn the mysterious, carefully kept secret of Our Lady's visit.

Tomorrow morning, Father Rosetti quietly thought to himself, he would go and see the first of the two girls.

The Irish girl.

The virgin Colleen.

He completed the 225-kilometer trek from Dublin's O'Connell Street to Maam Cross in Galway—driving without really noticing the rolling saddle-brown and green country roads—in slightly less than four hours.

Easing into the almost-medieval village of Maam Cross, the Investigator was straightaway directed to the former estate house of a wealthy English landlord.

A very handsome and secure-looking stone building. The Holy Trinity School for Girls.

Abandoning his English Ford on a brown dirt bridle path, the priest slowly threaded his way along a winding fieldstone path with sinewy beech trees and elms thick on either side. Quite pretty territory. Uplifting.

Observing a class of girls in progress through a latticed window, hearing the familiar chant of Latin declensions, Father Rosetti found himself reciting the known facts of his investigation. . . .

A virgin in the Republic of Ireland, site of John Paul's mysterious visit in 1979, he thought to himself.

A girl eight months or more with child. . . . But which child?

A fourteen-year-old schoolgirl named Colleen Deirdre Galaher.

Rosetti absently lifted and released a heavy ring knocker on the convent school's front door. His heart was racing already.

A tall, very flat-chested teenager suddenly appeared. The Holy Trinity student wore a puffy white blouse with a gray pleated skirt, conservative black shoes, dark stockings, and a dickey. She performed an old-fashioned curtsy, then silently led Rosetti to the office of the Reverend Mother.

"It isn't often we're receiving visitors from the Archdiocese . . . much less from Rome," Sister Katherine Dominica said with a benedictory smile that made Father Rosetti instantly like her. She was undoubtedly nervous and curious about her student Colleen Galaher, about the high-ranking visitor from Rome. But Sister Katherine would ask no leading or probing questions. As a provincial Irish nun, Sister Katherine clearly knew her place in the Church's hierarchy.

"This term, Colleen Galaher has been studying her lessons at home," the Mother Superior told Father Rosetti. "The other students, and especially their parents—they haven't been kind about this unusual pregnancy. . . . Neither were we so charitable at first, Father. The Sisters here at Holy Trinity. Myself included."

Father Rosetti nodded. Then the strong-looking priest smiled gently. "I'm originally from a very small town, Sister. I think I know what has happened here so far. I once watched Sicilians cripple a pregnant fifteen-year-old."

"I'll take you to see Colleen, then," Sister Katherine finally said. "She's waiting in our library. Please come, Father. Please follow me."

The fourteen-year-old girl was seated in a high, uncomfortable-looking bishop's chair in the convent library that was warmed only by a small peat fire.

Seeing the Mother Superior and a priest, Colleen Galaher rose up like a rigidly disciplined soldier.

Ah, the Irish Catholics, Father Rosetti couldn't help thinking. *The last refuge on earth for the Church Militant, the Army of Christ.*

The unimaginably young girl standing before him was outfitted in a ragged but clean beige raincoat, with a red housedress underneath. She wore drooping white ankle socks and ancient school shoes with rips along the toes. She was obviously poor, but proud. And pretty. With the brightest emerald-green eyes in Galway.

Dear God in Heaven, she is so young, Father Rosetti was silently awed and astonished.

She's only a ninth-grader. The bulging stomach seems a brutal mistake on this waif of a girl. . . . The virgin Colleen.

Father Rosetti asked Colleen to sit, then he situated himself at the scrolled writing desk across from her.

After he got the young girl modestly comfortable and at ease with him, the Vatican priest began the lengthy and formalistic interview of the Congregation of Rites. The first test.

She is just a young child, fourteen and a half, who very innocently ascribes her mysterious condition to "the will of God the Father," Father Rosetti entered in his notes. *She is a classic convent-school girl!*

Later, Eduardo Rosetti found himself hurriedly, excitedly writing: *My prayers are with this young girl Colleen Galaher. There are definite signs of the promise of Fatima here. . . . But what of the other virgin girl? Clearly it is too soon to decide which girl will bear the Savior.*

And then: *This young Irish girl is the precise age of Mary of Nazareth when she bore Jesus! . . . Dear Lord, please help me. Holy Mother, help me please. The girl speaks calmly of visitations and great miracles!*

ANNE

The swishing, clicking windshield wipers were clearing a tight half-moon tunnel which fit snugly over the slick gray Interstate.

The late-afternoon rain drummed a hypnotic cadence on the roof of the St. Anthony's School station wagon.

Anne Feeney tried her best to concentrate on the blurred white stripes that sliced Route 128 South into curving, sliding, equal parts.

Fifty-eight, the red line of the speedometer said.

Fifty-seven.

Fifty-five.

A high-pitched whistle came from somewhere behind the dashboard wood paneling. The speedometer needle was hitting over sixty. Anne's loafer pressed down on the brake pedal.

In one of her worst Naturalist moods, suddenly Anne began to recall where much of her current religious skepticism had originated.

At the Archdiocesan Office in Boston, of all places.

As she hurried toward her important new assignment, Anne found herself thinking back to those early days in Boston, wondering about their relation to the present.

When Anne had first been assigned to the Chancery

Office on Commonwealth Avenue, she had been astounded by the number of young, bright, and very progressive priests and nuns who were working there.

After particularly trying days at the Church Office, Anne would sometimes go with them to a favorite bar on Beacon Street called Jackie Doulin's. Clustered around one or more of the dark, musty booths in the back, the fathers and sisters from the Archdiocesan Office would gather and often the conversation would turn into a long, serious discussion. They talked about controversial subjects like the Church someday dispersing its great wealth, or the complex problems of racism in Southey, the Christian theology of sexuality, the possiblity or impossibility of the ordination of women.

They ate Doulin's sharp cheese with mustard and drank watery sodas or beers. It was a great opportunity to test ideas and share the frustrations and problems of their lives.

Late one spring afternoon at the Archdiocesan Office Anne was summoned to Cardinal Rooney's office. The subject of her audience—Anne was warned ahead of time by an unpleasant lay secretary—was to be the infamous gatherings at Jackie Doulin's Bar & Grill.

Cardinal Rooney's office turned out to be an unexpectedly bright and cheerful haven. There were framed posters from classical concerts and Boston Garden sporting events on one wall. A lot of matching red-mahogany and leather furniture. A fine Oriental rug which added necessary warmth and stateliness to the informal room.

In addition, the large room had a splendid four-window view over the Commonwealth Car Barn, Boston College, Cleveland Circle.

And on John Cardinal Rooney's desk, Anne couldn't help noticing, there were two sparkling-clean pilsner glasses, two uncapped bottles of Carling Black Label beer.

"Ah, Sister Anne," the tall, white-haired Cardinal rose from his cluttered work area. "I've heard so much about you. I'm glad you could make it this afternoon."

Anne's heart began to sink hopelessly. It was moving

to a new location somewhere down below her knees. She
had no idea what was going to happen next, but she was
certain that Cardinal Rooney knew the most flagrant
details of her past visits to Doulin's Bar & Grill.

"Please sit down, Sister Anne. Please." Cardinal
Rooney gestured to a red-leather chair right beside his
huge, scarred desk.

"I can see by looking into your eyes that you've
misjudged my intentions this afternoon," the Cardinal
continued. "Let me just say this as a preamble, Sister. My
one and only speech for this afternoon. Promise . . . I
approve with all my failing heart of the little meetings
which have been going on for months now in Jack Doulin's tavern. Right under my proverbial nose, as they say.
I would prefer that our priests wouldn't wear their collars
into Doulin's, but that is my only substantial complaint.

"Now *please* relax, Sister. Enjoy a sip of beer with
me. Let me prove to you that I'm not all gas and garters,
as they say out in the parishes."

For the next two hours the young Dominican Sister
and the Cardinal of Boston sat and talked. He asked her
views on a whole variety of topics and when she talked he
listened carefully.

The informal conversation completely changed the
impressions Anne had had about John Cardinal Rooney.
This priest, who had seemed somewhat narrow-minded
and open to charges of old Irish cronyism, was actually
extremely aware of the needs of his people. Moreover,
Cardinal Rooney was actively *doing* things to change
some of the unforgivably bad habits developed within the
Church.

"Two or three centuries ago," the Cardinal told
Anne at one juncture, "when I was a young priest at St.
Margaret's—this is over in Attleboro, Anne—I was overwhelmed by grave, terrifying doubts about the Church. At
one low point I was so thoroughly confused that I left St.
Margaret's and went on a five-week toot. A sabbatical
you'd call it if you wanted to be kind. In general, I
conducted myself rather badly during those weeks . . . but
I finally came back to St. Margaret's.

"And I came back with a faith twice as strong and alive as the one I had thought enough of to make me a priest in the first place."

The Cardinal's grayish-green eyes seemed to remain back in Attleboro, Massachusetts, for a moment. Suddenly then, John Cardinal Rooney laughed out loud. He took a long pull on his beer.

"Needless to say, the pastor of St. Margaret's kicked me right back out on my ear. No prodigal-son nonsense for that fierce old bird. Good man! Terrific priest of the old school. I made him a bishop when he was seventy-six years old. Wonderful how life works out, isn't it, Anne?

"At any rate, my point is that we must ask difficult, even threatening questions. We must! The women of our Church especially!

"Ask those damning questions! Why are there no women leaders in the Church? Why does the Church treat women so shabbily? *I* know they do; *you* certainly know it. Is that honestly the way you believe Christ planned it? Can something be done about it? *Who's* going to do it, Sister Anne?"

Anne was feeling such a surge of emotion, such hopefulness for the Archdiocese, that she was afraid to stop and think about it right then.

"Cardinal Rooney?" she finally asked. "What if I ask the right questions and lose my faith entirely?"

"You won't lose your faith by asking questions." John Cardinal Rooney smiled at Sister Anne. "Don't you know that yet, Sister? That's the secret! Your *questions* are the whole *basis* of your faith."

The day after their long and complicated talk, Sister Anne received a letter from the Chancery Office. It was a request from Cardinal Rooney. Asking her to assume a new position. She was to be the new special assistant to Cardinal Rooney himself. Anne was to be the first non-priest ever given that job—the first woman. *That* was why Cardinal Rooney had wanted to talk with her the day before. Sister Anne Feeney was obviously marked for important things in the Archdiocese of Boston.

Just north of Lexington and Concord, Anne pulled
off the highway in search of gas and something filling to
eat. In daylight and better weather this was a pretty area
of Massachusetts, she remembered from past Sunday
drives. The people of the surrounding towns were into
preserving and restoring historic homes, barns, taverns.

Inside, at the mercilessly bright counter of a Howard
Johnson's, Anne sat on one of the orange vinyl stools and
gently spun thirty degrees from side to side.

She savored a brimming mug of steaming black
coffee.

Beginning to relax a little, Anne allowed herself to
think back to her talk that morning with Monsignor John
Maher. Staring at her reflection in the restaurant mirror,
she could almost hear Monsignor's voice:

Cardinal Rooney has asked for you specifically,
Monsignor Maher had said. *Anne, he wants you to be a
sort of companion for this young woman.*

There is a *possibility of a virgin birth,* Cardinal
Rooney had very clearly implied. *In Newport, Rhode
Island.*

Anne found herself nearly repeating the amazing
evidence out loud at the crowded restaurant counter.

Anne tried to logically think through the idea of the
virgin birth. Her body shuddered and she had to put
down her jiggling coffee cup.

An incredible miracle was being secretly investigated
... *seriously investigated,* Anne considered. The Vatican
was already involved. The Cardinal of Boston was personally involved.

The birth of a divine child in the twentieth century!

The sort of thing that used to happen—or perhaps
didn't use to happen—nearly two thousand years ago?

No. Anne's mind had to reject the impossible idea.
Things like that can't happen in our age.

It had to be a hoax somehow. A bizarre and complex fraud. Definitely to be taken with a grain of salt.
Cum grano salis.

Cardinal Rooney was sending for her because he

knew she had a good background in Mariology, Anne considered.

And because I have a background with disturbed teenage girls? she wondered.

All of a sudden, Sister Anne Feeney couldn't wait to meet young Kathleen Beavier.

THREE

THE VIRGIN KATHLEEN

At a few minutes past five A.M., seventeen-year-old Kathleen Beavier was busily opening and snapping closed antique kitchen cabinets, humming an old James Taylor song, "Sweet Baby James," rustling up a breakfast of orange sections with honey, tofu and sprouts cooked in saffron oil, camomile tea.

Kathleen had been eating natural foods since she'd first read about the bad effects of preservatives, red dyes, hydrogenated fats.

The seventeen-year-old had become especially careful now that she was sure she was going to have a baby.

After breakfast, and still before the day's sunrise, Kathleen adventured out for an early morning walk. She headed down toward the rocky shoreline fronting her parents' house in Newport, Rhode Island.

As she tiptoed over lichen-covered rocks, then down a steep flight of bleached wooden stairs, she was still humming "Sweet Baby James." Trying to keep her chin up. Sinking just a little bit.

Kathleen began to think about all of the crazy happenings, the odd, weird circumstances of the past few months. As usual, she was completely overwhelmed.

The young girl watched a crack drill team of sandpipers scrambling in and out of the frothy surf on tiny matchstick legs. The gray and white birds *watched* her right back.

It was incredible enough suddenly to be pregnant at seventeen. To be a virgin too—well, that took the experience into provinces too rarefied for her even to speculate on.

Just relax, she thought to herself. *Enjoy the morning before everyone gets up.* It's beautiful out here. . . .

There were other nagging side effects, though. Things like the very serious involvement of the Archdiocese of Boston. And the arrival of Father Martin Milsap to *live* at their house until the birth. And the nervous, *embarrassed* looks everybody gave her now. Even her own parents.

Kathleen brushed through a plain of high faded yellow dune grass. She saw a bushy red squirrel watching her. The little creature was cocking its bony head at an extreme angle. Staring at Kathleen with one frozen, gleaming eye.

"*Bon matin,* Monsieur Le Squirrel!" Kathleen spoke her first words of the new day. Talking to the animals, for heaven's sake! Reminding herself of Saint Francis of Assisi.

As Kathleen glanced back toward her beautiful home, she noticed a second red squirrel. *Staring at her.* Then another. And a big gray fellow standing upright like a bear over near the stairs. *Watching.*

The young blonde girl then heard a distracting screeching voice over her head. She looked up. She saw flapping white wings. Six or seven circling gulls. Swooping. Kiting. Sailing like rudderless ships over the gray beach.

The birds seemed to be keeping an eye on her too, Kathleen suddenly had a notion. *Watching.*

What is this nonsense? Hey, what's going on here?

Kathleen thought she noticed an increase in the whirring, the buzzing of insects in the waving dune grass. *She was certain of it.*

A cloud of black flies appeared. A rash of the pestering black creeps.

"Go 'way! Get *out* of here now!" Kathleen started to cough. She waved both hands in front of her face. The young girl started to be afraid.

What is this?

On a straight line down the beach, two usually friendly golden retrievers began to stand their ground and bark at her. Other neighborhood dogs took up the howling, yelping, whining, baying.

Kathleen's stomach tightened. Her heartbeat quickened. She thought she might be sick.

What is going on? Please make this stop. Now!

The squirrels. The screeching gulls. The dogs. The black flies. . . . They all seemed to be gathering in a tightening ring around Kathleen.

Watching the teenage mother-to-be.

Waiting.

"Stop it!"

Both hands cradled under her swollen stomach, Kathleen Beavier finally began to run back to her house. The teenage girl was crying: sobbing. Everything seemed to be watching her, menacing, waiting.

Just as she slammed the heavy front door, the morning's sunrise majestically, peacefully peeked up over the sea.

ANNE

On the ocean side of her bedroom suite, Sister Anne stood behind matching large-bellied bay windows and surveyed a choppy, navy-blue Atlantic.

Out in the channel, three Alden racing sloops, their halyards snapping crisply against aluminum masts, were already kiting across the water in the September winds.

Just outside the window, the northwest air rattled crisp oak leaves like a new kind of shaker instrument.

At nine-thirty the previous night Anne had arrived at the imposing Beavier house—what local people call "cottages" in Newport. Kathleen had already retired to her room with stomach cramps, Anne was told. Anne was then shown to her own suite with its lovely sea views.

As she stood at her window the following morning, still dressed in a woolen gown, Anne heard a polite knock behind her at the door.

"Yes? Who is it, please?" she called.

A soft mumble came from outside in the hallway. "It's Mrs. Ida Walsh. I've come to draw your bath, Sister."

It almost seemed to be a statement of fact, Anne thought to herself. Draw my bath? Was that how these people lived?

"Come in, please, Mrs. Walsh."

A slight woman with the curliest snow-white cap of hair appeared in the doorway, nodded hello, smiled most cordially, then scurried directly to the adjoining bathroom. Whistling some obscure Rhode Island–Irish chanty, she began sprinkling Floris oil under the waterfall created by full twists of four inlaid porcelain cocks.

Anne stook awkwardly at the open door and watched the happily whistling woman, feeling she should help somehow.

Mrs. Walsh eventually appeared out of the bathroom again. Behind her, great puffy clouds of steam were rising to the elaborately molded ceiling.

"Your bath is ready."

"Thank you very much," Anne whispered. It *is* a dream, she thought. No one really lives like this.

Mrs. Walsh left the room, and Anne slowly entered the large and handsome bathroom.

Her eyes took in Victorian towel racks and mirrors, dainty bibelots all over the available shelf space, wood-paneled glass cabinets overflowing with clean linen and fluffy towels.

The bathwater itself was tingly hot, smelling strongly of jasmine. As Anne slipped off her gown and stepped in, it immediately turned her flesh pink.

"Jesus, Mary, whoever else is listening . . ." Anne had to smile as she settled into the wonderful tub. "Thank you all very, very much. I think that I might need this before the day is through."

Feeling very badly out of place—almost as awkward and uncomfortable as she had once been going to a Bob Dylan "Save the Hudson River" concert in her medieval Dominican nun's robes—Anne peeked her face into a sunlight-dominated library room.

"Good morning, Sister Anne." She heard a tinkling woman's voice from the far right—a bright wall of leaded, floor-to-ceiling windows which looked out on side lawns rolling down to the sea.

Walking farther into the room, Anne saw Carolyn and Charles Beavier, both of whom she had met briefly the night before. Mr. and Mrs. Beavier were seated together on a grand old couch covered with cabbage rose and wisteria.

Carolyn Beavier was an attractive well-kept woman —in her late forties, Anne would have guessed. She had an elegant oval face, prominent cheekbones, piercing blue eyes. Her blonde silver-streaked hair was long and flowing.

Her husband Charles was an impressive silver-haired man. That morning Mr. Beavier was dressed in a basic British charcoal business suit; he had on a crisp white shirt and a striped gray- and red-silk tie. Anne thought that he could have dressed himself in the mirrors of his shining black shoes.

The other person in the library room was Father Martin Milsap, a thin, gray man in a wrinkled soutane, the official representative from the Archdiocesan Office in Boston.

Father Milsap was bent over a handsome writing

desk, trying to look busy and important as he unlatched a solemn black briefcase. It was Father Milsap who had summoned Anne to the library, to discuss formally what her duties would be at Sun Cottage.

"Charles and Carolyn," the priest began to speak as soon as Anne had seated herself in a striped Regency chair near the sofa, "you will find that Sister Anne has impeccable credentials for serving as Kathleen's companion during these final days of the pregnancy.

"Sister has a master's degree in psychology. She has a minor in Mariology, the study of the Blessed Virgin. Less than a year ago, Sister Anne was one of Cardinal Rooney's executive assistants in Boston. Since then, she has worked extensively with teenage girls. . . . Sister Anne has even been present at the delivery of a child at St. Anthony's School."

Casting an appraising eye toward Sister Anne Feeney, Mrs. Carolyn Beavier considered that her important first impression was good. Very good. Her instincts told her that Anne and her daughter Kathleen would get along well.

In a minor way, that realization made Carolyn sad. Mrs. Beavier wished that she was closer to Kathleen, that she had made more time in her life for her young daughter. A little less of the Newport—Boston—New York social whirl; a little more finding out who her daughter truly was. . . . It wasn't that she and Kathleen didn't love each other. They did. It was just that they weren't as close friends as Carolyn would have liked. Especially now. Right at this moment, Mrs. Carolyn Beavier desperately wished that she could be her daughter's *friend*.

Listening to Father Milsap, whom she knew faintly from her years in Boston, Anne suddenly decided that she absolutely couldn't stand the man. Milsap seemed to be suggesting that if she wasn't completely satisfactory to the Beaviers, she could easily be replaced by another nun from the Church's vast storeroom. . . .

"Father Martin, Father Martin," Carolyn Beavier finally waved for the priest to halt his businesslike presentation. "I'm sure Sister Anne wouldn't be here if she wasn't a very special woman. Isn't that so?

"Sister," the slender silver-blonde woman walked over to Anne and took her hand. "I'm certain you'll get along very well with Kathleen. She's a very nice girl. She's very considerate and loving. Of course I'm wildly prejudiced. Welcome to our home, Sister."

"Yes, we're very glad you're here," Charles Beavier added, still sitting on the sofa. "If there's anything you want or need, just ask. We want you to be entirely comfortable here."

Anne began to smile.

"Thank you both very much," she said, responding to their warmth and quick acceptance.

"Could you possibly tell me a little bit about Kathleen before I meet her? When did you first find out about Kathleen's special condition, for instance?"

Charles Beavier reached for his wife's hand. "Let me take you from the beginning. As much as we know about the beginning anyway."

As well as he could, Charles Beavier tried to explain.

The first days had been incredibly difficult for both him and his wife. That had been the worst time by far. They had always trusted Kathleen—there had never been a reason not to trust her. Still the pregnancy had been such a jolting surprise. . . . Then, Kathleen had stubbornly insisted that she was still a virgin. For a moment Charles and Carolyn had worried that Kathleen might be going into shock over the incident. A virgin birth? . . . How was one supposed to handle it now, only weeks before the actual event? *Did Sister Anne understand?* Charles Beavier asked with fearful, glistening eyes.

Suddenly another voice came from behind them in the library.

"I would like to try and answer Sister Anne's questions. I don't know if I can, but I would like to try."

Anne twisted around and looked back toward the open library door leading to the parlor.

A teenage girl was standing beside a huge glass-fronted bookcase overflowing with jacketless hardbacks.

The girl had long blonde hair and a very striking,

pretty face. Her features were slender, except for her grand swelling belly, the stomach of a woman easily eight months pregnant. She was wearing an oversized red- and black-checked lumberman's shirt, sandals, jeans. She looked very much the way high-school and college girls look all over New England.

"Hello, Sister Anne Feeney," Kathleen Beavier smiled quite wonderfully.

What struck Anne most about the young girl was the fresh, chaste look she had. Kathleen had an aura of almost radiant innocence. It was a little frightening.

"I'm Kathleen, as you can probably tell by *this*." She patted her huge stomach.

"Hello, Kathleen," Anne smiled. At the same time, though, she found that she was actually clutching the fabric on the arm of her chair.

Anne couldn't take her eyes away from the young blonde girl's face.

Did no one else see what she saw there?

For the first time really, Sister Anne Feeney actually *felt* that something quite extraordinary might be going to happen. Anne thought that she suddenly understood part of what all the excitement and confusion was about.

She understood exactly why they had taken her out of St. Anthony's and rushed her to Newport.

The lovely face of Kathleen Beavier was in the image and likeness of the Blessed Virgin Mary herself.

KATHLEEN AND ANNE

At one time the picturesque Beavier estate had been a working farm operated by a former English millowner, his wife, three daughters, and two strong-backed sons.

There were still antique animal stalls and gnarled corrals made from driftwood spotted everywhere around the stunning grounds. There was also a much newer stable for Charles Beavier's expensive thoroughbred show horses. Occasionally, families of deer would be seen loping along down on the white sand beach.

"It's very idyllic here," Anne said as she and Kathleen walked down in the direction of the beach. "My father's house is near the Sound in New York. I love it close by the water."

Anne kept turning and looking back at the main house. Sun Cottage had been named by the daughter of a Boston attorney who had used the house just six weeks a year during the blast-furnace stretch of summer in the 1920s. The cottage was a truly beautiful and special structure, with four imposing wings added onto an impressive Victorian shell. The house had twenty-eight rooms and twelve full baths. Quiet, formal elegance was the best description that came to Anne's mind.

"It's not exactly a humble stable in Bethlehem," Anne heard Kathleen say.

She turned and saw that the blonde girl was smiling. "I thought someone ought to break the ice," Kathleen shrugged. "Maybe we should talk a little now. We could get into what you know about me, and what you don't know. A little, anyway."

"All right," Anne said. She found herself taking a deep breath first. All of this had happened so fast, she suddenly realized. "The obvious thing—I'm told that you are a virgin but that you're also pregnant."

"Strange, but true."

"I know that the Church is concerned about your condition. I know they are trying to keep all of this very quiet, which is understandable. . . . One thing I don't know is why and how the Archdiocese became involved in the first place."

Kathleen nodded. "Okay . . . first of all, though, one minor correction. . . . You said the Church was concerned. I would have to say the Church is concerned but more frightened than anything. Cardinal Rooney can't look into my eyes without having to lower his. The same with Father Milsap. That's strange. I think it is, anyway. They won't tell me anything, either.

"Secondly, my mother was a personal friend of Cardinal Rooney's for a long time before any of this happened. After she found out that I was pregnant, but also a virgin, she contacted the Cardinal. She would never tell me this, but I think she talked to him about an abortion.

"A little while after that, Father Milsap came from Boston to stay with us. I was examined by a Boston specialist who does work for the Archdiocese. Then I was examined at Harvard University. After that all these different priests began to come to the house. They all wanted to talk about the *possibility* that something very holy and special might be going to happen. But no one will tell me *why* they think so."

As she listened to Kathleen, Anne found that she was beginning to sympathize, almost to identify with much of what the young girl was telling her.

Anne understood from her own experience how the Church attempted to know everything about you, while revealing so very few of its own secrets. Anne also knew how the Church traditionally chose to deal with its women members.

Women were to be seen at Mass and Sodality; women were not to be heard from when the time came for decision-making—even decisions that very dramatically affected their lives.

"Kathleen, will you tell me how all of this began?" Anne asked the girl. "I've heard little bits and pieces about a day last January. A day nearly nine months ago. You had gone out with a boy from town after a school prom? What was that all about?"

Kathleen's blue eyes suddenly dropped away from contact with Anne's. The brief trust between the two of them seemed to dissolve; it was as if a door had closed between them.

"I'm sorry," Kathleen said quietly but firmly. "I can't tell you about that. I can't tell anyone about that night."

Tears suddenly glistened in Kathleen's eyes. She put her hand up to her forehead; she seemed both confused and in some kind of real, physical pain.

"I'm so afraid," she finally spoke. *"I'm so alone and afraid.* No one will be able to understand. Please help me, Sister."

Anne reached her arms out to the badly shaking young girl. It was a little like being back at St. Anthony's, she thought for a moment. Young fears; terrible loneliness.

She could feel the girl's shivering and her quiet sobs. She could feel Kathleen's pulsing stomach pressing against her own.

For several moments, Sister Anne Feeney and Kathleen Beavier just held one another on the lonely ash-gray beach.

ANNE AND JUSTIN

Very late that evening, Anne stood with her cheek, her whole right side, flush against the cool glass of a drafty bay window in her bedroom.

She watched smoking blue-black clouds sliding, almost seeming to be racing one another, past the crusted face of the moon.

Anne's mind was reeling with strange new ideas and conflicting impressions of Sun Cottage.

Besides that, she couldn't get the innocent face of Kathleen Beavier out of her mind. That New England schoolgirl freshness. The simple beauty of the girl—*the virgin Kathleen.*

Finally Anne began to whisper her evening prayers. She left her window lookout, turned down her bed's counterpane, and quietly slipped in between fresh-smelling linen sheets.

She was feeling so terribly alone and afraid—just the way Kathleen had described it that morning down on the beach. Anne thought that her mind was quickly becoming overloaded with unanswerable questions.

Not just about Kathleen Beavier, Anne realized, but about herself.

At seventeen, Kathleen's age in fact, Anne Feeney had graduated second in her class at the very competitive Sacred Heart Academy in Westchester. She had been accepted at nearby Sarah Lawrence College and also at the College of New Rochelle.

The summer before she was to begin college, Anne had taken a job at the Schuyler Hotel on Lake George. Both Anne and her mother had insisted on the job, against her father's well-intentioned wishes that she simply have a good time the summer before school began.

During her ten weeks working at the Schuyler, Anne forced herself to go out on a steady parade of dates. The end result of the dates was remarkably the same, Anne soon discovered. The boys and men found Anne pretty enough (clothes-shopping restricted to Peck & Peck and Arnold Constable kept her a little too conservative-looking), but they also found Anne what they considered to be stuckup and very prudish.

For her part, Anne discovered that most of the men were incredibly insensitive and quite overbearing. Worse, though, they were absolutely demeaning to women in their obsession with sexual conquest.

After her summer at the Schuyler Hotel, Anne was more certain than ever that she wasn't like most other girls, or at least her impression then of what other young women were like.

In early September she failed to appear at her first English Rhetoric class at the College of New Rochelle. At the exact hour of the English-class meeting, Anne was one of twenty young women kneeling in the prayer chapel at Mount St. Mary's Novitiate in Newburgh, New York, sixty miles up the Hudson from New York City.

Anne had officially entered the Dominican Order of Teaching Sisters in late August. Admittedly, part of her decision had to do with her feelings of social incompatibility, but Anne also felt that she had a strong and true vocation.

For twelve years in the Dominicans, Anne seemed to have made the right choice.

Then something completely unexpected happened.

Sister Anne met and fell in love with Father Justin O'Carroll from County Cork, Ireland.

The first time she had seen Father O'Carroll, he was a case worker for Catholic Charities in South Boston. Both of them were attached to Cardinal Rooney's office, the main archdiocesan office on Commonwealth Avenue in Boston.

She had never met a priest quite like Father O'Carroll. He was disturbingly young and handsome—all of the sisters working at the Chancery thought so. He had a slender, muscular body, long black curls that casually fell over his Roman collar, the most intense green eyes Anne thought she had ever seen. . . . But Anne had resisted purely physical temptation before. Even as a Sister, attractive men had come on to her. Fathers of her students, a few of the high-school boys themselves, men on the street who couldn't tell she was a nun.

No—at first it was something else about Father Justin O'Carroll. Something less obvious. Something much more troubling than just a physical attraction.

There was an unmistakable inner strength about Father Justin that was unusual and intriguing to Anne. It was a trait one sometimes found among men and women in small New England towns, self-reliance and individuality. A seeming indifference toward the rude ways of the world. Moreover, Father Justin was articulate on a variety of subjects ranging from Irish sociology to classical art and music to American politics; he was educated and intelligent, but not vain as far as Anne could tell.

And Father Justin was so very serious about life, serious and sensitive. . . . Maybe that was what it was at first: the rough-edged good looks in combination with a quiet, sensitive temperament. Whatever the cause, the effect was terrifying and terrible. At the same time, it was wonderful and exhilarating. Anne had never experienced anything like it before.

In the prescribed Irish-Catholic manner, the frustrating state of affairs went on undiscussed for over a year.

Then Anne went away from Boston for two weeks, traveling to an international conference on Church Unity being held in Washington.

One night during her second week boarding at Georgetown University, she received a midnight phone call in the Sisters' dormitory.

It was Father Justin O'Carroll.

Anne's first thought was that Cardinal Rooney had suffered another heart attack back in Boston. Hearing Justin's difficulty speaking she became certain that Cardinal Rooney was dead.

"Will you please tell me what is wrong?" Anne finally had to ask Justin.

"Only one thing is wrong that I can think of," she heard the faraway priest's lilting brogue. "It's that you're in Washington, I'm here in Boston, and I'm missing you terribly. I feel like a fool, Anne, but I do miss you and I had to call."

Suddenly Anne became very flustered, hot, and dizzy inside the phone booth at Georgetown. Her heart was pounding uncontrollably.

Because she had been missing Justin too. She had been missing him terribly. Constant thoughts about Justin had been destroying her concentration all week. All month. All year.

When Anne got back to Boston, she went to her Mother Superior. In the Mother's sparsely decorated office, Anne honestly and forthrightly explained that she was having serious difficulties with one of the young priests. Anne then asked for, and received, an immediate transfer out of Boston.

Two very hectic and painful days later, Anne found herself living among nineteen black and Hispanic teenage girls at St. Anthony's in Holts Corners, New Hampshire. She had done it more for Justin than for herself, Anne believed in her heart. She knew many Dominican Sisters who had left the order by that time. In the United States, more than six thousand nuns were leaving their orders every year. But the situation with the Holy Ghost Fathers of Ireland was radically, dramatically, different. If it had come to Justin leaving, he would have been the first ever in that order. Ireland would lose a very good priest, potentially a leader. Worse though, Justin's family would be badly disgraced in its village. His father would very possibly lose his job; his mother and sisters would be severely chastened for what Justin had done.

During their first months apart, Father Justin seemed to understand Anne's decision. He didn't try to write or phone Anne at first. There was literally nothing communicated between them for over three months.

Very, very slowly, Anne found her faith and some of her commitment to the Dominican order returning. Then one afternoon Justin was waiting for her outside Hope Cottage. "I can't give you up," he told her. "I tried every way that I could possibly think of, but I can't give you up, Annie."

They went for a long, painful walk that afternoon. They tried to talk reasonably and ended up arguing. Finally, Anne told Justin that she never wanted to see him again.

I lied, Anne thought to herself now.

Sitting in the darkened bedroom suite in Newport, Anne found that she desperately wanted to talk to Justin right then. She wanted to hear his reaction to Kathleen Beavier's incredible story. She wanted to try to explain to Justin exactly why she had sent him away in New Hampshire. Maybe she could even admit to herself why she was afraid to be with him.

As Anne Feeney lay down that night, her mind drifted to a very curious, and at that moment anyway, powerful idea.

The idea was that she was close to entering her thirties now, and she was still a virgin herself.

FATHER ROSETTI

Two white pins of light playfully danced down pitch-black Foxland Road some twenty kilometers north of Shannon Airport.

Black magic was everywhere in the air.

The boxlike shape of Father Eduardo Rosetti's rented English Ford finally bowled into view in back of the flickering headlamps. The dark car was hurrying back from Maam Cross and the visit with Colleen Galaher. Now the Vatican priest would go to Shannon, then on to America—to see the second young virgin girl.

Behind the mud- and rain-smeared windshield, Father Rosetti was stirred from a slight driving daze by two

more rolling globes of light on the road. Two swerving,
flashing lights approaching from the rear.

As the glowing eyes came closer, Rosetti saw that
this wasn't a single vehicle behind him.

There were two vehicles—two careening backfiring
motorcycles.

Then suddenly, absurdly, one of the gleaming lights
slid right into the rear of his Cortina.

Bump. Bump.

"You damned fool!" Rosetti swung around angrily
in his seat.

The priest's car was immediately struck by the second bike. The taillight shattered. Rosetti's chest slammed
hard into the steering wheel.

The English Ford was struck again!

The two motorcycles continued to crash into his car.

Purposely.

Insanely.

Rosetti now saw that there were priests on the black
bikes. Both priests wore Roman hats like black saucers
on their heads.

Bump!

Bump! Bump!

Bump!

Father Rosetti had seen this dizzying roller-coaster
in some adventure movie somewhere before in his life.
The endless S curve of this road. The dark trees and the
mountain face itself rushing at his eyes. Then disappear-
ing in a blur on either side of his head.

It was like falling into a deep well.

Like hurtling down a perpendicular tunnel.

The car's red-striped speedometer stabbed at 61, 62,
65. It did this on a twisting road where 40 was pushing
it.

Bump!

Bump! Bump!

Why? Who were these insane priests?

Two unbelievable words finally formed themselves in
Father Eduardo Rosetti's fevered mind. An impossible
idea. A frightening medieval concept that could not be
happening here in the twentieth century.

Demon assassins, Father Rosetti thought. Then: *I am going to die. Who will find and protect the Virgin?*

Now both motorcycles struck his car repeatedly from the right side only. They were trying to force him over. Over the sheer cliffs of the mountain road to certain, instant death.

Father Rosetti tried to stamp down on his brakes.

Bump! Then a loud, new sound like *fwap, fwap, fwap* as something tore loose from the car's underside.

Both motorcycles struck his right side at almost exactly the same staggering instant. The small Ford was far out to the left on the narrow road. Rosetti saw nothing but the blackness of sky, the glint of white stars straight ahead of him.

Miraculously, the rented car clung to the narrow edge of the road. The car didn't go over the edge this time. The speedometer quivered at 68. The tires shrieked continuously.

Oh my God I am heartily sorry for having offended Thee. Father Rosetti prayed. *Protect the child. Please, good Father.*

The Italian priest suddenly flipped off the car's headlights. He strained at the wheel, twisting it as far right as he possibly could. At the same time, he stamped down hard on the brakes. His speed finally began to drop.

As the two motorcycles swept past him, Father Rosetti accelerated again.

Now he jerked the steering wheel to the extreme left. A terrible crunching, splintering sound came.

Father Rosetti had sideswiped the motorcycles at an extremely sharp angle. He watched as they spun off the road like toys. Exactly what they had hoped to do to him. Unreal. Pinwheeling. The bikes suddenly went head over wheels. Both motorcycles and their riders flipped over the steep cliffs on the high mountain road.

Father Rosetti finally brought his car to a stop. His heart in his throat, gagging badly, the priest staggered from the car.

He was able to watch the final unbelievable seconds of the motorcycles' descent. The last few tumbles and the ultimate crash.

Undoubtedly the two priests were dead, Father Rosetti thought and felt sick. He began to say a silent prayer. He began to pray for the two lost souls.

And then Father Rosetti saw the most incredible thing.

The Italian priest began to scream on the dark, lonely mountainside.

Two large horseshoe bats were slowly rising from the blazing flames down below. They were coming straight up the cliffside toward Father Eduardo Rosetti.

FOUR

COLLEEN GALAHER

The village boys and girls of Maam Cross could be
cruel without pity or remorse. They called fourteen-year-
old Colleen Galaher "the little whore of Liffey Glade."
They painted a fierce red sign on the greasy whitewashed
walls of the Catholic Social Club: COLLEEN IS A HUSSY!

Once a week, nevertheless, Colleen had to come into
town to do the shopping for herself and her mother, an
invalid because of a stroke. Somehow, she and her mother managed to live on just fifty pounds a month, their
allotment from State and Church.

DONAL MACCORMACK, FAMILY GROCER was third
in a row of dirty one-story storefronts at the village
crossroads. Over the slate roof a chimney pot puffed gray

smoke. Displayed in the market's grimy window was half
the bloody torso of a calf.

Colleen bought no beef that week at MacCormack's
(she and her mother tried to have meat twice a month if
they possibly could). She did buy a half-dozen eggs, flour
to make biscuits and bread, salted herring, praties, milk,
honey, a hunk of farmer's cheese.

As she was leaving the family grocer's, terribly con-
scious of the female clerk's knowing eyes burning into her
back, struggling with her parcels, her bulging stomach,
the badly sticking door—Colleen stepped directly into the
path of Michael Colom Sheedy.

"Oh, bloody excuse me, Missus," Michael feigned a
polite smile and pulled off his tweed cap. "Well, would
you believe this!" The sixteen-year-old St. Ignatius Boys'
student suddenly thrust his hand onto his wiry hips. "It's
wee Colleen Galaher . . . with her big, shameful belly."

Colleen's eyes quickly moved from Michael to the
others in his mob. Still dressed in their gray trousers and
blue school blazers, there were Johno Sullivan, Finton
Cleary, Liam McInnie, and also Michael's girl, Ginny
Anne Drury. All lolling in front of the Sweets Shop.

"Please, Michael, my mother is very sick today. I
have to go home."

"Aye, Colleen. This won't take a minute. We'd just
like a bit of group discussion here."

Very suddenly Michael Sheedy lifted tiny Colleen
and her shopping bundles right off the sidewalk. Way up
toward the sinking red sun over the village roofs.

"Oh, dear God, no, Michael Sheedy!"

Colleen's face turned incredibly pale. Tears slipped
out of her soft green eyes. Her heart was in her throat.

"Oh, dear God, no, Michael Sheedy!" the village
boy mimed in a high-pitched, mocking voice.

As his lads fell into laughter, the head bully-boy
passed Colleen down the line like a sack of squirming
cats.

"Quick think, Johno. Don't drop the ball now."

Johno Sullivan, a sodden boy already over two hundred pounds at sixteen, nearly did drop Colleen.

At the last juggling second, he shuffled her along to

Liam McInnie, Michael's chief lieutenant, flatterer, and imitator.

"Please, Liam," Colleen trembled and cried out. "Ginny Anne, please! Make them stop! *I didn't hurt anyone. I'm pregnant!*"

The freckled Irish farm boy held Colleen up over his head of flopping red hair. He screamed out a loud Croke Park football cheer. The others were nearly on the ground with laughter and howls.

"Aye, ye whore! Ye little whore, Colleen! *Never give me a date!*"

Very suddenly, then, the most peculiar thing happened on the desolate main street of Maam Cross. The strangest thing ever in the ancient Druids' village.

A brown-and-yellow thrush screeched once. Then the bird caromed off the side of Liam McInnie's sweaty head. The Irish boy instinctively put Colleen down. Both his hands then flew to his face. He covered his stricken eyes. Moaned horribly.

"Bloody fucker!" Liam McInnie screamed out. "Oh, you bloody fucker! My eyes! Oh Jaysus! My eyes!"

As Colleen slipped away from the terrifying scene, she saw Liam finally lower his hands. The tall, farm-boy's face was badly blood-streaked. Ragged strips of red and pink flesh were hanging from the boy's cheek. The bird that had attacked Liam was now nowhere to be seen. Nowhere.

Colleen Galaher whispered an astonished, terrified prayer. Then the young girl decided she'd better hurry on out of Maam Cross.

That night one of the Sisters from Holy Trinity finally came to stay with Colleen and her sick ma.

The Mother Superior, Sister Katherine Dominica, came herself.

THE SIGNS

Father Eduardo Rosetti sat with his eyes tightly closed on board an Aer Lingus 747 brushing across the night skies between Shannon and New York City. He kept seeing viscous explosions of fire. The infernal flying motorcycles, the screeching bats.

At first, the physically and mentally exhausted priest tried to sleep, to empty his brimming mind, to restore his body's lost strength and energy. . . . He suddenly remembered the mysterious attack on the Via di Porta Angelico in Rome. The powerful warning.

Less than an hour into the flight, Rosetti switched on the overhead reading lamp. He unbuckled the black satchel which held all his work on the virgin investigation. His hands were shaking badly.

The most recent evidence and documentation sat at the top of his bulging bag. A nineteen-page deposition on the meeting with young Colleen Galaher in Maam Cross. The amazing fourteen-year-old Irish virgin.

Next came a packet of two- and three-day-old newspaper clippings. Pieces from *The Times* of London, the *Los Angeles Times,* the *Observer,* the *Irish Press* and others.

Rosetti felt his neck beginning to stiffen. Tension seeping in. *Please let me rest.*

All of the news stories elaborated on a strange, very chilling medical drama. A very real nightmare unfolding on the West Coast of the United States.

Another part of the baroque message of Fatima, Rosetti knew. A warning from the Lady of Sorrows. What Father Rosetti called and classified in his notes as *the Signs.*

A story he'd pulled from the London *Observer* told of an American team of nervous-system specialists, rushed to Los Angeles by the State of California Health Board working with the Federal Center for the Control of Diseases. The doctors' job was immediately to create a vaccine that would be effective against a frighteningly powerful new strain of influenza. A killer disease called Polio-Venice because the first case had been reported at Venice Beach in California.

The signs were clear.

The prophecy was being fulfilled.

Father Rosetti could feel his mind beginning to cloud over.

The terrifying warning of Fatima. Kept secret for nearly seventy years.

The signs of the Apocalypse.

The Investigator began to review a story from the *Irish Press:*

> Polio-Venice is a crippling infection of the central nervous system which seems to combine symptoms of both polio and multiple sclerosis. It was first reported in Venice Beach, southwest of Los Angeles. Since last July, the killer virus has been responsible for over seven thousand deaths spread across the American West Coast in a puzzling, random, non-pattern. No immediate cure seems forthcoming.

Rosetti scanned a column from *The New York Times:*

> Strains of the powerful new virus are usually found in the nose, mouth, and excreta. When it strikes a victim full force, Polio-Venice severely cripples the arms and legs. In nearly half of all cases, Polio-Venice eventually paralyzes the muscles of breathing and swallowing.

The most current news was in a front-page story Rosetti had clipped from the *Los Angeles Times:*

POLIO-VENICE KILLS RECORD 122 IN A DAY, the news headline jumped out in the harsh airplane reading light. *People of Los Angeles are once again urged to avoid movie theaters, museums, department stores, and other crowded areas.*

No . . . Lord, please!

Father Rosetti reached over his head and snapped off the reading lamp. For several moments he stared into the dark oval window, seeing his own pale reflection, feeling incredibly tired and helpless now.

The signs . . . from all over the world . . . portents of the near future.

Less than an hour out of New York, the weary priest finally slept.

ELIZABETH SMITH PORTER

Beneath the damp, steaming concrete of West 43rd Street in New York, down in a cavernous two-story basement, a smudged red starter button was being jabbed repeatedly by the head printer of *The New York Times*.

Eighteen twenty-five ton presses began to roll off the second of four editions of the next day's *Times*. Each of the presses would spin off forty thousand papers an hour, completely folded and counted, ready to be sent just about everywhere in the known world.

At nine thirty-nine the phone on the desk of *Times* reporter Elizabeth Porter jangled once and was immediately picked up. The desk was located on the far right of the National News bullpen. Its closeness to the office of National News Editor Thomas McGoey signaled the influence of the slightly built mother of four on the News Editor's decisions.

"Can you give me any other confirmation of what you're saying? Anything at all? Anyone? I have two confirmations now. On this story, I'd like to have even more. Please . . ."

Liz Porter's hand was cupped over the telephone's mouthpiece. She was trying to speak and listen over the impossible din of copy boys, of ringing phones, of chattering UPI and AP tickers.

"All right, Monsignor. Yes, yes. I understand your problems. Listen to me. . . . Listen to what *I'm* saying, Monsignor. . . . I'm going to talk with our News Editor right now. His background is high Episcopalian, by the way. *Almost* Catholic. He'll have to clear this with the Managing Editor, I'm sure. You will stay near your telephone, won't you? All right. Yes, Monsignor. Now please, stay by your phone. We will do an honest and fair job with this. I promise you we will."

Liz Porter slapped down her phone receiver and took a moment to think this one through. She nervously lit a filter cigarette. "First things first," she mumbled to herself.

She quickly put in a call to Thomas Lapinsky, one

of the *Times'* stringers in Boston. She told Tom he had to take a drive over to Commonwealth Avenue, the Catholic Church's Archdiocesan Office.

"Of course right now, Tom. I'm sorry that you're having a bridge party. I'm sorry that it's Saturday night. I need a face-to-face confirmation. This is a very, very important story. Go to the Chancery. Have Monsignor John Brennan tell you the whole thing again. He's reluctant, but he knows the story is coming out one way or the other. I'm sorry to foul up your evening, Tom. I really am. Tom, I swear this is a huge story. Potentially, it's enormous."

After the phone call, Elizabeth took her buzzing head into the News Editor's office. She carefully shut McGoey's glass door. Then Elizabeth Porter attempted to explain the incredible story that had just been confirmed by Monsignor John Brennan of the Boston Archdiocesan Office. A story that had first come to her attention through a strange, anonymous phone call from Newport, Rhode Island.

When he had heard everything, the bleary-eyed, perpetually harried News Editor picked up his hot line to the Managing Editor. McGoey now began to tell Howard Geller the amazing story he'd just heard.

Finally McGoey hung up the phone. He turned to Elizabeth Porter.

"Frankly, he doesn't know what to make of it either. Just coming out of the Cardinal's office, it's a story. The fact that they won't deny the rumor. He wants to see some copy, Liz."

Elizabeth Porter nodded, then hurried back to her desk. She began to type out the story on the steel-gray computer terminal sitting in front of her.

In the meantime, Thomas McGoey was alerting his make-up editor about a possible front-page hold. McGoey told the editor that he didn't want to go the route of a very expensive lobster-shift job, but to definitely hold space on page one.

Fifteen minutes later, the Managing Editor called McGoey. Howard Geller had pushed a button on his own computer terminal. He now had Elizabeth Porter's story in front of him on the small pale-gray screen.

"I don't like her saying *imminent* in the story. That suggests we're making some kind of half-assed prediction about the birth of this . . . *child*. I want you to underplay this thing, Tom. Make it seem as if the story could be about the great hoax aspect of this thing. The strangeness. But keep it on page one. Tell make-up to leave a hole for six hundred words or so."

McGoey set down the phone and looked up at Elizabeth Porter. "You've got fifteen minutes for a rewrite. He hates the use of the word *imminent*. Loves the rest of it."

At eleven forty-five, the felt green scoreboard in *The New York Times* composing room showed that there were additional news stories coming for pages one, nineteen, and thirty-two.

At eleven fifty-nine, the head union printer pressed the dirty red starter button once again.

The midnight edition of the *Times* began to roll.

Six hundred thousand copies due to reach homes all over the metropolitan area by breakfast.

At twelve sixteen the last of the late-page plates had been cast. All the monster presses were screaming. The maintenance crew was busily filling and refilling the huge black wells that greased all moving parts; they were checking the ink fountains; they were making sure all the papers were in position.

Beside each printing press was a pressman-in-charge and a crew of journeymen. Each pressman wore a square paper cap to protect his hair against flying grease and ink spray. The shirts and arms of the pressmen were covered with printer's ink. In less than an hour they would come home to families in Queens and Brooklyn, looking dirtier than the average auto mechanic after eight hours. Very unusual for these men, some of them would actually wake their wives to show them one of the front-page stories written late that night.

The morning *Times* was powering out of the brawny presses, ten completed papers every second. The papers then climbed on spring-wire escalators to the mailroom, one floor up at street level. The newspapers were automatically stacked there, tied into neat bundles, whisked by conveyors to the loading platforms.

Less than ten minutes later, the first-off-white— and — blue-piped *New York Times* truck was pounding down 43rd Street to deliver the final edition.

ALL THE NEWS THAT'S FIT TO PRINT said the side panel of the truck.

Leaving the Times building a little after twelve-thirty, Elizabeth Smith Porter carried a fresh new paper under her arm.

Ten minutes later she collapsed into the familiar surroundings of the Cafe des Artistes bar, two blocks up the street from her apartment in the Prasada. She unfolded her newspaper and looked at it in the dim yellow light.

Elizabeth Porter reread her byline, then her front-page story:

CATHOLIC CHURCH CLOSELY WATCHING
A VIRGIN PREGNANCY IN NEWPORT

"A divine child," she muttered in the baroque, buzzing des Artistes. "My good God."

The chaos was beginning in America.

Great Holiness . . . Great Unholiness.

The essence of choice and temptation.

FIVE

FATHER ROSETTI

St. John of the Cross in Saugerties was a tan-and-gray cluster of castlelike buildings in a wooded compound ninety miles north of New York City.

Jolting up the rutted drive, Father Eduardo Rosetti was struck first by the natural beauty of the grounds, then by the hundred-year-old estate building and sandstone cottages which housed the deranged and melancholy priests and lay brothers from the Archdiocese of New York. It was at this unusual rest home that Rosetti hoped to answer a vital question about his investigation of the virgin.

Inside the almost medieval estate-home, a crew-cut monk, Brother Thomas Brendan, led the visiting Roman

priest down stone-block corridors that echoed and amplified their voices and footsteps like pistol volleys. Along
the way, Father Rosetti observed mostly older priests, but
also a few who were surprisingly young.

The monk finally swung open one of the dark oak
doors. Father Rosetti was suddenly face to face with
Monsignor Joseph Stingley, silenced in 1978, supposedly
because of his radical "fire-and-brimstone" teachings, Eduardo Rosetti's former mentor and confessor at the Lat-
eran in Rome: *a scholar of the Apocalypse.*

Rosetti took in an impression of the Monsignor's
room at St. John's. Bookshelves had been constructed on
all of the walls. Next to the larger of two casement
windows there was an unmade daybed and busy work
table. All around the room were Joseph Stingley's familiar collections of Chinese, Greek, and Far-Eastern statu-
ettes.

"Edward, how are you?" Monsignor Stingley em-
braced Father Rosetti. "Brother Thomas told me you
were coming, but I couldn't quite believe him. I told
Brother that he had surely joined the ranks of the 'sancti-
fied' here at St. John's."

"I've come because I've finally thought of the answer to your question once posed about Anselm's proof
of God's existence."

The silver-haired Monsignor's thin, pinched face
broke into a smile. *"That,* Father Rosetti, I sincerely
doubt. I think not."

The two sat down at the cluttered work table. Out
the window, the Hudson was like a smooth gray highway.

"Enough humoring of hospital shut-ins, Father," Joseph Stingley finally said. "I understand you're the man
over at the Congregation of Rites now. That's very impressive to an old Vatican campaigner like myself. How is
it that you think I can help you? What brings the Chief
Investigator to America for the first time since Mother
Seton's appraisal?"

Father Eduardo Rosetti stared into the familiar
steel-blue eyes.

"Monsignor, I know that *you* know the secret of

Fatima. The message of the Virgin. The Virgin's promise
. . . and the warning."

Joseph Stingley said nothing in response. His eyes
showed nothing.

"You were with Paul VI much of the time he was ill.
He spoke of Fatima and you were there. You heard it all,
Monsignor."

An unpleasant look came over Monsignor Stingley's
face. "Why come to see me if we both share the same
information?"

Sitting in the small room at St. John's, Father Rosetti had a vivid flash of the crippling attack on the streets
of Rome. He saw the fiery motorcycles once again. The
screeching bats . . .

"Monsignor, please, I need to know how it is going
to be. My investigation. The search for the Virgin. The
Apocalyptic trial. I want you to tell me exactly how it's
going to be. . . . This descent into Hell that I've already
begun."

Monsignor Stingley stood up over the littered work
table and Eduardo Rosetti. He shuffled away, heading
toward one of his overflowing book cabinets. Abruptly his
entire body sagged. He felt a chill.

"The very worst thing, *at first*. . . . This will be the
loss of control, the loss of free will that you will experience. You will find that you have no free choices left. No
freedom of thought. No freedom of action. That's the
beginning. Do you know what that will be like? *To lose
all control over your own will?*

"Next you will feel a physical decaying of your
body, your mind, your soul. You will lose *all* hope,
Father Rosetti. And that rotting hopelessness, that abject
feeling of pointlessness and futility, will be the most
defeating of all possible human experiences. Worse than
you can begin to imagine.

"When this happens, when there is nothing in your
mind and soul except that abysmal black hopelessness,
then you know you are *about to take the first ignominious
step into Hell.*"

Joseph Stingley stood at the bright blue window, his

back to the Vatican priest. He almost seemed afraid to face Eduardo Rosetti at this point.

"Father, right now I would beseech God the Father to have infinite mercy on you. But that would mean deceiving you with false hope. Father Rosetti, don't go any farther on this terrible investigation of yours! You mustn't!"

Monsignor Stingley turned . . . and his room was quite empty.

Father Eduardo Rosetti was out in the long, echoing hallway again. Passing muttering priests.

Walking very fast.

Walking faster still.

Running out of St. John's of the Cross.

"I beg of you, Father!" he heard the shouts at his back.

"No man has the right to ask this of you! Not even the Pope has the right to ask this of you!

"NOT TO DAMN YOURSELF TO AN ETERNITY IN HELL!"

JOHN CARDINAL ROONEY

Sunday was a rousingly cold day in Boston. All day across the Bay City, thin plumes of gray-blue smoke rose determinedly and blended with the high, subtly warring skies. All day the story of a possible virgin birth in New England had been gaining momentum at an unprecedented rate of speed amidst hysterical excitement.

Late on Sunday afternoon, Archbishop of Boston John Cardinal Rooney issued a tense statement from his office high over Commonwealth Avenue: ·

IN RESPONSE TO THE GATHERING INTEREST IN THE PREGNANCY OF KATHLEEN BEAVIER, THERE WILL BE A LIMITED PRESS CONFERENCE ON MONDAY.

    THE CONFERENCE WILL BE HELD AT SUN COTTAGE, THE BEAVIER HOME IN NEWPORT. KATHLEEN BEAVIER HERSELF WILL BE PRESENT TO ANSWER QUESTIONS.

ADMITTANCE WILL BE BY INVITATION ONLY. UN-
TIL MONDAY, GOD BLESS ALL OF YOU. YOU REMAIN
IN MY PRAYERS.

MONDAY MORNING

For his nine o'clock Monday class at Providence
College Dr. Leonard Caputo, an eager and enthusiastic
lay professor of theology, decided to talk about the virgin.

"Do any of you learned gentlemen know anything
about Sir James Frazier's *The Golden Bough?*" Dr. Caputo began.

There wasn't a word of response from his sleepy-
eyed seniors, most of them physical education and business majors.

"It's a classic book that deals with ancient myths,"
one of the young men finally volunteered.

More silence.

Finally a loud sigh from Dr. Leonard Caputo. "In
the fourth century A.D."—Caputo decided to begin his
lecture with something other than Sir James Frazier—"St.
Ursula set off on a famous and quite hair-raising pilgrimage to Rome. It was a pilgrimage of eleven thousand
virgins."

That engaging thought, perhaps the imagery,
brought vague life signs from up and down rows of
scarred wooden desks in the classroom. Red-rimmed eyes
popped open. Someone even whistled.

"Exactly so. The virgins were attacked and ravaged
by an army of Huns," said Caputo, now beginning to
warm to his subject.

"Gentlemen. What do you think about this virgin
girl in Newport? Seriously. The Cardinal of Boston is
traveling to Newport today. He's to make a statement
about a possible virgin birth in the twentieth century.
What does this mean to young Christian men today?"

Two other twenty-year-old men, local gas jockeys in
Newport, were talking about the virgin down at the Mobil
station on Thames Street in Newport.

"Neal . . . do you know what I think would happen if Jesus Christ came back on earth again?" asked George Winters, a grumpy mechanic's apprentice wearing a faded red Red Sox cap.

"If I knew what you thought, *before* you told me . . . I'd be in as big trouble as you are."

"Yeah, well, I think they'd kill him all over again. Crucify him all over again."

Situated on a pretty sculpted hill less than a mile from the Mobil station, Sacred Heart was the picturesque church attended by President John and Jacqueline Kennedy when the summer White House had been at Newport's Hammersmith Farms nearly thirty years before.

Early on Monday morning, two elderly Newport women, Irene Goodman and Nettie Blatt, were chatting as they shuffled out of the graceful twin-spired church. The two old ladies were holding their hats on against the sea breeze as they created an alternate current with their own gusty conversation.

"Did you hear what I heard, Irene?" asked Nettie Blatt, one of the women.

"Well, I don't know that yet, dear. What did *you* hear?" Nettie's best friend, Irene Goodman, was a perpetually grieving woman who still worked as a filing secretary in the offices of the Beattie and Grum Insurance Company.

"It seems . . . the Bea-vayay girl was out on this big secret date. She was out with some local admirer one night in March. About nine months back, Nettie. She got herself in trouble, they say. It's all over Rogers High School that way."

"And how did *you* hear that, love?"

"Betty Brown's daughter happens to have told her. *Her* daughter Reenie. She *attends* Rogers."

"Hmpp," Nettie Blatt made a sound. "Well then, I'm just dying to hear the story they're cooking up at the Beavier house out on Ocean Avenue."

"So am I, Nettie. I'll bet, I'll just bet it's going to be some terrific humdinger. Got the Cardinal down here and everything."

"Divine child, indeed," Nettie Blatt said, blessing herself anyway.

ANNE AND JUSTIN

Early on the delicate blue morning of Cardinal Rooney's press conference, Anne wandered down by the sea to think and to pray.

Balancing her morning's third cup of coffee in one hand, she cut a meandering path through the high dune grass which bordered the beach. Then she walked beside the lolling water, letting the lazy tide sneak up her bare ankles, letting it push the cream and salmon pebbles up between her toes.

Anne was thinking about Kathleen as she traced the curving water line with her footprints; she was trying to guess what Cardinal Rooney's personal involvement might mean now.

Most of all, Anne was trying to imagine what the Cardinal could possibly say at the important news conference now scheduled for five-thirty that afternoon. From what she had been able to gather so far, reporters from everywhere were arriving in Newport, very quickly filling up the resort's few hotels. One of the kitchen helpers who lived in town had told Anne that Thames Street had the look of the middle of summer that morning. At seven there had been a long line outside Poor Richard's coffee shop.

Scaling a ten-foot-high dune that waved beach grass and Scottish heather, Anne looked back toward the imposing main house.

Off to the east a bit, she saw an old black Buick Special bobbing along beside a row of scrub pines. The awful car was just being parked—like an ugly mistake on the well-groomed, white-pebbled Beavier driveway.

Anne's heart began to pound. She suddenly had trouble keeping her balance on legs that were rubbery and buckling. She could feel her whole body flushing red.

Father Justin O'Carroll had come to the Beavier house.

Shielding his eyes from the sun glare off the white house and even brighter sand dunes, Father Justin stepped from the prize '65 Buick Special he'd salvaged from the estate of a monsignor in Wilberham, Massachusetts.

Justin's six-foot-two frame rose above the streamlined automobile, his pride and joy in America. His curly salt-and-pepper hair and sturdy build suggested several possible occupations, none of them priest.

Justin had on a beaming, benedictory smile, but that was forced by the bright sun glare rather than any good feelings he had about the upcoming few minutes with Anne.

He watched Anne Feeney coming over the dunes toward him and he actually felt a little heartsick. Much too vulnerable already.

Her black hair was catching the morning sun. She was walking in slow motion, it seemed.

Finally, they stood facing one another in the driveway in front of the Beavier house.

Anne stayed more than an arm's length away from him. Her mind had gone blank for a moment. She didn't know what to say.

"I'm sorry about just coming like this," Justin finally spoke to her. "People are flocking into Newport today. Almost as bad as the America's Cup crowd. Pilgrims coming to see the virgin miracle, Anne. I'm here as one of them, Anne. I've come to see the virgin mother."

Anne suddenly found herself smiling at the Irish priest. She held out her hand to him. "I am glad you came, Justin. I've been wanting to talk to you ever since this happened. Does your old car have a few more miles left in it?"

"At least a hundred thousand."

"Let's take a drive, then. I'll tell you what I think is going on. I'd love to have your opinion. We have a lot to talk about."

Justin's luck held, and there was a parking space on Newport's tour-busy Thames Street. He and Anne then waded through snarled, honking traffic to Bowen's and Bannister's Wharfs.

Since the mid-1970s, the former marketplace of Colonial Newport had been the site of a successful minimall by the sea. The area was full of arts-and-crafts shops, cute little outdoor cafés, a few fancier restaurants. Justin and Anne walked past the Black Pearl and Clarke Cooke House restaurants; a place for buying scrimshaw jewelry called HMS *Bliss;* the Eastbourne Gallery for nautical paintings; the Spring Pottery Store, where a real kiln was already fired up and working.

Just beyond the pottery store was the Ezra More Café, a buzzing place where Anne and Justin stopped for coffee and to talk—and to be petrified about being alone together.

At first Anne tried to talk about what had happened between the two of them; what had happened in New Hampshire; what had happened in Boston when she had suddenly left Justin. When that proved absolutely impossible to discuss, too painful for either of them, they began to talk about Kathleen Beavier only. They both completely avoided the other subject, almost as if their past had never existed.

"Last night after dinner," Anne was saying as the mugs of coffee arrived, "I talked to the family doctor, who comes to the house for Kathleen's checkups."

"He was the one who originally confirmed that Kathleen is a virgin?" Justin asked.

"Yes. Dr. Armstrong also happens to be a Catholic himself. He eventually got into some interesting side points about the birth with me. He suggested that there was a possibility of an outside agent, perhaps a virus, triggering the duplication of chromosomes. That happens fairly regularly, Dr. Armstrong said."

"Parthenogenesis. I've read a little about it," Justin nodded.

"Doctor Armstrong thought it was unlikely in Kathleen's case, though," Anne went on. "None of the tests he made confirmed it. . . . He brought up another point, though. As Dr. Armstrong sees it, a major unresolved issue is whether Kathleen can remain intact after child-birth."

"The Vatican won't even investigate the birth unless she remains a virgin," Justin said. "I don't imagine they would anyway."

"As a woman," Anne said, "I've always felt that the Church's position on that was degrading to all mothers who have given birth in the natural way. It suggests that childbirth, and women, are unclean, unworthy."

"I have this crazy thought logged in my memory," Justin suddenly shook his head. "Something about women becoming pregnant because of semen present in a bath-tub."

"An old wive's tale. Dr. Armstrong said that exact body temperature controls the lifespan of semen. He discounts all of those stories about girls becoming pregnant in swimming pools and bathtubs. Listen to this one, though.

"A woman can be intact, but there is still a small opening through which she menstruates. If Kathleen was drugged, or in a dead faint, Dr. Armstrong suggested, it's possible that a man could attempt to have intercourse with her. He could deposit semen by coming too fast, then disconnect without actual penetration. She could still be a virgin. She might not even know *how* she had become pregnant."

"What a detective you would make," Justin grinned. "Our Church's version of Rabbi David Small—that man in *Friday the Rabbi Did This or That* . . . Is that how Dr. Armstrong thinks it might have happened, Anne?"

"No. Not really. Dr. Armstrong believes there is going to be a divine birth here in Newport."

ELIZABETH SMITH PORTER

From her wide double bed in the Newport Goat Island Sheraton, Elizabeth Porter had a splendid view of the gently arching Jamestown Bridge.

"What hath God and the *Times* wrought," she whispered as she watched the conspicuous traffic jam of *what?* Believers? Nonbelievers? Curiosity seekers? Ambulance-chasers?

Elizabeth's virgin-birth story was what newspaper people over forty still called hot copy. It had the necessary ingredients to remain on the front page for an extended period of time: mystery, controversy, religion, sex.

It was the kind of jarring news that seemed to put people off balance. Consequently they talked about it during coffee breaks at work, on theater lines, over their evening meals at home.

Liz Porter hurried from her motel room to get out to the Beavier house on time. Striding across the Sheraton's parking lot she found herself doing something she couldn't remember doing for fifteen or twenty years.

Elizabeth Smith Porter was actually saying the Our Father.

It wasn't so much that she believed in the virgin; it was just that Liz couldn't quite *not* believe.

MR. AND MRS. BEAVIER

Charles Beavier came over to the ornate mirror where Carolyn was absently running a comb through her hair. He thought that his wife still looked undeniably beautiful at forty-eight. Even under the impossible strain and pressure of Kathleen's virgin pregnancy, Carolyn seemed brave and in control.

He put his arms around her slender waist. "Do you know what I realized about you today? Something I've been thinking about quite a lot lately."

Carolyn looked up at Charles in her mirror. She smiled warmly. "What new realization could you possibly have made about me?"

"Well, twenty-five years after our wedding . . . I still love you as much as ever. More, I think."

Carolyn Beavier had to lower her eyes. "I wouldn't trade our years together for anything. I do love you so, Charles," she whispered. Mrs. Beavier turned around to face her husband.

These past few months, the last few weeks especially, had been horrible and terrifying beyond any description. Their daughter—the girl they had lived with, and brought up, and raised so dearly for seventeen years—was suddenly completely different. Not that Kathy herself had changed. But the circumstances had been altered so drastically. This birth. This incredible virgin birth. The Church's suspicion that Kathy might become the mother of God. . . . How could that possibly, possibly be? What would it all mean to her and Charles? What would happen to Kathy when the child was born?

"Charles, have we given enough of ourselves to Kathy? Sometimes I become afraid she might have been left out of the whirl of our lives. I wish that she and I were closer. I . . . I do love Kathy very much."

"Do you tell *her* that?" Charles asked.

"Not enough up until now. I think I can get much better at it. I will. I hope it isn't too late."

"It isn't. Everything will be fine. I'm sure it will."

"I pray that everything will be all right today. My God, this is hard. This is absolute hell we've been thrown into."

"Let's go downstairs, dear," Charles whispered softly. "I love you very, very much."

"My legs are actually shaking . . . Charles, will you please hold my hand?"

KATHLEEN

The housekeeper, Mrs. Walsh, was making up Sister Anne Feeney's room when she thought she heard Kathleen's voice. Ida Walsh stopped working, then she slipped out into the shadow-filled hallway. Her ears pricked up under the cap of her white hair.

"Sweet Sacred Heart of Jesus, Mary, and Joseph!" Mrs. Walsh whispered.

Was the young girl reciting her prayers aloud before the important meeting with the newspeople?

Ida Walsh couldn't clearly make out the words. But *no,* Kathleen sounded like she was talking to someone.

Not her mother or her father. Not Sister Anne or

Father Milsap either, the housekeeper considered. Who could it be then?

Mrs. Walsh took a cautious step closer to the girl's room.

She got herself in perfect position so she could see Kathleen's reflection in her vanity mirror. . . . Now shift over to the right a bit and she'd be able to see exactly who else was there. . . .

Sweet Sacred Heart of Jesus!

The housekeeper took a step backward. Her right hand went flying up to her breasts. Mrs. Ida Walsh stared in silent confusion and horror.

Kathleen Beavier was talking to someone all right. Talking out loud. Gesturing with great animation.

Only there was absolutely no one else in the bedroom.

And in the young girl's mirror—the housekeeper was sure that she saw—*rising, licking, gold and crimson flames.*

FATHER ROSETTI

Father Eduardo Rosetti hurried down New York's crowded Eighth Avenue, wondering where he could watch the important press conference.

His reaction to the break of the Kathleen Beavier story was shock and despair. It was a grievous error for this news to be released in America. There was little if anything he could do now though. He had to get to Newport to see Kathleen Beavier as soon as possible. He had to keep the news of the second virgin in Ireland a secret. Whatever happened, it must be the will of God, Father Rosetti prayed.

Five thirty-five; Father Rosetti looked down at his watch. He had to find a television set. Right now. The conference in Newport would be coming on any minute.

Father Rosetti actually had to see the virgin; he had to hear her voice and look into her eyes for the truth.

Beginning to run now, Rosetti threaded his way through the stumbling and despairing on Eighth Avenue.

Finally he saw what he needed. Inside a battered storefront with the sign MARTIN'S GRILL. A television throwing out garish blue and red light.

Stepping into the bar, the Vatican priest was struck by the mixture of boiling cabbage, stale beer, and Irish sausage. He heard complaints that a Yankee playoff game had been interrupted for the special news broadcast.

The line-up of faces at the bar slowly turned toward the open front door.

"Here's the very dude can lodge a complaint for us." A bar comedian gestured toward the priest.

"No, no. This is very important. This news conference," Father Rosetti said. The priest's eyes rose to the large color-television screen.

The Boston Cardinal was being shown from the waist up. Then there was a shot of the beautiful seaside house where the girl lived. As he watched, Father Rosetti's mind went back to his meeting with Colleen Galaher. The virgin Colleen.

Then, suddenly, he was looking up at Kathleen Beavier on the color television set.

He stared at the blonde American virgin. He silently urged the television cameras to move in closer. To show Kathleen's face. To let him see Kathleen's eyes. Father Eduardo Rosetti began to pray in the ruins of the Eighth Avenue bar.

Soon the Holy Child will come for all of us. Very soon now.

KATHLEEN
5:30 P.M., September 30, 1987.

A wet gray fog was beginning to wash over Sun Cottage as Kathleen was led down the rasping back porch steps.

Overhead, the sky was painted in ash grays, streaked with long purple slashes. The lamps in the living-room windows were glittering in the warm-yellow way house lights can on late fall and winter nights.

Kathleen shivered involuntarily as several cameras flashed out across the darkening lawns.

Her family and the clergy formed a tightly protective pocket two deep behind the wedge of microphones and lights set up on a twenty-foot-long banquet table.

On the opposite side of the table were a hundred or more news reporters, many of them recognizable faces.

Kathleen stared out into the brightly lit, unreal scene and shivered again. Her pulse shifted into a higher, racing gear.

More cameras flashed and popped in her eyes. Tape-recording machines whirred to readiness. Reporters and cameramen nudged and tugged at one another for a better position to view the young virgin.

Kathleen was unconsciously grabbing and squeezing handfuls of her simple white dress. She was extremely nervous and afraid now. She couldn't help wondering what all these men and women thought about her.

Did the newspeople think she was a terrible liar? Did they consider her a freak? Kathleen could get no idea looking out into this sea of wet, shiny eyes staring at her. It was like gazing into a ghostly one-way mirror.

"Thank you all for coming. Thank you for coming here on short notice."

Tall and visibly imposing in his courtly red clerical robes, John Cardinal Rooney was beginning to speak in the most engaging man-of-the-people tones.

"Will you please join me in a brief prayer? The Hail Mary." Cardinal Rooney folded his hands and bowed his head. Then, in a strong, practiced voice, he began to pray: "Hail Mary, full of grace, the Lord is with thee, blessed art thou among women, and blessed is the fruit of Thy womb, Jesus. Holy Mary, Mother of God, pray for us sinners, now and at the hour of our death. Amen."

After the prayer and a prudently brief introduction, the Archbishop of Boston opened the conference for any background information questions the newspeople might have. Following this question-and-answer period, Cardinal Rooney promised, he would issue a statement about the virgin and the Church's position on the upcoming birth. A rail-thin man in a tan Burberry began the questions.

Charles Swerdlow, Chicago Sun-Times:

"At this time, it seems to me and many others I speak to that the Church is going through a difficult, some say an extinguishing, period." The reporter spoke with a pleasant Midwestern accent. "Now we read about the upcoming Christus Synod in Rome. An important worldwide Church meeting where vast changes are quite likely. We hear rumors that a schism is possible, even likely between the Conservatives and the Communists inside the Church. Is there any connection between these political difficulties and what is happening here in Newport?"

Cardinal Rooney spoke in a confidential manner, first to the Chicago reporter, then to his captivated audience at large.

"I don't want to sound apologetic—the apologetic period for the Church is over now, I think—but there really shouldn't be such disappointment and concern when the leaders of the Church are struggling. The Church is human. That is its flaw. But that is also its strength and its beauty. The Church is always trying to live up to the teachings of Christ.

"As to Church politics and Kathleen Beavier, to my knowledge there is no connection between what is happening here and the upcoming Christus Synod. The birth of this child is not a political act, I can assure you."

Jean French, ABC News:

"Cardinal Rooney, does this conference represent the official position taken by the Church? Has His Holiness Pope Pius been consulted about what is to be said here?"

"I am not speaking ex cathedra." Cardinal Rooney squinted out at the familiar sandy- and gray-haired woman he had seen so many times on television. "Only the Holy Father himself can speak with infallibility, with divine guidance, I suppose you could call it. But yes, Pius has been consulted about what I mean to say here.

"The fact is, the Church *is* interested in the birth of Kathleen Beavier's child. Otherwise, I wouldn't be here. . . . Officially, I wasn't to say very much more than that today."

Cardinal Rooney paused for a sip of water. He then smiled out at the reporters, admiring their restraint and tact thus far.

"Allow me to say a few more words in answer to this last question. And please, understand that I am personally struggling and searching for answers too. Try to understand what I alluded to before—we are fallible human beings in the Church. We are trying, most of us, to do the best job that we possibly can. We are aware of the Church's faults in the past, but these errors mustn't come to overshadow the ministry of Our Lord Jesus Christ."

Cardinal Rooney's deep, impressive voice hung over the crowd.

"A great and a very troubling mystery within a mystery is involved here. It is a complex problem which only Pope Pius, and before him Pope John Paul, Pope Paul, and John XXIII could fully explain to you.

"In nineteen sixty, you may recall that Pope John XXIII privately opened a secret message sent by Our Lady of Fatima through the young Portuguese girl Lucia dos Santos. Only Pope John and the popes who have succeeded him know the content of that message. Even the College of Cardinals has never been fully informed about the secret.

"I myself know only that there is a relationship between the miracle of Fatima in nineteen seventeen and the birth of Kathleen Beavier's child.

"I know that Pius XIII is watching the birth with interest and with his prayers. If it was in my power to tell you any more than that, believe me, I would. Please believe that!"

Elizabeth Smith Porter, The New York Times:

"Cardinal Rooney, I have a question for Miss Beavier herself, if that is permitted. Could Kathleen please give us some of the background information from *her* perspective. There is a great deal of conjecture and surmise right now. I think we would all like to hear the story in Kathleen's own words."

The Boston Cardinal now gestured for Kathleen to come forward. The crowd tensed, inching closer yet to the microphones to hear Kathleen's words.

"I don't know what to say," Kathleen whispered to him as Cardinal Rooney moved to change places with her.

"Just answer their questions honestly," the Cardinal said, gently squeezing the young girl's hand. "You're going to be wonderful."

Once again the squad of cameras began to pop and flash in her eyes. Kathleen felt as if her entire body had gone numb, as if fog was being pumped into her exhausted brain.

For a few seconds she suffered through one of those embarrassing periods where the mind goes perfectly blank.

"I've never spoken to a large group like this," Kathleen finally managed in a thin ribbon of a voice.

"Please forgive me if I'm not very good at this. My friend Sister Anne and I did a little bit of practicing in the house before and I was terrible."

Kathleen finally had to smile at her own obvious uncomfortableness. Many of the reporters smiled at her honesty and simplicity.

"Last spring," Kathleen went on, "I discovered that I was pregnant, though I was still a virgin. . . ."

She had been very frightened and confused, Kathleen went on to say. She had finally worked up the necessary courage to tell her parents. That same day, they had taken her to the family doctor, who confirmed that she was both pregnant and a virgin. Cardinal Rooney then heard about the situation from Kathleen's mother. There were more tests by doctors in Boston. There were a lot of questions by all sorts of priests. Finally the Vatican became involved, which Kathleen still didn't completely understand herself.

"That's really all I can say to you right now,"

Kathleen finished up her story. She didn't know whether she'd answered the question very well but she could feel that the reporters were receptive to her in some way. There was a strange shared intimacy about the moment. She felt so unreal and dreamy, though, almost completely separate from her body.

A reporter's voice floated up out of the crowd.

John Kamerer, Boston Record-American:

"There is more to your story then, Miss Beavier? You just said 'that is all I can say *right now.*' "

Kathleen hesitated on the makeshift dais. She looked out at all the curious, expectant faces. She wasn't sure whether to say what was on her mind or not.

"There is . . . *something* that happened to me on a night back in January," Kathleen finally whispered.

"Will you please tell us, Kathleen?"

This terrible feeling of unreality—the dizzy confusion of what was real and what wasn't was coming on so strongly now. Fears she had never imagined were sweeping over her. Kathleen felt as if she was speaking to all of them in a dream. As if they might be in a dream anyway.

She was surprised when she reached her hand forward and felt a real microphone there. Real metal. A loud, amplified *clunking* sound.

"I'm sorry," Kathleen shook her head. "There are some things that I can't tell you about. I . . . I'm sorry."

Kathleen nearly began to cry as the picture-taking accelerated. She didn't know what to say to them now. She couldn't tell them the truth, she just couldn't.

"I really don't mean to be this way . . . I'm sorry," Kathleen repeated.

Just then, Kathleen was distracted away from the reporters . . . *By a noise? . . . By an unseen, but felt movement out on the lawns?*

Something was happening.

Something was happening near a dark stand of pine trees that hovered like a giant sentry at the rear of the mass of reporters.

Kathleen's heart was beginning to pound terribly. For a moment she thought she felt the child moving inside—violently. Her face was turning incredibly red, she knew. She was feeling a strange heat sensation that she'd never experienced before. Her body, her dress, were wet.

"She's here."

Seventeen-year-old Kathleen Beavier suddenly raised her voice above the crowd. Reverberation screamed out across the lawns, seeming to be sucked out toward the sea.

Then there was a strange silence.

"She's here now," Kathleen said again, more softly.

The reporters began to turn. They slowly looked back to where the young blonde girl was pointing her arm.

"Our Lady has come. Please look behind you. The Gentlewoman is here."

Kathleen's soft blue eyes seemed to glaze over; they became distant and more peaceful. The young blonde girl stood pointing back over their heads, her face beaming with the most dazzling smile.

Obvious awe and lovely surprise were clearly etched on Kathleen's face.

Every camera eye moved in for a close-up of the remarkable young girl. They all tried to capture the astonishing innocence and rapture of her expression.

"Can't you all see her?" Kathleen suddenly whispered to them and began to tremble. Tears began to roll down her cheeks. Kathleen's whole body began to shake.

"Oh no. . . . Can't you please see her? Oh no, no. *You can't see her, can you?*" Kathleen Beavier quietly asked of them.

"Oh, please God, why me? . . . Why me alone?"

THE SIGNS

Judging by the immediate and startling reaction that evening, people all around the world badly needed to believe in something . . .

In anything . . .

Even in a look of startling innocence and honesty on a young girl's face.

"A miracle! . . . A miracle!" A roughneck Italian man danced and spun across the magnificent consecrated piazza of St. Peter's in Rome. The man was laughing at the Universe for trying to crush his wonderful faith into dust and insignificance over the past fifty years.

A divine child will come now, the man was convinced.

Finally a second divine child will come for the world.

Six-foot-wide gold bells began to toll across the majestic Basilica's cobblestone piazza. The rich, ageless sound of the bells held such a new and special meaning for more than ten thousand faithful gathered in the vast shadows cast by the world's largest church.

Christians everywhere had begun to pray; to cry out for their sins and for their immortal souls.

Everywhere, they were transfixed by the innocence they had seen in the eyes of the American virgin Kathleen Beavier.

A long ribbon of Germans trailed out of the waffle-like exterior of Berlin's famous cathedral the Kaiser-Wilhelm-Gedächtniskirche. The line extended far down the glittering Kurfürstendamm. As far as the eye could see. Wealthy Herren and Damen characterized by lean, well-chiseled features; lower-class Germans who tended toward broader and overweight faces—this cold night in Berlin they all stood together. They all sang the most beautiful, exalting hymns to the Blessed Mother Mary.

At St. Patrick's Cathedral in New York, Bishop Donald Browning celebrated an unscheduled High Mass at midnight. Nearly five thousand New Yorkers crowded into the Gothic cathedral.

In Dublin and Cork, white-and-yellow papal flags flew from the general post office on O'Connel Street, from all the restaurant and pub roofs, from the portal of the famous Gresham Hotel.

A second divine child, the word spread.

Another chance for the world.

At Notre Dame in Paris, the south tower's great

thirteen-ton bell sent the holy message out to the Left and Right Banks, to the nearby Sorbonne, the Marche aux Fleurs, Les Halles. Below the great towers in the Place du Parvis, the people-watchers, the lovers, the street entertainers and *clochards* actually stopped for an impressively quiet and solemn moment. The crowd offered a prayer for the young American girl Kathleen Beavier—who was after all of French descent.

In London's Westminster Cathedral, nearly five thousand attended a touching morning Mass before they trudged off to work. Up on the high, solid Cornish granite altar, Cardinal Hume offered the Mass himself, all the while thinking that there were more people here than he could have expected on Christmas Day. Why was it that the people were so affected now? Why were they so ready to believe, the Cardinal wondered? In the morning papers, Graham Greene said that he too was a little mystified by the startling popularity of the story or myth. He said that he was reminded of the way nearly one hundred thousand people had somehow traveled to Fatima to be on hand for that curious, largely unexplained miracle in the fall of 1917.

At midnight, great ceremonial cannons exploded across Bernini's magnificent meeting place in front of St. Peter's in Rome.

Ruffled birds took to the air from a thousand dark hiding nests.

The massive international crowd began to clap their hands respectfully, to light candles and matches in the purplish dark.

High up in a top-floor window of the gold-domed Apostolic Palace, a tiny figure in a white gown and skullcap finally appeared. The Holy Father now extended his frail arms out over the people. He offered a short, tentative benediction and then prayed along with the faithful himself.

People in the crowd began to wave and call out to the distant papal figure. "Papa, Papa," they called.

The powerful bells inside St. Peter's began to peal thunderously once again.

Crimson-plumed sentries from the Swiss Guard now appeared at every archway in their colorful Michelangelo-styled uniforms.

"Holy Mary, Mother of God," Pius solemnly intoned. "Pray for us sinners."

The Roman Catholic Church with its seven hundred million faithful seemed more alive and filled with promise that night than it had in more than a thousand years.

BOOK II

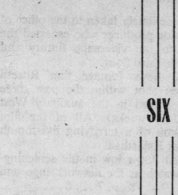

SIX

THE SIGNS

Briskly swinging his bulging satchel, walking fast with a dark, distracted scowl across his face, Father Eduardo Rosetti hurried down the busy New York City block near Lincoln Center.

He flashed past a dozen sparkling windows in the WABC-TV building on Columbus Avenue. In the shining panes Rosetti caught the mirrored reflections of Chipp's Pub, Dimitri, McGlade's Café across the traffic-blurred street. He saw a black-and-white marquee for an ABC studio theater where something called *All My Children* was playing.

Finally the priest plunged in past the glowing neon SEVEN in the front door of the West Side ABC building.

Father Rosetti was immediately taken to the office of an *ABC Evening News* senior producer who escorted the important Vatican visitor to the videotape library and private screening room on the third floor.

The unreleased ABC news footage that Rosetti wished to see had all been shot within the past three weeks (fresh footage was stored in the auxiliary West Side building for up to four weeks). All of the film portrayed the ongoing drama of a terrifying five-month drought in the Indian state of Rajasthan.

Father Rosetti slumped down low in the screening-room chair. He began to watch as the network logo and film leader appeared. 10 . . . 9 . . . 8 . . . 7 . . . 6 . . .

The time is close at hand, the priest thought. *Too close.*

The first grainy film image was a wide traveling shot flashing through a grotesquely impoverished Indian village, Sirsa. An unbelievable, seething hellhole, with an average daily temperature of 115 degrees.

The accompanying narration was provided by Jean French, ABC's best-known newswoman, also a participant at the Sun Cottage press conference the past Monday evening.

In much of modern-day India [Mrs. French's familiar voice came with picture], life is not as you or I may have seen it portrayed in movies about the British East Indian Company or the Bengal Lancers.

The state of Rajasthan, in particular, is sometimes called the Great Indian Desert because of its vast arid plains; because of its relentless sirroccos and simoons. This Indian state, with a population of ninety million, is commonly known as the worst drought and famine area in all of the world.

From April until July, a feverish white-hot sun literally bakes the smoldering land and the people like an angry, demonic acetylene torch. Dust accumulates for miles. Hot suffocating winds will sometimes blow the dust and meal chaff as far north as New Delhi. Villages are like smoking furnaces, reeking and blistering to the naked eye, silent in their unspeakable misery. The great, motionless sand dunes are almost tawny to the eye. They

actually become evil presences as you stare at them.
You begin to feel that ancient, primordial, evil
presences are there in the Indian desert.

As of September seventh of this year, the
terrible drought has persisted two full months longer than ever before. This entire Indian state now
subsists as a smoldering pyre for its own dead.

The Indian government has been unable to send
enough doctors, or even sufficient medical supplies
to the doomed disaster area. The British and now
the American Red Cross are trying to help, but it
is much too little, too late.

Six hundred thousand men, women, and children have already died here since April! Over six
thousand more die each day! If there is such a place
as hell on earth, then it is clearly located here in
pitiful Rajasthan.

As he watched the dancing, flickering images cast
before him, Father Rosetti was overcome with pity and
revulsion.

He viewed the rotting human corpses littering the
streets of Sirsa and then Pushkar India. Scenes too severe,
too true for network television release. . . . Women and
babies stacked like inconsequential piles of cordwood at
an intersection of a village. Four inhumanly thin school-
age girls weeping beside the sun-blackened body of their
mother. The gentle tinkling of ankle bells. The clinking of
bracelets. Tight shots of suffering human faces.

Everywhere, the clear signs of the Beast's presence
in this valley of death.

Gehenna, Rosetti thought.

Six hundred thousand dead.

Father Eduardo Rosetti finally had to turn away
from the screen. The Vatican priest tried to scribble notes
for his important depositions. To create order out of the
chaos he had witnessed. He began to enumerate:

The drought in the state of Rajasthan, the unspeakable famine in India.

Polio-Venice crippling the West Coast of America.

A burgeoning plague apparent in southern France,
flowering near the miraculous shrine of Lourdes.

The Enemy.

Just as it had been foretold at Fatima. . . . It was coming true.

The promise and the terrifying warning!

The two virgin mothers.

One so pure and good. . . . One so evil; destructive . . . But which was which?

Which virgin was which?

Father Rosetti's eyes were finally pulled back to the screen by a sudden darkening in the room, an unusual sound whining from the speakers.

It was twilight in the movie. Tens of thousands of Indian people were cast across a great flat plain near the golden capital city of Jaipur. The people were praying in unison with a saintly Hindu priest. The grand sound of the human voices filled the sky like a hard physical object.

The Indian people, wealthy Rajputs and peasants alike, all prayed together for an end to the terrifying five-month drought and famine.

Father Rosetti bowed his head and prayed along with them.

The people prayed with touching faith to the one eternal God of all Goodness and Life: *Brahma.*

The people prayed for *chamaltkar*—what Christians call a miracle.

COLLEEN

The idyllic spot widely known around Maam Cross as the Liffey Glade was a grottolike clearing caressed by a copse of feathery evergreen trees.

The glade had been a natural shrine long before the Christians, even before the Druids. It was to Liffey Glade that Colleen Galaher came when she wanted to be alone. Just to think off by herself. Or to pray to the Lord.

A brisk-flowing, clear stream bubbled through the grotto on its way to the Lough Corrib. The pine and spruce trees hunched over the nibble of water like a huddle of conspirators. High up at the top branches, a

jagged hole like a church's rose window exposed a patch
of the deepest blue sky.

It was here in Liffey Glade that young Colleen
Galaher had undergone what she now considered a mystical experience nearly nine months earlier *on January
twenty-third*. The day of the baby's conception.

Before that night, before she'd become heavy with
child, Colleen had been known around Maam Cross as a
very quiet and well-mannered scholarship student at Holy
Trinity. The girl's shyness came, most villagers imagined,
because of all the time Colleen spent caring for her sick
mother, because of the isolation of their cottage miles
outside the village.

Colleen was liked well enough at school, but she was
never fully accepted by most of her schoolmates. She was
appreciated best by the Sisters at the convent school, who
perhaps saw an image of themselves in the quiet and
reflective girl who was usually near the top of all her
classes.

That was how it was until the child began to show
anyway. Then young Colleen Galaher was ostracized and
cruelly insulted by all of them. She was isolated at just
the time when she so badly needed loving support. She
effectively became a nonperson in Maam Cross.

This particular smoky morning of October first, Colleen carefully and gently rode her mother's stiff-legged
horse, Gray Lady, down across the sodden cow pastures
that sloped behind their cottage. At Liffey Glade she
tethered the horse to the trunk of one of the tall ferns.
Colleen then pushed her way through wet, rustling
branches. She entered the private little outdoor
chapel.

The young girl immediately knelt down on the soft
carpet of pine needles and duff. Diffused rays of faded
yellow sunlight were beginning to slant in through the
highest tree branches. *How lovely it always was here*.

Colleen lowered her head of gleaming black hair.
The girl humbly prayed in a soft, whispery chant.

"Dear Father in Heaven, I am your servant. You are
the only one who understands me. But Father, I am so
lonely now. I am so terribly lonely these nine months."

Which was a most ironic thing to say at that particular moment . . .

Because in among the feathered branches of the glade, several dark beady buttons were beginning to appear.

Four gleaming eyes . . . then six eyes . . . eight eyes . . .

Slowly inching toward the small praying figure of Colleen Galaher.

Watching.

Waiting.

Still on her knees, Colleen looked straight up at the blue hole at the top of the dark towering trees.

"It isn't fair," she called out. "I'm too young . . . and I don't even have a proper husband!"

The gleaming eyes watched . . . and they listened.

JUSTIN

"A Father Justin O'Carroll, Your Eminence . . ."

As Justin was shown up to the second floor of the spotless mansion, the young priest was as nervous as he remembered being two years before, when he had first met Cardinal Rooney, when he had first come to the city of Boston.

On entering the handsome mahogany-and-leather study, Justin's wit, his Irish charm, and easy smile deserted him like the false friends he had always known they were.

Observing the young priest's fidgeting hands, the way his black loafers were shuffling back and forth on the Bokhara carpet, Cardinal Rooney remembered to let down his own imperious guard.

"Father O'Carroll! This is a pleasant surprise. How are you? How are you, Father?" the Cardinal took the young priest's hand and shook it warmly.

He asked the housekeeper if they might have coffee, then he took Justin and sat with him in a cozy nook overlooking the sea.

"I feel so strange now that I'm here," Justin said

after the two of them had exchanged a few pleasantries. "Your Eminence, have you ever . . . worked out a scene satisfactorily in your mind, thought that you were relatively comfortable with it, then found that the actuality was completely different from what you had imagined it would be? Something on that order is happening inside of me right now . . ."

Cardinal Rooney's lips parted in a smile. Among other things, he was remembering how pleasant it had been to have Justin around to talk with before he'd been transferred out of the Chancery office.

"I've experienced that feeling you described many times," the Cardinal said, "the most recent example being last night with young Kathleen.

"Let me see if I can possibly make this a little easier for you, Father Justin. . . . You came to Newport yesterday because as a priest, as a thinking Christian adult, there was no way you could be kept away from witnessing this, this . . . grand mystery, I'll call it for the moment."

"Yes, I had to come," Justin nodded and smiled. "Boston is so close. It seemed impossible not to come and see it myself."

Cardinal Rooney nodded. He truly did like this young priest's spunk.

"Is Kathleen Beavier really a holy virgin?" Justin suddenly asked. "I haven't been able to stop wondering— did she actually see a vision last night? The look on her face said that she did! The lovely innocence of her face."

The eminent Cardinal stared into Father O'Carroll's eyes. The question was so straightforward, Father O'Carroll so intense that Cardinal Rooney was taken aback a little.

"Father, I honestly don't know," he finally said. "I know that Rome believes something very important is happening in America. I also know that my usual Boston-Irish skepticism isn't operating at its normally high level right now. As you said, there is *something* about the face of that young girl. Somehow, I can't believe that she is lying to us, and I can't believe she is mad. Like yourself, I am incredibly eager to learn the truth."

Cardinal Rooney watched Justin's hand comb back

through his black curls. Father O'Carroll was obviously still anxious, still upset about something.

"Cardinal Rooney, you've known me for two years. You know I have to speak my mind."

"I sometimes get that impression." The white-haired Cardinal smiled.

"The reason I've come to you, Your Eminence . . . I would like to remain here in Newport for the birth.

"I know, or at least imagine that every single priest in the diocese would also like to be here. I see no reason for my being given special treatment . . . but I must ask you to consider my request. I have a very strong feeling about this young girl, about the birth. I feel that I must be here."

Cardinal Rooney eyed young O'Carroll closely; he quickly evaluated the young priest's petition.

"I believe I owe Cardinal Neeland in Dublin that much at least," the Cardinal said. "I'm sure he would not approve if I didn't allow his protégé to be present for the birth of Kathleen Beavier's child. Whatever the outcome!

"Yes, you may stay, Father. To make yourself useful to me, I would like you to assist Father Milsap in anything and everything he needs. There will be a great deal more work for him after yesterday. Too much for one priest to handle, anyway."

The Cardinal stared away out the den's window. A snow-haired groundskeeper was merrily crossing the lawn on a small red mower. Finally Cardinal Rooney smiled and looked back at Justin O'Carroll.

"Actually, I don't owe Cardinal Neeland in Dublin a nickel cigar at the horse races. The reason I want you to stay is that you had the courage to come here and ask me. Not one other of my priests has had the nerve to do that. What's wrong with them? My God, don't they believe in miracles?"

Justin suddenly knelt in the den and asked Cardinal Rooney for his blessing.

"Thank you, Your Eminence," the young priest said in a hushed, reverent voice.

. . . *And please forgive me for not telling you the*

*entire truth about why I have to stay here with or without
your permission . . .*

ANNE AND JUSTIN

Cliffwalk-by-the-sea is a slender, three-and-a-half-
mile footpath that fits like a choker around Newport's
graceful southeastern shore.

Here William Barkhouse Astor once walked with his
lady, the "Queen of the Four Hundred"; John Kennedy
courted Jacqueline Bouvier on Cliffwalk while he was in
the navy and she was Newport's debutante of the year;
Robert Redford and Mia Farrow promenaded along Cliffwalk in the most recent film of *The Great Gatsby.*

Now it was Anne Feeney and Justin O'Carroll's turn
along the historic path.

Justin's green eyes were twinkling as he looked out
over the rolling lines of whitecaps.

He is so crafty and utterly outrageous for a priest,
Anne was thinking as they walked along. Clearly, Father
Justin O'Carroll was powerfully moved by both good and
evil.

Why was it that so many beautiful Irish boys still
fled into the priesthood, Anne found herself musing as she
and Justin traipsed along the high winding path. It must
still be like the eighteenth century over on that fanatical
little island. . . . If Justin had been born in America, say
in Southey, or New York City's Yorkville, surely he
wouldn't have become a priest. Not with his looks. And
smarts. Maybe he would have become a doctor. Or a
stage actor. Or maybe a three-piece-suit businessman. . . .
Not a priest, though. Not today in America . . .

At that very moment, Justin himself was trying to
beat back a strong surge of good old-fashioned Irish-
Catholic guilt. On account of the incredible virgin-birth
situation—the unprecedented drama and emotional pres-
sures—Justin now found that he wanted to be with Anne
more than ever. Several times in the past day and a half
they had taken long walks or drives. Ostensibly they were
sightseeing in Newport. But not really.

They hadn't touched one another, not yet; but the urge was there. That these feelings were aroused at such a holy time almost seemed a sacrilege, blasphemy, Justin thought. He was a Holy Ghost father. Anne was a Dominican. He still solemnly respected all of the reasons he had taken his vows and holy orders. At heart, he still loved being a priest. . . . It was just that he loved something else too. He loved Anne Elizabeth Feeney, Sister or not.

Finally he offered up a silent, anguished prayer for help. He prayed that he was doing the right thing.

Dear Father in heaven . . . Give me the strength . . . Give me the fortitude and wisdom . . . Don't let me hurt Anne. Don't let me hurt the Church we both love.

Justin finally looked over at Anne.

"What are you thinking about?"

A faint smile brushed across her lips. She shrugged her shoulders.

"Oh, I don't know . . . I was just observing . . . how wonderfully idiosyncratic many of these houses are. Don't you think so?"

Justin didn't believe that the Newport houses were the only thing that had been on Anne's mind.

Anne continued to speak.

"There's something a little depressing about the passing away of this sort of, well, dream house. Conveniently forgetting the unpleasant socioeconomic realities for the moment, I love the idea of men and women building these homes. Building the cathedrals and palaces in their minds."

"I do too," Justin agreed. "Especially the cathedrals . . ."

"I guess I don't much like the abstractions that they're building nowadays. The shopping centers and this or that city's trade towers. I don't know, Justin . . . am I a closet romantic?"

A pleasant, ironic smile spread across Justin O'Carroll's face.

"No, Annie, I don't think I would ever characterize you as a romantic. Actually, some people might say that you deny yourself the romantic side of life."

"Let's not." Anne touched the sleeve of his red Boston College windbreaker. "Please. It's been a long two days. Cliffwalk is too nice to spoil. By the way, though, when will you have to be heading back to Boston? Your pastor certainly seems the understanding type."

Justin slid both hands into his deep khaki-trouser pockets. He shrugged in answer to Anne's question. He wasn't ready to talk to her about his meeting with Cardinal Rooney yet. He hadn't figured out an acceptable way to tell Anne that he wasn't going to be heading back to Boston right away. Not until after the birth of Kathleen Beavier's child.

The two of them continued to walk along a winding stretch of Cliffwalk overgrown with berry bushes, and the incredibly overgrown Newport mansions of course.

They were passing directly behind Millionaire's Row, the place where, locals swore, Henry James was said to have coined the phrase *white elephants*.

Here was The Breakers; Stanford White's Rosecliff; Beechwood; Richard Hunt's obsessive Marble House.

As they passed one after the other of these incredible homes, Justin was off in another world, thinking that he just couldn't help himself in this terrible affair with Anne.

No matter how hard he tried, he couldn't keep his true feelings buried inside. Somehow, to stop pursuing Anne, to give her up now, seemed terribly wrong, almost cowardly. It was contrary to everything he felt so strongly in his heart.

"You know, Annie," he began to speak again, "sometimes I think that you have a strange image of the person you are. I think you view yourself as this awfully shy and retiring and inadequate lady. As a *girl* of sorts, who could never begin to measure up to her very strong and socially successful mother."

Anne's face instantly began to stiffen. She felt terribly hurt—so much hurt that she had difficulty speaking.

"I took a vow of humility," she managed. "If that's what you mean by *shy and retiring*."

Justin really didn't want to say anything more on the

subject. He couldn't help himself, though; he loved her so much he couldn't help himself at all.

"I think it would be a good thing if you broke your vow of humility," he offered. "I think you ought to become *absolutely vainglorious* for a while. Discover who it is that you are as a woman," Justin said.

"Annie, whether you love me or you don't love me, you are still a woman with an unusual and beautiful passion for life. I must say that. I've seen it in practice again and again. At the Archdiocesan Office. Here in Newport with Kathleen. . . . You truly believe in the wonder and the grand individuality of people.

"It's a beautiful, beautiful attribute—which you generously ascribe to me—but you're the one who has it. *You're* the one, Anne. You're so much better than all the formalistic religious vows in the world. Everyone but you seems to know that you're a very, very special woman," Justin said. "Now I'll keep my big mouth shut. And walk. And take in the gilded fantasies of nineteen-ten America."

All the while he had been talking, Justin had been afraid to look at Anne. Finally he did, and it nearly broke his heart.

Big, glistening tears were flowing down her cheeks.

He'd hurt her.

He could see that he'd hurt Anne very badly this time.

Why, for God's sake? He'd meant what he had said to be the finest compliment. He thought of Anne at the absolute pinnacle of everything important to him. All he had been trying to do was to tell her that adequately. Why couldn't he have expressed himself better?

Ever since they had first met in Boston, Justin had known in his heart that Anne wasn't like the women he'd known in Ireland. She was very strong-willed and independent. Anne was also, very clearly, emotionally troubled. She was openly struggling with her vocation in the confusion of modern-day America. She realized that her vocation was caricatured by many people who wouldn't even try to understand that there might be a spiritual side to this life. She obviously wanted to be a Sister—but she also desperately wanted to be recognized as a modern woman. Her dilemma struck a sympathetic chord with Justin. He could readily identify with the latter problem. Deeply so.

Almost instantly, Anne had affected Justin in ways, in areas where he hadn't even known he was vulnerable. He wanted to be with her constantly—walking in Boston Common, at a Celtics game with Catholic Charities, in chapel—and felt a strangely depressing emptiness whenever she wasn't there. Most troubling of all for Justin, he quickly developed a desire to go to bed with Anne. Fantasies that came to him at all times of the day. A two-year-long physical ache. Frustration that was even more painful. . . . Was it wrong of him? Justin supposed that it was. But years of repression and deprivation had to have some effect. All he knew was that he loved this woman, this lovely gentle nun, more than he'd ever loved anything in his entire life. . . . He loved her, Justin thought, but she didn't love him.

Anne suddenly broke away from his side and began to run up the vine-strewn path.

Justin just stood and helplessly watched her go. Feeling incredible confusion, he listened to her loafers clocking rapidly up Cliffwalk. Way up past the grandly romantic Grand Trianon replica called Rosecliff. Completely out of sight around high topiary evergreens and cedar trees.

Justin hadn't even gotten the chance to tell her the really bad news, he thought with irony. He hadn't told Anne that he was going to be working with Father Milsap in Newport.

Out on the lovely, tree-tented Bellevue Avenue meanwhile, Anne finally stopped running.

She stood under the towering, sweeping black gates of one of the fabulous mansions. She watched a bright yellow Albany tour bus loading and thought she knew exactly why she'd run away from Justin. At least she could admit the truth to herself, Anne considered.

She was still very much in love with Father Justin

O'Carroll. Infatuation. Fantasies. The whole bit. She was helplessly and what she considered tragically in love with the young Holy Ghost father.

That night Anne walked on the beach in front of the Beavier house. Her eyes followed some kind of ghostly jet liner effortlessly sailing through the dark skies.

Twenty minutes before, Father Milsap had told her that Father O'Carroll was going to be added to his staff in Newport.

It seemed too absurd to even begin to deal with, Anne was thinking as she slipped along the creamy lip of the sea.

She wondered how the events had transpired, and then decided she couldn't deal with it at all. Not tonight anyway.

All of a sudden Anne felt so very alone and frustrated at Sun Cottage. She felt selfish for some unexamined reason; she felt as confused as she'd ever been as a grown-up woman. She wanted to throw a very adolescent tantrum, but she knew she wouldn't, couldn't be that egocentric.

Justin was very right about one thing, Anne thought as she walked along the Newport beach. *She did love him very much.* She had never met anyone else even remotely like him; never anyone whom she consistently thought about, fantasized about.

Dear Lord, she finally began to pray in a conversational style she'd adopted since moving out of the convent in Boston.

Please help me to do the right thing now.

I'm confused. I'm very afraid. I'm lost in slightly unfamiliar territory. That's just the way it is.

Sometimes, for a whole host of complicated reasons, I feel that I can't believe as I once did.

I call myself Sister Anne still. But I don't know if I want to be Sister any more. I think that I love Father Justin O'Carroll, and I don't know what to do about that.

Please help me to help myself.

Anne was so involved with her own problems that

she didn't notice something strange about the moonlit beach scene.

Something that greatly disturbed and unnerved the two golden retrievers farther down the shoreline.

The bats had come.

MRS. WALSH

The housekeeper, Mrs. Walsh, was high up in her secluded bedroom near the attic of Sun Cottage.

Just a few minutes earlier, Ida Walsh thought that she'd witnessed a terrible, terrible fire.

A fire raging right inside her room.

Flames! Terrifying orange and red flames.

She had been in the bathroom brushing her teeth, and suddenly she'd *seen* all these poor people being burned alive. She had thrown down the bubbling brush and paste.

It was crazy, impossible, yet it seemed so real to her.

It was so real!

There was no one Ida Walsh recognized—just hundreds of poor souls screaming at her for help, trying to shake off the horrible, dancing flames of hellfire. Then she saw Michael; her deceased husband Michael was on fire; Michael was screaming right into her face.

Then it was gone.

She couldn't bring the nightmare vision back even when she tried.

The housekeeper found her way into the bedroom and lay down in a pathetic crumble. She held her head in both hands and moaned out loud in the semidark room. She thought about pushing the black switch on her night table which lit a box by her room number in the servant's pantry.

No. What could I tell them? She stopped herself from calling out for help.

That I've just seen terrible fires of Hell raging in my room?

That my already-dead husband Michael was dying in a fire in my very room?

Mrs. Ida Walsh swallowed two nerve pills without water. She was nearly certain that she was going mad. For the past few months, it had been building. What was most terrifying about it was that she couldn't control any of it.

The fire had simply *appeared* before her eyes. Out of nowhere, she'd heard the grotesque human screams as she stood over the sink in her bathroom. As she had looked into her own eyes, she'd seen the suffering face of poor Michael.

But if I think I'm going crazy—if I can still tell the difference—that means that I'm not mad yet, the housekeeper thought.

"Please stop. Don't scare me like this. Sacred Heart of Jesus, I'm just a poor old woman. Please stop, or I'll go mad."

As Mrs. Ida Walsh hugged herself tightly and began to sob, an even more horrifying thought came into her mind. Much like the fire, it just flashed into her head without any forewarning.

A voice.

A powerful, irresistible voice was speaking to her.

The priest knows the truth, she heard at first and didn't understand.

The priest from Rome knows the truth. Watch for the priest with the dark eyes.

Kathleen is not one of God's.

POPE PIUS XIII

Dressing in unconscious half-time to a phonograph record playing Vivaldi, Pius XIII slid a white damask cassock over a plain black business suit made by Gammarelli, the ecclesiastical tailors in Rome.

Pius then wrapped a richly embroidered Cardinal's red and gold stole around his narrow shoulders.

He tugged on the familiar fisherman's slippers.

He set a white silk skullcap, the *zuchetto,* way back on the crown of his head.

Ever since the nineteen forties, Pius considered as he shuffled out of his bedroom, the absolute power of the Church to influence and shape world affairs had been eroding terribly. . . . Perhaps an end to that condition was now in sight. Perhaps tonight would be said to represent a new beginning for the Church in the modern age.

At six o'clock, Pius rode a manually operated elevator down to the third floor of the Apostolic Palace.

There, in the library, he was to conduct the most important meeting of his life; probably the most important and dramatic audience any pope had given since the outbreak of World War II.

In the elegant papal library, fourteen expensively dressed men and women sat in armchairs deliberately grouped to suggest an informal conversation area.

In the first of the easy chairs, Pius recognized Parker Stevenson, the United States ambassador to Italy. Next to Stevenson sat Señora Maria Guerrero, the official Vatican representative from Spain. Next, Pius cordially acknowledged Sir William Palin from Great Britain, Premier Francisco Nicco of Italy, Wolfgang Ostermann from West Germany, Mrs. Ruth Downing, the U.S. representative to the Vatican.

As he sat down before his distinguished visitors, Pius bowed his head and prayed silently. He prayed for all people: for those represented in the papal library; for those whose countries would not or could not send representatives to the Vatican.

Pius finally looked up. His surprisingly clear and alert eyes met those of the others around the handsome room.

Pius began to speak in Latin, a trusted priest from his staff translating his words first into English, then into German.

"Vos omnes vix scientes raptim advocatos nocte advenire potuisse magnopere honestatus guadeo." Pius spoke calmly and impressively.

"I am greatly honored and pleased that you all could come tonight," the translator spoke, "on such short notice. With very inadequate explanation from us."

"Compertum habeo vos non fugisse qua in causa sit puella Catharina Beavier in America commorans."

"I am sure that you are aware of the situation involving the young girl Kathleen Beavier in America."

"I would like you to know first of all that the Church has chosen to take no official position on the possible divine birth in America," Pius continued. "There are extenuating circumstances which make this a very difficult decision for us.

"Each of your countries is now experiencing some form of unusual emergency. There is great turmoil, great confusion and suffering all around the world at this time.

"There is a polio epidemic which is taking many lives in the United States. There is a great locust and insect problem all through the central parts of Africa. A cruel drought is killing thousands each day in India.

"These are extraordinary natural disasters." Pius's eyes slowly went from face to face around the room. "For all of these things to be occurring at one time is difficult to accept or rationalize.

"This brings me to the point of my urgent message this evening. I am afraid it is a serious warning to your governments, to all of the people in your countries. . . . The warning is this. All of us most now prepare ourselves for the possibility of great change in the world, for possible chaos, even for an apocalyptic time—an end time.

"There is an evil presence in the world which is undeniably strong at this time. . . . If this sounds melodramatic, please consider that I am aware of how open to your ridicule I am right now. Under ordinary circumstances, I would not speak in such an unguarded manner.

"Please take my warning to heart. Please heed this warning first handed down in this century at Fatima in 1917. It is the warning given all through both the Old and the New Testaments: the warning of a Last Judgment for man which must come at some time."

Pius had finally stopped speaking. Letting his eyes go around the circle of armchairs, he saw their concern, the beginnings of fear.

He knew he must impress on them the significance

of the events taking place. He must voice the warning . . .
as preordained:

A pope's warning of widespread chaos.

The possibility of the Apocalypse.

A reminder of the secret messages of Fatima.

The continuing mystery of Kathleen Beavier in America.

"May I please give you my blessing?" Pius asked in the gentlest voice, a voice that reminded the visitors that they were in the presence of a great holy man.

"Good Father, please look over these men and women in the work they must do," Pius intoned. "All the power of Satan shall not prevail against us."

"Res Diabolo nos ne vincant," whispered the Holy Father.

"We shall not be overcome by Satan."

SEVEN

COLLEEN

A thousand crows masked the horizon with black flapping wings, calling to one another in raspy early-morning voices.

Outside the rattling Galaher barn, it was easily twenty degrees colder than the day before. The smell of punishing Irish winters was already in the air, Colleen noticed as she led the horse into the pale green light of morning. Ground that had been soft and springy just the past week was now partially frozen. A slick icing was beginning to hang in the grass tufts, and Gray Lady's hoofs made a clicking sound against the hard turf.

"Now this is goin' to be a real short and sweet ride," Colleen whispered softly to her mother's horse. "Just

101

enough of a jog to strut your stuff, dearie. Ya look pretty this mornin' by the way."

On account of the snapping chill, the old mare was especially frisky, Colleen saw. Her ears were standing up. Lady kept throwing her head way back and snorting white smoke like a locomotive.

Colleen carefully held Gray Lady back in a gentle canter at first. Then the small dark-haired girl began to sit into her horse's forward movement. A feeling of exquisite freedom began to spread through Colleen's body. A beautiful pleasure like no other the country girl knew.

Finally, Colleen let the horse have its own way—to run.

Head all the way forward, heavy tail out perfectly straight, Gray Lady began to thunder over the dull brown-and-green cow pastures. All four of the mare's legs would suddenly lift off the ground at once.

Colleen was blowing out half as much smoke as her horse. She was suddenly working hard. Beginning to perspire. Feeling a release finally. Feeling momentarily free of all her concern, and worries about having the wee baby.

Following the exhilarating run, Colleen got down off Gray Lady to let her breathe. As she walked Lady down near the Liffey Glade, Colleen couldn't help reviewing and in a way reliving much of what had happened during the past few months. The terrible first shock of the pregnancy ... The truly awful reactions of the people in Maam Cross ... And then the strange visitor all the way from Rome. Father Rosetti, who said he would come back to help her.

A quick, furtive movement in the glen suddenly caught Colleen's eye. Then Colleen saw them.

Michael Sheedy, Johno, Liam McInnie, Finton Cleary.

The young girl's heart sank. She moaned softly. Tears came into her green eyes.

"Mornin', Colleen. Cool turn in the weather, no?" Michael called.

Without speaking a word to the boyos, the very frightened young girl began to climb back up on her horse. Colleen was already beginning to tremble badly. *It was so isolated and lonely down near the glen. These boys had been waiting for her. They must have been waiting. Why?*

"Don't try to run from me. Don't you dare it, Colleen! I'll only warn you once," Michael cried out.

Colleen tried to weigh all the terrifying possibilities, the consequences one way or the other. Michael Sheedy meant to harm her, she was certain.

Finally, Colleen shouted out a loud command. Lady began to move.

Then, suddenly, the old horse bucked. Gray Lady's front legs lifted surprisingly high off the ground.

Michael Sheedy had struck the horse with a sharp rock.

"Oh, please no!"

Both Johno Sullivan and Liam McInnie now fired rocks. Johno's pitch clipped Lady's shinbone, cracking hard. Liam's hit in the hind quarters.

"I warned you, harlot!"

"Whore! Village pump!"

Colleen meanwhile was beginning to scream above the harsh, whistling wind. "Easy Lady! Lady!"

The terrified horse reared high a second time. Then Lady broke into a full gallop through the thick underbrush of the dark glen.

Scrub pines and stone fences flashed by on either side of Colleen. Gray Lady was weaving and cutting through the bramble like a fox under heavy pursuit. A prickling bush raked the right side of Colleen's tender face.

All of a sudden the young girl thought of how she had been saved from Liam McInnie before.

The strange and mysterious bird in Maam Cross. The magical thrush.

"Holy Father, please help me," Colleen prayed out loud.

"Please don't let my baby be hurt!"

Just then the exhausted horse stumbled badly against a fallen tree stump. Gray Lady's head and torso dipped to less than a foot above the flashing ground, just above a low bank of flowering montbretea.

Then a loud snap like a thunderbolt in the crisp, fall
air.

A branch?

A leg?

My God, Lady is going over.

Please, please Lord!

Straining her leg and thigh and chest muscles, the
horse tried to stop its fall. It was too little, too late.

Then Colleen was spinning, twisting, falling sideways
through the cold, gray air. Her thin white arms were
rigidly outstretched in front of her. She was desperately
trying to shield herself. To protect the baby inside.

"Please don't let my baby die. Oh please! . . ."

The girl's small hands ripped into something all
scratchy and bristling wet.

Probing hands and fingers were everywhere on her
body.

Then the softest imaginable impact came in the
hundred arms and hands of thick evergreen branches.
Colleen Galaher had been caught by a blue-green pine.

The young girl's fall was cushioned.

She was saved.

A miracle had quietly happened in Maam Cross.

A sign.

ANNE

Kathleen and her mother visited the girl's obstetri-
cian in Boston the following day. For the first time since
she had come to Sun Cottage, Anne found that she had
the better part of a day to herself.

In the morning, Anne sat up in Charles Beavier's
study and read or reread selected books about the Blessed
Virgin: *Our Lady in the Gospels, Our Lady of Fatima,
Woman's Mysteries: Ancient and Modern, a* wonderfully
contemporary book called *Alone of All Her Sex,* which
offered so many true ideas, some of which Anne had
experienced herself.

"The Virgin, sublime model of chastity," Marina Warner, the author of *Alone of All Her Sex* had written, "remained for me the most holy being I could every contemplate, and so potent was her spell that for some years I could not enter a church without pain at all the safety and beauty of the salvation I had forsaken. I remember visiting Notre Dame in Paris and standing in the nave, tears starting in my eyes."

It was so true, Anne thought to herself. *This was the way faith worked, the way it felt.*

Further on in her book, Marina Warner remarked that the Virgin "is one of the few female figures to have attained the stature of myth." *Another important point to keep in mind.* Anne considered.

In a later section of the book, Warner quoted Henry Adams, who had written "The study of Our Lady leads directly back to Eve, and lays bare the whole subject of sex."

Anne spent a solid four hours at Charles Beavier's desk.

The main trouble—there just wasn't that much historical evidence about Mary. Two major theories, based on what scholars loosely called "Christian tradition," were usually accepted in theological circles.

The first was that Mary was the product of an immaculate conception herself; that is, Mary supposedly had been conceived "immaculately," inside the womb of her mother—she had been born without the stigma of original sin.

The second accepted theory was that when Mary had died (perhaps in the ancient city of Ephesus in western Asia Minor; once again, the biblical facts were sketchy), her body had ascended directly into heaven: the Assumption of the Blessed Virgin this was called.

On bright yellow foolscap, Anne wrote.

The Blessed Virgin Mary is the least known, by far the most mysterious, of all major historical figures!

Why was that? Anne considered.

Even as her mind posed the question, however, Anne felt that she had the answer.

Once again, she scribbled on her pad:

Is it because Mary was a woman, a mother, and all of the major Scripture writers were men?

Walking out on the sun-flooded grounds of Sun Cottage around noon, Anne came upon Justin playing tennis with Father Milsap.

To his honor and credit, Justin had completely thrown himself into his work assisting Milsap in every possible way—usually still at it as late as eleven or twelve in the evening. Also, since their unfortunate talk on Cliff-walk Justin had stayed clear of Anne, offering little more than a quiet hello when they occasionally passed inside the Beavier house.

Justin was not a good tennis player. Anne observed the action down on the pretty, red-clay court. Neither of the priests played well.

Their serves were like the opening, wrist-snapping strokes in badminton; their foreheads were strong but as likely to knock the ball over the outside fence as the net; their backhands were more swipes than actual tennis strokes.

Anne found herself smiling at the game, and Justin finally saw her standing on a little nub of lawn.

"Don't laugh," the young priest called out with a smile. "This is not tennis, actually."

"I can see that," Anne started to laugh out loud.

"No. It's an entirely new game invented by Father Milsap and myself. You're the first spectator to actually witness an official match."

"What do you think, Sister?" Father Milsap smiled and waved his racquet like a triumphant flyswatter.

"I think you've both gone mad."

"Mad?" Justin complained. "Our game serves as a very necessary emotional release during our day. Besides, priests shouldn't play either tennis or golf well. That only helps to support our unfortunate current country-club image."

Justin swung and popped one of the fuzzy green Dunlap balls in Anne's direction. Quick as Jimmy Connors, he scooted around the outside fence to retrieve it.

"I think that's about all for me, Father," Justin called back to Father Milsap. "My most accurate shot of the match," he said in a lower voice to Anne.

"I just wanted to apologize for the other afternoon," he continued before Anne had a chance to say anything. "I had no right to offer my egotistical opinion of your life. I'm very sorry, Annie. I really am."

"That's very nice of you to say," Anne stared into Justin's bright green eyes. "Apology accepted," she said.

Anne then walked away from the dripping, over-heated, and red-faced priest. Not really wanting to leave Justin—but doing it anyway. Doing it like a very good Catholic, Anne thought to herself.

At the wheel of the Beaviers' tan Mercedes station wagon that same afternoon, Anne swept along past Newport's famous Bellevue Avenue, heading west on Memorial Boulevard.

Anne was returning from a most stimulating little adventure. She had just explored—she'd walked the complete mile-and-a-half length of Sachuest Park—where Kathleen Beavier had apparently gone parking with some boy nearly nine months before in January.

The mysterious, perhaps mystical evening of January 23.

In a lot of ways, Anne thought to herself as she effortlessly piloted the smooth-riding car, she was feeling more frustrated and confused about Kathleen than she ever had.

The more time she had to think about the particulars of the Newport situation, the less Anne was ready blindly to accept the virgin birth. And yet nothing she came up with could explain away the troubling facts of the story. Nothing made any better logical sense than what was being offered so far.

For one thing, there was Cardinal Rooney's apparent acceptance of the virgin facts.

Anne knew that the Cardinal was a sarcastically brilliant, cynical, and tough-minded priest of the old school. That is to say, Cardinal Rooney wouldn't have been fooled easily. Not by a clever hoax of some kind.

Not by the most elaborate set of coincidences, even if they went all the way back to the Old Testament . . . and John Cardinal Rooney *did* believe in Kathleen Beavier. Cardinal Rooney did believe a holy child was about to be born.

Next, there was the matter of Kathleen herself. Kathleen *was* a virgin, and she was certainly very pregnant. Kathleen said that she'd seen Mary—actually seen the Blessed Virgin—and Anne couldn't *not* believe this young girl she liked so much and also trusted.

Finally, there was a very complex historical perspective to consider, Anne understood.

Christianity was firmly based in a belief in miracles. At the very least, a Christian ought to believe that Jesus Christ, the Son of God, had become man.

As many as a billion people were said to believe this.

And if a miracle was possible two thousand years before, Anne asked herself, wasn't another extraordinary miracle at least possible today?

So why was it so difficult for her truly to believe in the virgin birth right now?

Why did she keep searching for the overlooked logic catch?

As she continued down Memorial Boulevard, Anne saw a gold-and-blue sign pointing to the left just past Spring Street. ROGERS HIGH SCHOOL the sign said. She hit the left-turn signal and made the turn.

Anne had decided to go and see the only other person who might logically know something that could cast some new light on the fantastic puzzle.

She was going to see Kathleen's thus-far anonymous date for the night of January 23.

JAMES JORDAN

His name was James Jordan III.

He was a senior at Rogers High School.

Those were the only two sure facts about the boy that Anne knew. She thought about the implications as the

Beavier station wagon glided down the colorful tunnel of maple and oak trees that was called School Street.

She parked in front of a handsome colonial farm-house, right out of Currier & Ives. She climbed out of the station wagon letting her eyes wander over the house. In a way, she thought, she would have loved to live in a house like that.

Once she got up close to Rogers High School, Anne waited out front with some young mechanic types apparently waiting for their friends to get out.

It was 2:40 on her black-banded wristwatch. Some long-haired boys and girls finally wandered out of the faded red-brick high school. There were still a few minutes until the main bell and total chaos. . . . And hopefully James Jordan.

Her heart beginning to pound, Anne stopped one of the high-school girls as she was coming down the hedge-bordered front walk.

"Excuse me, I'm sorry for bothering you," Anne said to the girl, a redhead with a short tartan skirt and long, freckled legs. "Do you happen to know who James Jordan is?"

The high-school girl's name was Katherine Mahoney and she told Anne that James was usually called Jaime. Katherine then said that she'd seen Jaime during first-period homeroom so he was probably around somewhere.

Perhaps in the mob of students just beginning to squeeze and stampede out of the high school's eight glass doors? Anne suddenly thought.

An electric bell had finally begun to clamor. The noise of joyous youth filled the crisp fall air. An over-inflated football wobbled out away from the sedate, co-lonial-styled school building.

"Is this about the Beavier thing?" Katherine Mahoney asked as she and Anne both turned to face the onrushing crowd.

"Yes it is." Anne had to raise her voice over the crowd noise. "Do they talk about it very much here? The students and teachers?"

"Are you kidding?" Katherine began to put on an orange shade of lipstick which didn't work very well with her bright hair. "That's the *only* thing anybody talks about. If you haven't noticed, this whole town has temporarily flipped out over the virgin thing."

Anne looked at the great barbarous horde of capes, woodchopper's vests, GI caps, all varieties of wool jacshirts. She tried to imagine what a Jaime Jordan III might look like. She tried to guess which of these young men Kathleen might have wanted to date.

"What does everyone think about the virgin?" Anne asked the girl. "What do you think?"

The girl shrugged and shook her head. "Lately, for the last few weeks anyway, Jaime has been telling *everyone* that he slept with Kathleen Beavier. Personally, I don't know or care very much. A lot of kids I know don't really care. Jaime is definitely the kiss-and-tell type, by the way. He has an ego as big as all outdoors. . . . Hey! There he is. That's Jaime Jordan." The redheaded girl pointed a freckled finger toward a noisy pack of seventeen- and eighteen-year-olds slowly aproaching on the crowded sidewalk.

"See the red down vest? Red-checkered wool shirt? That's Jaime."

Anne stared into the mass of shaggy haircuts and lumberman's stag jackets. Her eyes finally settled on a young boy with a bright shock of blond hair. He was tall, lean, a little more in possession of himself than most of the others in the crowd. He had a kind of unconscious swagger about him, Anne thought.

"I don't know if this is a terrific idea," Anne muttered to Katherine, her eyes still on Jaime.

"What's that?"

"I wonder. . . . All right . . . Thank you. Really. Thank you a lot for talking to me," Anne said to the girl.

As she waded into the shrill, frolicking crowd—like trying to avoid rough breakers walking into the ocean—Anne was feeling very uneasy. She was thinking that maybe this wasn't a very good idea after all.

"Hello, my name is Anne Feeney," she said as she came up to a tall, slender boy with blond hair and fine

Chippendale features. "I was told that you're Jaime Jordan."

There was no immediate answer from the handsome boy, just a cool, appraising smile.

"I guess that means you're Jaime," Anne forced a smile, feeling more and more unsure of herself. *This is getting worse by the minute,* she was thinking.

The boy tapped out a cigarette from a red-and-white pack.

"Yeah, I'm Jaime. Why?"

"Would you please walk with me for just a few minutes?" Anne asked the boy. She could feel that her face was turning bright red. "I would like to talk with you alone. I'm not from a magazine or any newspaper. Actually I'm a little nervous and frightened right now. Will you please walk with me?"

Jaime Jordan looked at his friends first. They all smiled and snickered group approval. They were checking out Anne's breasts, her long, slim legs.

"Okay," Jaime finally said. "Let's walk."

"Actually . . . I'm a nun," Anne said as soon as they were out of hearing distance from the others.

Jaime Jordan remained cool, maybe vaguely amused.

"Yeah. Actually, I'm not a student here. I'm really with the Federal Bureau of Narcotics."

Anne started to laugh. She was reminded a little of the girls back at St. Anthony's: their crazy bravado.

"It does sound a little unlikely," Anne smiled at the boy. "People still think of flying nuns, black habits, Sally Fields. Actually, it happens to be true. My part."

"Okay," Jaime said. "You have my attention anyway. What's up Ss-sister? That's the way they say it over at Salve Regina . . ."

"This past spring," Anne said, "you went out with Kathleen Beavier."

"I knew this was coming," Jaime Jordan shook his head. "Okay. I went out with Kathleen Beavier once. One official date. Plus a few trips to get a frappe or something after school."

"How come there was only one date?" Anne asked.

At the same time she couldn't help thinking that they would have made quite a striking couple together.

"How come only one date? Well, we can't spread the boy around too thin, can we?"

Anne controlled a frown. Boys will be boys, she thought.

"Could you be very straight with me for one minute?" she said in her best Hope Cottage voice of authority. "This is really pretty serious, Jaime. It is for me, anyway. I couldn't have gotten the courage together to walk up to you and your friends if it wasn't important."

The blond boy's look softened slightly.

"Hey, I'm walking with you, aren't I?"

"Jaime, will you please tell me exactly what happened back on January twenty-third? I know that you took Kathy to a formal dance at Salve Regina. Please tell me what happened after the dance? Kathleen won't, and it could be important to a lot of people."

A look of anger, maybe even a look of hurt, flashed across Jaime Jordan's face.

"Listen, goddammit, I don't care what she says! *We made it* the night of the big school dance. Everybody knows we made it. Kathy Beavier was like a dead fish I'll admit, but that doesn't make her the blessed virgin. *And she knows that!*"

"Jaime." Anne purposely lowered her voice. "I've seen the doctor's reports. Kathleen is still a virgin. Kathleen Beavier has never made it with *anyone!*"

Jaime Jordan's hands suddenly flew up out of the pockets of his red vest. For a second, Anne was afraid she was going to get punched out right there on School Row.

"Hey bullshit!" he screamed at her instead. "I had her, with *this!*"

Jaime Jordan grabbed himself hard between the long legs of his faded jeans. Then he whirled around and walked away from Anne.

"Oh, dammit," Anne muttered as students continued to pass on both sides of her, nudging, some of them staring at the misplaced older woman, two girls boldly lighting up twisted marijuana cigarettes.

Anne was beginning to tremble now. She thought she could use a cigarette herself. She couldn't really believe what she'd just done—talked to Jaime Jordan all on her own authority.

At the same time, she was thinking that either Jaime Jordan was a terrible psychopathic liar, what they called a sociopath at St. Anthony's . . .

Or Kathleen Beavier was.

ANNE AND KATHLEEN

Anne watched closely, curiously, as Kathleen fingered an old rag doll that was something like a combination between Charlie McCarthy and Huckleberry Finn.

When she had been seven or eight years old, Kathleen had made the clever doll herself.

The face was a flesh-colored stocking stuffed with rolled-up paper towels. The doll had dotty black eyes, a big bulbous nose, a knitted-on smile, eyeglasses made from electrician's wire. The doll wore one of her father's bow ties. It had a real hankie in the pocket of a real little boy's shirt. The doll's suspenders were made of plaid ribbons; they held up walking shorts, large argyle socks, real little Buster Brown shoes . . . Kathleen had named the homemade doll Mr. Fibs.

"I made it myself," Kathleen suddenly looked up at the bedroom doorway where she'd sensed that someone was standing and watching her.

"I must have been a smart little whip when I was a little girl."

"Don't you feel smart any more? . . . my old lady of seventeen!"

"No." Kathleen smiled at Anne. "I'm afraid the magic is all gone. No more magic."

Anne walked farther into Kathleen's cozy, honey-yellow bedroom. She noted stacks of rock and classical records. Glossy *Lord of the Rings* posters. A fairly normal seventeen-year-old's room.

"Kathy, I came up here . . . to ask you kind of an important question."

Anne sat in a yellow pine rocker beside Kathleen's canopy bed. "Do you really trust me, Kathy? I mean really and truly?"

"Is *that* the important question?"

Anne cleared her throat and took a deep breath. She let the air out very slowly.

"No . . . but do you?"

Kathleen smiled. That incredibly innocent and infectious smile of hers; an absolutely charismatic smile, Anne thought once again.

"I trust you very much . . ." Kathleen's eyes looked down at the childhood doll instead of at Anne's face. "I . . . I also love you, Anne."

Anne found that she had to reach down deep, right into the pit of her stomach, for her next breath. *Why was it that Kathleen could affect her like that?* Kathleen could knock the wind out of her just about any time she wanted to with a few specially chosen words. With a look. A smile.

"Kathleen . . . will you please tell me about Jaime Jordan?" Anne finally asked. "I went and I saw him today. I spoke with Jaime. Kathy, he said that . . ."

"He said we had intercourse. He tells that to people because he thinks that's what they expect from him. I feel so sorry for Jaime Jordan. His whole macho fantasy."

Kathleen held the precious rag doll in her thin arms. She looked like such a frightened little girl holding the doll. Like a strange modern-day madonna. Her face was so incredibly innocent, Anne thought to herself.

"We didn't make love. We didn't even kiss. Jaime took me to go parking out on Sachuest Park Road, but I wouldn't do anything. I didn't love him; he didn't love me. He was like an ugly animal. He became like that. That's everything there is to tell right now," the young blonde girl said.

She looked up into Anne Feeney's eyes and Kathleen felt so bad. She felt terrible about half-lying to Anne . . . She did love her! There was something about Anne's generosity; her openness and honesty.

"Don't you believe me, Anne?" Kathleen asked. "Please believe me, Sister Anne. If no one believes . . . what will happen to me? What will happen to the child?"

KATHLEEN

Kathleen could feel a terrible hammer-heavy pounding inside the most sensitive creases of her forehead. Her head felt as if powerful hands were trying to rip it into halves.

Even before anything actually happened, she felt the intense pressure, the foreboding that something really bad was starting now at Sun Cottage.

She tiptoed to her bedroom window and pulled back the lacy chintz curtains. Kathleen didn't even know exactly *why* she had gone to the window.

She could see her breath, a pale, ghostly gray film on the black windowpane.

Outside was the fuzzy cold light of carriage lamps strung up the driveway toward Ocean Avenue. Private security guards in dark fur-collared parkas were standing at the front gate, the way soldiers do sentry duty on army posts.

Looking straight down beneath her window, Kathleen saw him.

He was being greeted by Cardinal Rooney's assistant, Father Milsap, as well as by the young Irish priest, Father O'Carroll.

He was wearing a black fedora hat with the brim severely pointed down. He carried a shiny black satchel filled to bursting.

His shoulders were all rounded and bent—carrying the weight of the world, no doubt.

Just before he entered Sun Cottage, he looked up at the dimly glowing window on the second floor.

Father Rosetti looked right into my eyes, Kathleen thought with a shudder. He already knows the truth, but he hasn't the faith to believe it.

The priest with the dark eyes had finally arrived.

FATHER EDUARDO ROSETTI

The first meeting was held that night in one of the handsome double parlors on the first floor of Sun Cottage.

Kathleen sat on a rigid hardbacked chair, her protruding stomach ready to burst open from the look of it.

Sister Anne Feeney sat on one side of the teenage blonde girl. Mr. and Mrs. Beavier, seeming very tense and nervous, were on the other side. The maid, Mrs. Walsh, was hovering about, serving tea and coffee. Fathers Milsap and O'Carroll sat closest to the sliding oak doors, both of them in flowing black soutanes which seemed to be from another age entirely.

Father Eduardo Rosetti appeared nervous and troubled as he stood before them in the elegant room.

Father Rosetti continually clasped and unclasped his large, horned workman's hands. His eyes were surprisingly gentle, though, surprisingly relaxed. His infrequent smile was warm, even intimate.

When it came, his voice was soft, patient, very easy to listen to.

"I have been sent here by the Vatican," Father Rosetti said to them. "My official title is Chief Investigator for the Congregation of Rites. Sometimes I've played the role of the Devil's Disciple or Postulator of the Cause.

"This Congregation of Rites is the sacred body within the Church that investigates miracles, all varieties of supernatural phenomena, claims of sainthood. I am under the direct supervision and orders of His Holiness Pope Pius XIII."

Father Rosetti looked into Kathleen Beavier's soft blue eyes.

"I'm like a . . . a tax investigator of the supernatural." The broad-faced priest smiled. "I can be a huge pain in the neck. But I'm really quite a harmless bureaucrat. You don't have to be afraid of me. Please don't be."

"I'm not," the blonde teenager shook her head. "I'm not afraid of you, Father."

Kathleen did appear physically ill, however. She seemed pallid on the outside, possibly bruised inside. Kathleen looked as if she might have the baby right there.

"Kathleen . . . is the Blessed Virgin Mary here with us tonight?" the priest from the Vatican suddenly asked.

Father Rosetti put forth the idea informally, as if the strange, leading question was small talk to be bantered about.

Kathleen took a deep breath that pushed her upright against the straining hardbacked chair. Her stomach swelled out like a gas balloon curtained in pale blue. She pushed back a wisp of beautiful silken hair.

"She is here. Yes," Kathleen said in a soft whisper.

"Inside the house?" the priest asked, one of his bushy black eyebrows curving upward.

"Yes, inside the house. She's here."

"In this very room with us, Kathleen?"

"Yes. Right inside this room, Father."

"I'm sorry, Kathleen," Father Rosetti said softly, "I suppose I am just not used to having Our Blessed Mother around . . . Is she quite beautiful? Is she standing up, Kathleen? Is she sitting over in that blue chair, perhaps?"

"Father Rosetti," Kathleen said. "I know what you're trying to do, but please don't. Our Lady is here with us. In appearance she is like a beautiful gentlewoman. You must act as you would, if you *could* believe in her."

"Kathleen, I'm concerned only with what *you* believe," the Vatican priest said softly. "Let us go on. Please."

During his exchange with Kathleen, the parlor had grown uncomfortably silent.

"Ever since I was a boy in the schools of Sicily," Father Rosetti now looked around to the others in the parlor, "I have heard the consecrated representatives of Our Lord . . . his priests . . . using such meaningless and trite phrases as 'Our Lord functions in strange and mysterious ways, my son.' I always resented that sort of loose

talk very, very much. It was a sham, I felt, deep inside
me. It was false and destructive talk. It told me that the
inner beliefs of these priests were very shallow.

"I would like to explain why I have come here very
plainly and clearly, therefore. My coming here to America is not at all mysterious. It can be very logically
explained, I think.

"The Vatican is greatly interested in the birth of
your child, Kathleen. . . . Many people all around the
world are already calling it the second Virgin Birth.

"Newspapers, television, radio, everyone is watching
the Church once again. Great hopes and expectations are
being raised. People are actually re-examining and evalu-
ating their ideas about God."

The Vatican priest's strong face was beginning to
show tension and worry. He was pacing in front of a case
filled with Charles Beavier's hunting rifles. The parlor
scene was becoming more and more uncomfortable for
everyone.

"Now I must tell you the most extraordinary news."

The Chief Investigator for the Congregation of Rites
bowed his head first. He finally looked up.

He said the next few words to Kathleen alone.

"One of the things I have uncovered thus far. One of
the few things I'm truly sure about," Father Eduardo
Rosetti said in his soft but firm and impressive voice, "is
that there are actually . . . *two* virgins."

"I know that there are two of us. At least two,"
Kathleen said so softly that only Father Rosetti could
hear her.

"How do you know it?" the Vatican priest asked, his
brown eyes narrowing to slits, his great chest beginning to
heave. "Kathleen, you must tell me how you know that.
Please tell me everything that you know about all this.
Kathleen, this is so important."

While Kathleen and Father Rosetti whispered all the
others in the formal sitting room began to talk at once, it
seemed. Two virgins? Who was this Roman priest? What
did he want from them? From Kathleen?

"Father Rosetti? Sir? Will you please tell us what all

of this means?" Mr. Charles Beavier finally stood up to
be heard in the buzzing room. "Please, Father."

"I said I would tell you everything that I know,"
Rosetti turned to the father of Kathleen Beavier. "I would
like to tell you now. Everything I know about this deeply
troubling affair. Please sit down. Listen for a moment
more.

"In July," the Italian priest remained in front of the
case of expensive rifles, "I was summoned from my apartment near the Porta Angelico to the Apostolic Palace,
where the Holy Father lives.

"Since I had never seen Pius XIII in anything more
than an audience with a hundred other priests—all acting
like immature gawking schoolboys, I must say—you
might be able to imagine my great surprise and trepida-
tion previous to the visit.

"I finally walked to the Apostolic hall after the
dinner hour that afternoon. Then, at the Apostolic Palace
itself, I received my second numbing surprise. Not only
was I to meet with Pope Pius, I was to see him alone
inside his private apartment, an honor that only a handful
of cardinals have ever received.

"Pius, it turned out, knew a great deal about my
work as Chief Investigator for the Congregation of Rites.
Essentially what I do is to track down the true facts about
possible miracles and claims of sainthood. I record and
document the facts. It is very much like an investigation
before a jury trial."

Father Rosetti paused and let his eyes slowly, effectively wander around the large room. They were all
listening intently to him now—listening in awe to this
strange dark priest who had met in private with Pope
Pius.

"The Holy Father and I talked about incidental
matters for what must have been fifteen or twenty minutes. Then Pius began to tell me a long and amazing story
about the famous miracle which occurred at Fatima in
October of 1917.

"When I noticed the time again, more than three
hours had passed . . . I'm not attempting to be a good

storyteller either. That is exactly as it happened. The time
flew by like a very few minutes. . . . The main point in all
that Pope Pius had told me seemed to be that at Fatima,
Lucia dos Santos had received an enormously important
and controversial message from the person the little girl
called the Gentlewoman.

"Only four men have read this message in the last
twenty-seven years—Pope John XXIII, Paul VI, Pope
John Paul, Pius himself. . . . None of the popes has ever
been able to reveal the seventy-year-old-message to a
single other person. John and Paul VI did hint at the
message's great importance. Both popes spoke of two
parts to the message of Fatima. First, a terrible warning
for all of us on earth. Second, a great and hopeful
promise from this Gentlewoman.

"This past summer in Rome, Pope Pius XIII told
me the message of Fatima revealed that there were two
virgins, perhaps more than two. He told me that I must
investigate the virgins in the same way that I would
investigate a great and very important miracle. 'One of
these young women may give birth to a very special
child,' Pope Pius said to me. A *divine child,* the Holy
Father said."

After many, many questions had been answered in
the parlor of Sun Cottage, Anne found that a rather
important one still remained unasked.

"Father Rosetti," Anne finally succeeded in getting
the attention of the Vatican priest. "You said before that
you were going to tell us why you've come here to
Newport. I'm not exactly sure that you have told us. Not
in a particular sense anyway."

Kathleen suddenly sat forward in her chair. Her
wide blue eyes went from Anne to Father Rosetti. In turn,
she spoke to each of them.

"Father Rosetti has come here to attempt to find out
which of us is the true virgin," Kathleen said.

The Vatican priest looked into the eyes of the innocent and very pretty American girl. He solemnly nodded
his large head. His eyes never left Kathleen's.

Nor did the eyes of Kathleen's parents, Sister Anne

Feeney, Fathers O'Carroll and Milsap, or those of the family maid Mrs. Walsh.

Nor the legions of eyes gathering outside on the night grounds of Sun Cottage.

Gleaming eyes watching . . . waiting . . . beginning to scream and screech in unison.

EIGHT

COLLEEN

At four-thirty on the morning of October sixth a single hard knock came against the thick bedroom door of Father Eduardo Rosetti.

Then a loud knocking came at the door of Father Justin O'Carroll.

Finally, a persistent knock at the door of Sister Anne Feeney.

By five they were all dressed and had come downstairs to the Beavier library, where they were met by Father Martin Milsap and by Mrs. Walsh with a tray of hot coffee and buttered toast.

"Father Rosetti has asked me to speak to you for

him," Father Milsap finally spoke, looking at Anne first, then at Father O'Carroll.

"It seems that a visit to the second virgin, a young girl in Ireland, is necessary at this time. Father Rosetti has questions to ask the girl. He has an important physical examination which must be made as well.

"It seems reasonable that someone else go to offer a second opinion about the girl. To help Father in any way we possibly can. On account of the complications here in Newport, I don't see how I can go myself. On the other hand, Sister . . . you know the virgin situation very well.

"You are actually *from* Ireland, Father O'Carroll . . . Father Rosetti suggested that the two of you might accompany him."

Anne and Justin quickly exchanged glances.

"I would like to meet the other girl," Anne finally said.

"Of course I'll go," Justin nodded.

Father Eduardo Rosetti suddenly smiled—a surprisingly warm and open smile.

"Very good," he said in a hearty voice somewhat inappropriate for the hour. "We'll leave here in an hour. I think you will find Colleen Galaher extraordinary. Quite extraordinary."

The British Airways Concorde to Shannon Airport in Ireland was a decent restaurant which happened to fly, which made up for other deficiencies by offering an overabundance of medium-good food and first-class drink.

A large piping-hot breakfast was hurried to Fathers Rosetti and O'Carroll and Sister Anne Feeney following the hook-nosed jet's controversial supersonic takeoff.

After breakfast, hot perfumed towels and a kit containing slippers and a sleeping mask were brought.

Both Anne and Justin, meanwhile, were staring wide-eyed out the jet's book-sized windows. Because the Concorde flies so high, they could actually see the curvature of the earth at one point. It was quite something to look at; they felt like astronauts for a short time.

A handsomely arranged brunch was brought next. Before the meal could possibly be digested, however, the

Concorde was falling out of a thick cloud bank, gliding down toward the glinting metal roof of Shannon.

The first part of their journey to see the second virgin had been completed in record time and comfort.

During the lengthy car ride from Shannon, Father Rosetti couldn't say enough about how fortunate it was that Father O'Carroll was a native of Ireland; how it must be Divine Providence working in their favor.

After nearly two hours driving through low, striking hills that must have shown a hundred different shades of green, they came upon the most incredible textured brown quilt of barley and oat fields.

Next came a vivid hill of ferns and evergreens that was like a dark roller coaster on the horizon.

A glassy black streak appeared and was soon recognized to be a crystalline river.

Then up popped the quaint village of Maam Cross; like some dim, ancient, fairy-tale city, it seemed to Anne.

There was a wooden gray-and-white road marker for the town. Next to the name itself, *God's Country* was scrawled in bright red.

Turning down a narrow paved lane, Anne, Justin, and Father Rosetti began to see the most anachronistic druids, village men all dressed in earthy browns. There were perhaps twenty men wearing brown suits; twenty plaid caps; twenty pairs of black boots, obviously the work of the same cobbler.

"This is the last real peasantry in all of Western Europe," Justin said with a shy smile that expressed either pride or moderate embarrassment.

I believe we've just officially entered Maam Cross," Father Rosetti said, seeming to be ignoring any of the culture shock.

There were a few one-room stores on the main street of the Irish village. Antique advertising posters: *Player's Please, Guinness for Greatness*. A livery stable and garage housed in one building. A row of sagging stone cottages too tasteless to be called charming.

Inside each of the cottages there would be a standard family room, Justin explained as they slowly passed through the town. This room would be the store-area for souvenirs, a television, numerous religious pictures; it would also be the place for having tea when the priest called. The bedrooms would all be cramped and tiny. There would be bad lighting in all the rooms. Also present would be the heavy smell of a turf fire, perhaps the odor of mackintoshes drying over hard wooden chairs.

Anne said that she found it impossible to believe that she was actually in Ireland for the day.

The home of Colleen Galaher was a mile or so east of town, just beyond a Bushmill's factory.

It was a respectable whitewashed cottage with mortarless walls and a thatched roof made from long rushes. Perhaps because the Irish girl was so isolated—perhaps because of God's will—the story of Colleen's special condition hadn't attracted any attention outside of cruel gossipy Maam Cross itself.

"That's a peat fire you smell," Justin explained as the three of them climbed out of their rented car. "All smoored up and alive. You won't forget that smell."

Anne looked over at Justin and she could see that he was greatly affected by the renewed sights and smells of his native country. She couldn't help but be pleased for him. Anne even wondered if Justin would have been better off if he'd never left Ireland.

"Colleen Galaher's father died a year or so back. A regular Finn McCool sort of man," Father Rosetti commented as they walked toward the cottage. "Her mother has had a stroke. She's forced to stay in her bed most days—the doctors out here are not terribly sophisticated. It's not the best situation for the girl. Much, much different than at the Beaviers'."

As they came through the gate of the low stone wall surrounding the cottage, the door suddenly swung open.

They all saw a nun; a severe-looking woman, her black habit blowing in the soft Irish breeze.

"Father Rosetti, you're back to see us," the nun called out in a friendly voice. She waved and smiled brightly at the Vatican priest.

"Sister Katherine Dominica. . . . This is Father Justin O'Carroll. Father O'Carroll is a native of County Cork. This is Sister Anne Elizabeth Feeney."

The Irish nun bowed her head in the direction of the visitors from America. Dun-colored hairs peeked out from under her stiff white cap. "Hello, hello," she whispered, ushering them inside.

As they all stood inside the door, a dark-haired girl in a white smock stood up from a low stool by the fire.

"*Hello*, Father Rosetti!" she said with obvious delight and surprise.

"Ah, here's Colleen." Father Rosetti smiled, and it was like the sun peeking through the darkest thunderheads. "The prettiest girl in Eire."

Colleen Galaher most definitely looked eight and a half months pregnant, both Anne and Justin saw at once. Her great, convex stomach seemed a terrible mistake— not only according to the laws of biology, but to those of physics as well.

Like Kathleen Beavier, she seemed so impossibly young and innocent. She had large, pale green eyes; healthy, rosy cheeks; a long delicate neck like a pretty flower stem.

She was such a small, delicate child . . . to be pregnant.

Fourteen years old, Anne couldn't help thinking. *The exact age of Mary of Nazareth when Jesus was born.*

"Could I get tea for anyone?" the Irish girl asked in a sweet, shy voice. "Some homemade soda bread after your long journey?"

In a small corner of her mind, Anne almost felt that she was betraying poor Kathleen. She liked the Irish girl quite a lot; she was thinking. Why in God's name were there two virgins? Anne wondered now more than ever.

After tea, Father Justin O'Carroll wandered out beyond a pale rim of trampled-down hay circling the Galaher cottage. His hands were unconsciously clenched, thrust into the deep pockets of his woolen trousers.

A coarse wind was raising dust across the low pas-

ture of reeds and dark red wild flowers. The wind squared
back Justin's hair in front. It lifted the soft black curls off
his overcoat collar. Made him look like a young, handsome sailor of the plains.

He was suddenly feeling overwhelmed by gathering
doubts and emotions. . . . It was one thing to be three
thousand miles across the Atlantic in Boston. It was quite
another thing to be home, fully confronting the direction
and intent of his vocation and life.

Now he could all too easily picture the pious scorn
of his superiors in Dublin; the legitimate disappointment
of his friends and sponsors throughout his order. Even
more serious, Justin considered, there was the damage his
leaving the Holy Ghost Fathers could bring to his family
back in Cork. There was no way that his mother and
father, his brothers and sisters, could begin to understand
what the past two years had been like in Boston. No
priest in their limited experience had ever openly taken up
with a woman, much less a Sister.

And yet . . . and yet . . . Justin thought.

He could feel that his love and respect for Anne had
never been greater. The contradictions were maddening!
The guilt was a physical, tangible horror. His betrayal of
trusts and sacred vows, of others' hopes and dreams for
him, was a living nightmare.

*My God, I am heartily sorry . . . . For offending Thee.
For offending all who have placed great trust in me. . . .
For offending myself, I think. . . .*

He hiked his dark collar up against the damp cold.
His whole body felt the flush of fear and shame. He
shivered involuntarily.

Damn it, he didn't want to hurt anyone in the Holy
Ghost order. Justin thought that he would do almost
anything to avoid hurting those proud and holy men. He
didn't want to become a profane example for other young
priests to follow, either.

More than anything else, Justin didn't want to see
his family harmed. He couldn't stand to have them slan-
dered and vilified, much as young Colleen Galaher was
cruelly taunted here in Maam Cross.

For the first time in over a year, Justin thought that he might be able to give Anne up. He could see no other way out of the problem. No other answer at that moment.

The tall dark-haired priest swung around in the direction of the small off-white cottage.

"Lord, why have you brought me here?" the young priest prayed softly under the whistling wind. *"Why have you brought me home again?"*

After Colleen had served tea and bread to everyone, she and Father Eduardo Rosetti went for a walk down the solitary brown path that twisted along behind the Galaher cottage. It was more like a muddy stream than a proper road, really. It was a dull, uneven seam sewn into the otherwise bright green countryside.

Eventually they came upon the idyllic Liffey Glade.

Once inside the evergreen glen, Colleen finally told Father Rosetti what had happened to her on the night of January twenty-third. The young girl's secret related in very important ways to the message of Fatima. For the first time Eduardo Rosetti thought that he might know some of the truth about the two young virgins.

JAIME JORDAN

Jaime Jordan III, Chris Grimwood, and Peter Schweitzer were a classic, textbook example of how male bonding in America hasn't changed in the last thirty years.

The three young men had been best friends, just about inseparable buddies since their grammar-school days in Newport. They had been coming to Neely's Long Bar in Portsmouth since the summer of their sophomore year, when they'd all worked as painters and go-fers at Mr. Grimwood's boatyard.

The Long Bar was typical of a special breed of tank bar in most small American towns: the "kiddie bar" it's called. Proof of age is checked only by an occasional visiting state trooper. The bar usually has a special corner reserved for the schoolies, as Tom Neely affectionately called his youngest patrons.

In front of Chris Grimwood and Peter Schweitzer were three cold, foaming drafts of Narragansett beer. On the color TV over the bar, the blue- and red-clad Rangers were pulverizing the local-favorite Boston Bruins. Behind the bar, hizzoner Tom Neely was politely listening to the stale patter of ethnic jokes and tall tales that were mostly ego trips rather than entertainment.

"I don't like what's been happening to our boy," Chrissie Grimwood was saying while Jaime made a quick run into the men's room. "He's very spacy. He's whacking down ludes like they were Flintstone vitamins. You know, he's coming to Neely's for liquid lunches on schooldays now. Old Tom told me before. Even he's concerned."

Peter Schweitzer thoughtfully plucked at the tufts of his new red beard. "Hey! Wait a minute, now. Hold on there. How would you feel being the prospective father of you-know-who?"

"Hey, I mean it, Peter. He's been having those migraine headaches. I'm really worried about Jaime. I shit you not."

Peter Schweitzer suddenly reached for his beer. "He's coming," he whispered into his bushy chin.

Jaime Jordan sauntered up to the crowded long bar with a wounded look on his face. He pushed his hand back through his long blond curls.

"You guys don't have to stop gossiping because I'm back. You can talk about me in front of my face. Chrissie? Schweitz?"

Chris Grimwood rolled his dark eyes back into his forehead. "Paranoid! Do you believe him, Schweitz?"

Jaime Jordan's face turned bright red. "Schweitzer, were you talking about me or what? If you weren't I'll buy the next round."

"Shots or beers?" Peter Schweitzer said, trying to relieve the potentially bad scene the best way he could.

"Hey, Jaime. This is Chris and Peter you're talking to."

"Yeah, and I asked the two of you a simple question."

"We happened to be trying to help you," Chris Grimwood finally said.

Which was when Jaime Jordan hit his friend hard in the chest with a closed fist. The dark-haired boy reeled off his chair in slow motion. He quietly slipped down onto the puckered linoleum floor.

Tom Neely grabbed for an old hardwood walking stick and waved it high over his bar. "You hoodlums cut the crap here or I'll brain the lot of ya!"

Neely's went dead quiet. The older working men all glared down toward the schoolies' corner. Part of the unspoken arrangement in the bar was that the young boys minded their manners.

Jaime Jordan spun away from the bar. He lunged forward toward the front door, bumping into ossified regulars who complained to one another rather than confront the tall, athletic youth himself.

Outside, with the sea breeze whipping across his face, Jaime Jordan thought about going right back in and wiping the floor with Schweitzer and Grimwood. *Oh hell!* he finally thought and smacked his palm hard. *Kathleen Beavier was the one he ought to wipe out.*

Walking to his car, Jaime remembered how he'd had to get down on his knees and beg for a date with her. He'd driven over to Salve Regina to meet the Catholic schoolgirls getting out of class on four different afternoons. He'd even worn his best Shetland sweaters and ironed levis. There was something special about Kathleen Beavier, he had to admit. Jaime had wanted her more than he'd ever wanted any girl. Not just for the sex, either. Jaime had wanted to be with her, to be around Kathleen.

Jaime fired up the motor of his '78 MG. He twisted the radio on full volume and jerked the neat red sports car out of Neely's parking lot.

As he motored up the steep cobblestone hill behind Neely's, Jaime Jordan began to think back to the night of January twenty-third. The night he'd taken Kathleen to the Salve Regina spring dance.

Jaime's parents were wealthy themselves, but Jaime had still felt intimidated as he'd driven up to the Beavier house that night the previous spring.

An old black with fuzzy white hair had answered the front door. The black man asked if he was Mr. Jordan come to escort Miss Kathleen to the dance? Jaime said that he was, and he was led into a handsome parlor filled with all kinds of antiques.

Just a few minutes later, Kathleen appeared at the parlor door. Not half an hour late, the way a lot of girls liked to make you wait around for them.

The sight of Kathleen actually took Jaime Jordan's breath away.

She was wearing a sleek white dress instead of one of the puffy gowns that made girls look so ridiculous on prom nights. Her long blonde hair was set simply and beautifully. She had a silver tiara on top of her curls, and she honestly looked like some kind of a queen, Jaime thought.

The dance at Salve Regina was almost as bad as Jaime had imagined it would be. The brand was a stiff, middle-aged quartet that played all of the Newport Club and debutante teas. Besides that, there was an old-fashioned wooden running track that circled the gym one story above the dance floor. Up on the running track, flocks of Carmelite nuns watched the dance from beginning to end. The nuns seemed to have a knack for laughing and tapping their feet at all the wrong times.

There was supposed to be a fancy party after the dance—engraved invitations had said "Come to a great bash at Elaine Scaparella's house." Outside in the parking area, Jaime talked Kathleen into going for a ride down near Second Beach and Sachuest Point.

SACHUEST POINT

That was where all the trouble had begun. Everything crazy and impossible to understand . . . the whole virgin-birth story.

As Jaime Jordan headed out past Second Beach on the night of October sixth, the high beams of his MG were glowing swords of light stabbing through the thick, dreamy fog.

Jaime was finally driving back to Sachuest Point—where he had taken Kathleen Beavier almost nine months before.

The odd thing was—Jaime wasn't exactly sure *why* he was going back.

As he banked the sports car around a soft S curve, the handsome blond youth noticed that one of his bad headaches was coming on. *Oh Jesus, not already*, Jaime thought to himself. He wasn't even close to being finished for the night. Not by a long shot.

Jaime looked down at the MG's polished wood dashboard. The car's glowing clock said nine fifty-four. Jaime watched the clock's second hand twitch a beat, another beat. His head was splitting already. The headache was like a ringing and a pounding right at the top of his skull; it was simultaneous noise and pain.

Memorial Boulevard slimmed down into a ruler-straight two-lane blacktop as it approached Sachuest Point. There was a small wildlife refuge out there. Flocks of seagulls and a few heavyset gannets. In the spring and fall there were loads of fishermen casting for blues and stripers. And local high-school kids coming to park on dates, to watch the submarines go out from Portsmouth.

In his rear-view mirror Jaime could see the receding lights of southeastern Newport. All the glittery mansions on the coast ... almost like a big army camped on the side of a hill.

"I just want to be like ever-y-body else!" Billy Joel was singing his heart out on the radio. "Oh why can't I be like ever-y-body else?"

The day after the Salve Regina dance, Jaime was remembering, he had told Peter, Chris, a few other friends that he'd made love to Kathleen. "I broke a vagina from Salve Regina," he'd strutted and bragged. Chris Grimwood had eventually told his girlfriend, who happened to go to Salve Regina with Kathleen. ...

Jaime had finally seen Kathleen three or four days after the school dance. She had looked so hurt and incredibly sad, he could still remember. He had gone up to her, and Kathleen had said she would never talk to him again . . . never . . . not until the day she died.

But he *had* to talk with Kathleen, Jaime had finally decided. Right now. Tonight.

Jaime reached up and held his head with one hand.

The pain was so bad it was making him nauseated. He could feel icy fingers grabbing onto his spinal column. And it was getting worse.

Jaime Jordan finally put both hands up to try to hold the top of his head on, to stop the incredible piercing pain.

"Please God, I'm sorry for what I did," the teenage boy whispered. "Please God, please God, please God."

The red MG swerved slightly to the left, just crossing the double white stripe.

Jaime's hands flew back to the steering wheel.

The sports car barely missed an oncoming station wagon, its fishing tackle waving wildly from the roof.

Chrome yellow headlights temporarily blinded Jaime.

An angry car horn trailed off into the thickening fog.

"Whew! Too close," Jaime said out loud, the beers he'd had at Neely's thickening his speech.

The MG was still skidding on the slick black road, though.

Then the small car's front wheels completely left the ground. The MG was shooting straight out with the centrifugal pull.

The car's headlamps picked up raw edges of mossy rock, dark waves crashing in from the sea, dust particles and insects in the air.

Eighteen-year-old Jaime Jordan screamed high above the music playing on the radio.

He never actually felt the crushing head-on collision with the sea wall.

Or the violent explosion as the MG burst into flames

that flickered and glowed in the dark night at Sachuest
Point.

KATHLEEN

The digital clock on Kathleen Beavier's night table
silently announced that it was 11:24:05, 11:24:06,
11:24:07. The inexorable march of time; faithfully re-
corded in the most important-looking stop-sign red nu-
merals.

Kathleen's hand slowly slid from under warm covers
which sloped down off the mound of her stomach. She
reached for the *bbrrrrrringing* telephone.

"Uhm . . . hello?"

Kathleen heard the uncertain distant-sounding voice
of her friend Jeanette Stewart.

"Oh Kathleen, I'm sorry to call this late. I made
them put me through to you."

"Jeanette? What's the matter, Jeanette?"

"Oh Kathy, Jaime Jordan cracked up his car. I just
heard it on WPRO." Jeanette Stewart suddenly began to
cry over the phone.

"Oh Kathy . . . *he's dead.*"

In a partial daze, crying, Kathleen began to tug on a
flannel shirt, jeans, heavy boots.

The young girl was feeling swimmingly nauseated.

She touched her cheek and her hand felt like a cold,
lifeless stone.

"Sweet Virgin, please help me right now . . . please."

A cup of golden light shimmered at the far end of
the upstairs hallway. Kathleen walked down toward the
inviting light, the house creaking like an old ship under
her feet. Mrs. Walsh was still up, which surprised Kathleen.

She passed through a small, dimly lit anteroom that
led to her father's bedroom.

Charles Beavier was sitting in a high-backed red
leather chair. A sheaf of business papers lay in his lap.

He had drifted off to sleep, still dressed in the white shirt and suit pants he'd worn into Boston that morning. *Poor daddy. He can never relax from his business,* Kathleen thought.

Charles Beavier opened his eyes as Kathleen entered the room. A look of concern crossed his face as he saw her.

"Daddy," Kathleen said, "there's been an accident." She could feel tears suddenly sliding down her cheeks. "The boy who took me to that dance last spring. Jaime Jordan. He had a car accident.

"I have to go there. I have this awful feeling that I'm responsible somehow. Will you please drive me, Daddy?"

Charles Beavier stared into his daughter's sad eyes for a moment, registering the shock and determination in her expression.

"Are you sure you should go, Kathy?"

Kathleen nodded her head. Her eyes were so gentle, so good. For weeks now, Charles Beavier had secretly been going to different churches in Boston; he had been sitting in the naves, staring at statues of the Blessed Virgin Mary. . . . Why did the eyes always seem to be the same? Why did Kathleen have those same sad, loving eyes? Almost like an exact imitation of the statues.

"I'll take you, then. If you must go."

To avoid the curiosity-seekers usually congregated at the front gate, Charles Beavier drove the Lincoln down over a gravel road that ran parallel to the beach, then twisted out of the beach bramble half a mile south of the main house.

Ocean Avenue was winter-slick, both Charles and Kathleen noticed immediately. The beachside road was like a twisting ribbon of shiny black glass.

"There's going to be more than one road accident tonight," Charles Beavier spoke in a soft, detached voice. Meanwhile, he kept both hands rigidly clasped onto the steering wheel; he kept his eyes fastened to the center stripe of the road.

"How do you feel, sweatheart?"

"I feel fine," Kathleen whispered into the collar of her parka. "I'm okay."

She was hugging herself and the baby tightly, though.

"Oh, Daddy," Kathleen finally cried out in the speeding car. "Daddy, I feel so bad. I don't want anything else to happen. I don't want to have this baby. Please make it stop."

Her father pulled the Lincoln onto a muddy bumpy shoulder off the ocean drive.

He slid across the leather seat and hugged his daughter tight against his overcoat. He held Kathleen against his heaving chest and Charles Beavier remembered the strange night of January twenty-third . . . the way he had found her . . . the look in her eyes.

They arrived at Sachuest Point a little past eleven-thirty.

The bleak, bald hillside which marked the beginning of the Wildlife Preserve was indirectly lit by the head-lamps of a long procession of cars which had come from the direction of town.

City of Newport and Portsmouth police vehicles were parked helter-skelter all over the hill.

Two shiny red fire-pumpers were balanced on the bluff down near the accident scene.

"I have to go down there," Kathleen said to her father. "This is exactly where it happened. This is where it all started in January."

There was a freezing wet wind slicing up from the ocean. Waves were crashing like thunder on the rocks just beyond the roadside.

Both the waves and the rocks were invisible, though, because of a thick bluish-gray fog that lay over the entire area.

At least a hundred people were loitering outside their cars, trying to get a better look at the accident, trying to grasp the newest twist in the story of Kathleen Beavier.

When Kathleen and her father got up close to the

automobile wreck, the Newport City Police Chief recognized Beavier first, then his daughter. Captain Walker Depew shook his head sadly. He took off his black-visored cap and stood nervously thumping it against his leg.

"I don't think this is a very good idea. There's nothing either of you can do here, sir. Believe me, there isn't. The boy is dead . . . we think he was driving while intoxicated, Mr. Beavier."

Kathleen didn't seem to be listening to the flustered, red-faced Police Chief.

She began to slowly walk forward again.

Kathleen walked toward the red MG awkwardly struck into the rocks, grille first, the way wooden airplanes crash-land.

When a few of the men and women saw who it was—Kathleen Beavier, the Virgin—a murmur rose and spread back among the white headlights and shiny black-lit faces.

"*Hail Mary full of grace!*" A woman's voice rang out in the fog and drizzle.

Kathleen walked toward the harsh blue glow coming from two police emergency lamps set beside the over-turned car.

"No farther there, Miss."

A familiar-faced Newport policeman, a young trooper in a black leather jacket held out his bulky arm to stop the young girl.

Kathleen was less than thirty feet from Jaime Jordan now. She could see a swatch of his blond hair from where she stood. She saw where whipped foam had been sprayed a foot thick over the MG's engine, a precaution against another explosion.

Kathleen stared at the wrinkled slicker-yellow litter where Jaime Jordan's body lay. 403-R was stenciled in black on the body-bag.

It was so sad and unreal for him to be dead at eighteen years old.

Kathleen finally knelt down on the hard, freezing ground. She felt completely separate from the rest of the crowd—even from the policeman standing right beside her.

Kathleen began to pray for Jaime Jordan. She said the most intensely personal prayer—something between her and her God alone.

And as Kathleen Beavier knelt on the ground at Sachuest Point, a whirling golden light suddenly appeared in the night sky.

The amazing light flickered softly over the smoking automobile.

"It's a miracle!" A shrill voice rose out of the crowd. "It's a miracle, I say. I can see the miracle myself!"

"Oh my God, I can see it too."

"So can I. I see it."

The people crowded along the shoreline began to whisper to one another and point toward the light; they began to move closer to young Kathleen Beavier still kneeling in silent prayer.

Second by second, the shimmering light swept closer and closer through the dense fog bank.

The voices in the crowd grew louder, more excited and frenzied. "Jesus God Almighty, I *do* see it!"

The light rushed directly toward Kathleen Beavier as over a hundred eyewitnesses watched the incredible scene.

The light seemed to flex out and make golden aureoles, almost fiery halos. Tucked inside the halos were the thinnest spokes of burning red.

Kathleen felt such a warm glow of hope deep inside.

She began to pray out loud in a clear, beautiful voice. The mesmerized audience of tourists, firemen, policemen, fishers, began to pray along with her.

It was like the scene at Fatima nearly seventy years before in the hills of central Portugal. Only it was happening here in America.

Every spectator on the shoreline watched and waited in shock for the brilliant aureole of light to reach Kathleen.

They waited to see the Lady finally appear.

Policemen, townspeople, firemen all waited to be able to believe.

THE MIRACLE

Its silver wings beating hard in the Boston Bay winds, flashing hard-colored lights that conjured up emergencies and terrible airway accidents, Concorde flight 442 squatted as if to sit down on the rain-slicked tarmac at Logan Airport.

Moments later, as they walked through the shiny new international service terminal, both Anne and Justin were strangely silent, still reviewing and assessing their long day in Ireland with Colleen Galaher.

Like Kathleen Beavier, Colleen appeared to be a normal, extremely pleasant, and very understandably confused teenage girl.

Doctors' reports from Trinity Hospital in Cork confirmed that Colleen was still intact—and that she was going to have her baby on or around October the thirteenth . . . the feast of Our Lady of Fatima.

The girl herself had been sweet and charming; innocent and naïve; unassuming about the miraculous possibilities. Colleen had talked mostly about farm life, in fact; about the simple lifestyle in the Irish village where she lived and went to school. In that respect at least, the fourteen-year-old had seemed much more like Mary of Nazareth than Kathleen did.

At one-thirty A.M. the International Terminal at Logan was still surprisingly busy, still littered with dragging, bleary-eyed travelers trying to escape from unpleasant time warps. Porters were mechanically stacking luggage on dull-metal handcarts. Customs inspectors cursorily checked criminal-looking pieces of luggage.

"You know, Father, I just thought of something," Anne said as she and Father Rosetti waited for his black satchel to appear on the rumbling conveyor belt.

"In the couple of hundred years before the birth of Christ," Anne said, "weren't there a number of families claiming that their daughters had virgin births? That their babies were Emmanuel? . . . They were all trying to fulfill the ancient prophecy of Isaiah."

"I forget, Sister," the Vatican priest said; "you are our resident expert on Mariology."

Anne shook her head. "I didn't really specialize in Mary. I've always had a strong interest, though."

Father Eduardo Rosetti nodded politely. His attention wandered down the bumping conveyor.

Outside the rain-streaked glass doors of the terminal, rumors of New England winters were swirling and gusting across the vast concrete parking plains.

The Beavier limousine finally appeared. The long black car slid up in front of the door and the three religious hurried in out of the coldness and wet.

Inside the warm quiet-riding car, as they cruised toward Rhode Island, Anne slowly began to relax after the long, difficult day. Her mind played back entire scenes from the draining afternoon in Maam Cross; lengthy conversations came back to her. . . .

Something had happened to her over there, Anne thought as she stared into the darkness outside. Something besides the strange and amazing meeting with young Colleen Galaher.

Anne felt very different somehow. Maybe it was an emotional mood brought on by the constant pressure. Or maybe it was just being so completely exhausted.

Perhaps just being out of the shadow of the Archdiocese had contributed. She'd felt strangely, nicely independent and on her own all during the trip. . . .

As the limousine surged forward, Anne began to think about how she had tried to run away from her problem with Justin. That was really what the sudden transfer to Saint Anthony's in New Hampshire had been. It wasn't a change just to protect her vocation, Anne considered. It wasn't to protect Justin or the Holy Ghost Fathers. She had run because of petrified fear and panic. . . . Now, Anne thought that she couldn't run away again. No matter what else happened between her and Justin . . .

Sitting on the far side of the car, Justin suddenly

moved forward in his seat. He cocked his head strangely.

"Listen," he said to Father Rosetti and Anne. "My God, listen to the radio!"

He called up to the driver to please turn up the radio sound.

"James Jordan, eighteen, of Newport was fatally injured in the crash of his sports car. The Newport youth was dead when police and residents arrived at the scene in the Newport public beach area."

"That's the boy Kathleen went to the Salve Regina dance with," Anne whispered. She could actually see Jaime Jordan's boyish face, his blond hair, the adolescent swagger.

"That was far from the end of the night's drama in Newport, however. Word spread through the shore hotels and many trailer camps which have been set up for what has been called the 'Virgin Watch.' Pilgrims and local residents hurried out to the fogged-in scene of the fatal accident.

"Then, another bizarre development as young Kathleen Beavier arrived at the accident scene herself. The teenage girl approached the still-smoldering automobile wreck where one of her ex-boyfriends lay dead. And as Kathleen Beavier knelt to pray a bright light suddenly appeared over the crowd. Many in the crowd gathered on the shoreline began to chant 'Miracle . . . it's a miracle.' The strange light seemed to take on a halo effect, according to eyewitnesses. It kept coming closer and closer, directly toward Kathleen Beavier, the Virgin. The great miracle of Fatima came into the minds of many people.

"Alan Kerr of station WNPO in Newport gave this report directly from Second Beach Road."

Loud, interfering static preceded Kerr's report. Finally, a crisp, young-man's voice came in the unmistakably self-conscious style of local radio reportage.

"We all watched Kathleen Beavier kneeling at the scene of James Jordan's tragic and dramatic accident. It seemed a touching and moving gesture to most of us in the crowd.

"The young girl was approximately fifteen yards from the twisted wreckage and Jordan's body. The whole

Sachuest Park area was blanketed with a kind of grave-yard fog which contributed to the general eeriness of the scene.

"*A number of people began to pray out loud with Kathleen Beavier.*

"*One couldn't help thinking of the power and glory of the ancient Church.*

"*It was quite something to see and hear.*

"*This incredible gold light came and moved right in toward the Beavier girl. Some of the people became hysterical. Prayers and ejaculations were screamed out from the foggy hillside.*

"*Then suddenly we all saw the explanation . . . we saw the proof of our amazing miracle.*

"*The light was actually coming from a boat out on the water. The Castle Hill Coast Guard station's search and rescue boat, the 41, had been drawn to shore by the noise and car lights. The fog had covered her hull until she was up extremely close. The lights we had seen were the twin revolving searchlights on the starboard side of the 41's cabin.*

"*There was no miracle at Sachuest Point tonight. Many people here have begun to doubt whether there will be a miracle in the future, either . . . especially those who were out at bitterly cold and disappointing Sachuest Point with me tonight. This is Alan Kerr near Second Beach in Newport.*"

"Mary our Mother," Sister Anne Feeney whispered as the Beavier limousine surged ahead through the early morning darkness. "Please help Kathleen Beavier and Colleen Galaher. . . . Please help all of us right now in our moment of great need."

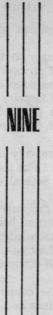

NINE

THE SIGNS

That night in Los Angeles Mrs. Rosemary Goodman was scheduled to be the last guest on the *Tonight* television show.

The attractive dark-haired woman was the most widely known, also possibly the most accurate and respected, psychic investigator and clairvoyant in America.

As she sat waiting for her stage call in the green room, Rosemary Goodman thought that she knew exactly what was going to happen next in her life. Which was, after all, her business ...

Sure enough, sure enough, with only five minutes remaining in the interminable show, a network page came into the empty lounge. The young, blond surfer type beckoned for Mrs. Goodman to follow him out to the studio.

So, Rosemary thought to herself, *they were giving her all of four minutes of network exposure!*

As she followed the page down a dismal, claustrophobic corridor, Mrs. Rosemary Goodman began to create a spontaneous little plan of her own. At least she would make the best of her inadequate few minutes on the program.

The studio orchestra very predictably began to play "That Old Black Magic." The harsh television stage lights effectively blinded her. Several of the NBC-TV cameras wheeled toward her.

Rosemary heard the affable talk-show host say something about California being "psychic-delia." She didn't even bother to acknowledge the host.

Instead, the tall, chestnut-haired woman walked toward the converging half-circle of powder-blue television cameras.

Selecting one of the cameras, Rosemary Goodman stared directly into the lens and began to tell her strange and powerful story to America.

"And now, the Rosemary Goodman Show!" the unflappable host quipped from a long table peopled with his cronies and a few hot stars of the moment.

"My dear friends," Mrs. Rosemary Goodman looked into the television camera, "I had another terrible dream last night."

As she spoke, tears came into the eyes of the clairvoyant.

"The world as we know it seems to be ending. I understand how that sounds strange and impossible, but it is what I saw. The forces of eternal salvation are preparing to meet the fearsome legions of destruction and despair. There is to be one final, horrifying battle across the face of the earth. Good against evil one last time. Right before our eyes.

"*They* won't tell you and me until it's too late. You know how they work. Please, please my friends, prepare your immortal souls for the kingdom of God!"

FROM THE SIGNS OF THE VIRGIN

October ninth exists in the mind as a strange linear sequence of dramatic events that rightfully should only have occurred in a dream.

What happened couldn't actually have taken place. Those who were there have told themselves that time after time.

There will never be satisfactory rational explanations for several of the peculiar events of that day.

Everything seemed to be turning toward a single focus—everything was becoming a grand question, one final test of faith.

Do you believe in something? a ritualistic exercise used at Trappist Order retreats begins.

Have you ever believed? Do you remember the feeling?

What is it that you really believe in?

In God?

In the absence of God?

In Evil?

In yourself?

In nothing at all?

What do you really believe in right at this very moment?

KATHLEEN

The morning after the Coast-Guard–boat incident at Sachuest Point, Kathleen Beavier woke as a band of sunlight, which had been slowly spreading across her quilt, finally reached her eyes.

Looking across her meticulously ordered room, blinking her eyes repeatedly, the teenage girl saw that her window was filled with the most gorgeous, sky-blue.

It was the kind of ebullient fall day that only happens once or twice a year in New England. The maple and oak trees were showing a hundred brilliant shades of

red and yellow. The smell of salty ocean and burning
leaves was everywhere in the air. . . . Somehow, that made
it all the worse for Kathleen. It was like being sick in bed
on a beautiful day, she thought.

The seventeen-year-old girl was feeling so very, very
wounded, ill, pregnant. She was incredibly, hopelessly
confused. Most of all, Kathleen was deeply saddened by
Jaime Jordan's death.

Climbing stiff-legged and lopsided from her bed,
Kathleen began the morning ritual she had been following
for the past six weeks or so.

First thing always, she had to go to the bathroom.
She had to go very badly.

Next came a storm of self-doubts and fears which
crashed down all around Kathleen.

There was one recurring, guilt-ridden vision that her
baby would be born deformed; there was another cruel
fantasy that the baby would come out of her and be some
kind of lurid monster. Kathleen didn't really believe that,
she couldn't let herself believe it, but the thoughts came
anyway—and because the thoughts kept coming so regularly, *that* frightened her.

Kathleen had other doubts too, practical doubts,
about what she would do after the baby was born, about
what her life would be like once she had a child.

And a more immediate question: Would she know
when she went into labor? The dramatic, ever-present
question of every first mother.

On that scary subject, Kathleen decided to review
the basic signals she'd learned from her doctor. The
loosing of the mucus plug, which she was going to feel,
supposedly. . . . A sharp uterine cramp somewhere
around the center of her pelvis . . . breaking water as the
membrane between the baby's head and the opening of
her cervix ruptured . . .

Ruptured . . .

Now that sounded scary and unpleasant, though Dr.
Armstrong said it wasn't too bad.

At any rate, none of the above seemed to be happening so far that morning. Knock on wood. Any trick to
deflect her true emotions.

Somewhat reassured, Kathleen Beavier began the arduous task of dressing her suddenly very delicate and sensitive body.

She didn't even want to have the baby, Kathleen began to think once again. *She wanted to tell all of them everything about the night of January twenty-third!*

Except, who would believe the truth? Kathleen thought and grew sadder and sadder.

Kathleen's soft blue eyes peeked up as the pine floorboards suddenly creaked sharply across her bedroom.

"Oh dear." She cupped her fist to her chest. "You scared me. I have to find some way to just calm myself down after last night. *Whew!* Hello."

Kathleen smiled up into the dark green eyes of the housekeeper, Mrs. Walsh.

Kathleen then immediately looked away. Ostensibly to locate her woolen socks, but really because she was afraid her eyes would betray what she was thinking. That Mrs. Walsh had been acting odd around her for a couple of weeks. Had the housekeeper come to talk it out now? Maybe to explain?

The upstairs part of the house was so quiet and still that morning. It made things even more uncomfortable between the two of them, Kathleen thought.

The girl dragged a pair of tan Squeejuns from under her bed. She began to pull on heavy wool argyle socks. God, how she needed to get away from all this, Kathleen was thinking.

"I'll be out of your way in here in just a minute. Two seconds," she said.

Mrs. Walsh hadn't really spoken to her yet, Kathleen noticed. *God, what could I have done to her?*

Finally, Kathleen looked up at the older woman.

The wool sock fluttered down out of her hand.

Mrs. Walsh had a horrifying double-edged knife clenched in her hand. A fillet knife, which they used to slice and gut fish down in the Beavier kitchen.

"In the name of Our Holy Father!" The housekeeper finally spoke, a harsh guttural rasp that was barely

recognizable to Kathleen. *"I cast out Satan and his fiendish child!"*

With no more explanation than that, her right arm slashed down very hard and fast toward Kathleen's huge stomach.

Kathleen couldn't make herself believe that this was happening. She tried to twist away from the flashing knife; at the same instant, she was trying to make sense of the unfathomable horror.

The stainless blade drove deep, parting cloth, slashing through the feather mattress and into the box spring. Kathleen jerked herself away from the bed. The housekeeper struggled to pull the knife free again.

"Please help me!"

Kathleen tried to run away but there was nowhere to go.

"You're not one of God's! You're not even Kathleen!" Mrs. Walsh screamed, her eyes fierce and red-rimmed.

"No, please . . . I am Kathleen!"

Kathleen was being forced into the bedroom's far left corner. There were two high windows there with billowing curtains. No doors out . . . no escape.

The young girl's screams echoed off the pretty, cream-yellow walls.

Kathleen screamed again.

Again.

"Someone please help me! Please God. Please help me now!"

ANNE

Anne heard the first, distant scream, but she didn't realize what it was. Seagulls, she thought. That oddly plaintive cry made by laughing gulls.

Anne had dug herself a snug windbreak among the small hunchback dunes rising and falling along the beach behind Sun Cottage.

She lay flat out on her back on a plaid wool blanket, letting the Indian summer sun warm her face, loosening all the achy muscles in her body. She breathed in the clean, crisp October air.

This is nearly perfect, Anne thought.

The moment alone.

Peacefulness.

Somewhere in James Joyce, in *Ulysses,* Anne thought she remembered, someone, probably Leopold Bloom, had sat out by the Irish Sea in a mackintosh and crazy derby. . . . It was an unappreciated, much-under-rated luxury—just plopping down and sunbathing in your clothes.

After a few minutes toasting her front side, Anne sat up and let the breeze coming off the ocean refresh her. The sky was such a perfect dark blue it made her want to live forever. The combination of warmth and cooling breeze was so soothing she was tempted to nap.

Anne heard the distant, crying seagull again . . . then a pleasure boat horn honked—like one of those odd hand horns she'd heard at football games.

As Anne looked out over the ocean, she heard another of the cries. A piercing, strangely familiar cry that seemed to be coming from the main house, from Sun Cottage itself.

"Oh my God, Kathleen!"

SATANAS LUCIFERI EXCELSI

Kathleen pushed the rattling bedroom window open wide and clumsily fell out into clear blue sky.

Feeling dreamy and unreal, she stepped down hard and immediately slid on the steep roof jutting out over the main dining room.

Then Kathleen was walking, tottering three stories over a flagstone patio that seemed to be pulsating with her heartbeat. The wind off the ocean blew right through her flannel shirt. Her bare feet clung tenuously to the loose, freezing-cold roof shingles.

"Can't somebody please help?" The girl's voice trailed away from the roof like wispy smoke from a chimney.

The housekeeper, meanwhile, was struggling out of the bedroom window in her billowing work dress. She started to come for Kathleen again, scrabbling along the steeply slanting roof like a land crab.

Two of the estate's groundsmen finally came running down below, pointing at the terrifying roof scene, not really believing what they saw up there.

"Please help me!" Kathleen screamed to the workmen, realizing it was no use, that they would never get there in time.

Protect the child. Somehow. The child. It became Kathleen's only thought.

Protect the child. You must. Somehow.

Nothing matters but the child.

Bent over with her arms down low, the housekeeper was nearly on all fours to keep her balance on the slick roof tiles. Her eyes were wide and blank. Her white hair was fanned out in the wind like Medusa's nest of snakes.

Down on the ground, Anne came racing up from the beach, screaming something that was forever lost in the winds.

Someone was yelling inside Kathleen's bedroom; then her mother was suddenly at the bedroom window, not believing, trying to get outside too.

Father Eduardo Rosetti burst through the French doors of the downstairs parlor, windows crashing as the door slammed into stucco walls.

Kathleen edged out away from this crazed woman on the roof with her. She went out as far as she could possibly go. Out to where the half-roof made a hundred-eighty-degree turn around a corner of the house.

She couldn't make it any farther without falling, Kathleen realized. She was sliding hopelessly on the loose shingles.

"Whoever you are—I command you to stop!" the young girl suddenly screamed out. "I command you!"

The housekeeper's bare white arm rose high in the air. Her elbow seemed to be touching a cloud. The woman's eyes were so lifeless and unreal.

Suddenly a jagged wound split open in the side of her neck. Blood sheeted down Ida Walsh's striped blue uniform. The woman moaned horribly, her face frozen in a rictus of shock and hatred.

A loud noise thundered, thundered, thundered, out away from Sun Cottage—an amazing sound that none of them would ever forget.

Then there was eerie, total quiet except for the distant roll of the sea.

Kathleen's eyes fell to the back lawns, where Father Eduardo Rosetti stood straight and tall, his legs spread wide and stiff.

The Chief Investigator for the Congregation of Rites still held one of Charles Beavier's hunting rifles to his eye.

Investigator!

The single word rang in Kathleen's mind.

Then the young girl thought—*he knows. He knows the secret of the virgins.*

The housekeeper's body dropped softly from the roof. The human shape trampolined off a green-and-gold awning, bouncing onto the patio concrete, where it lay in ugly spread-eagle.

"Satanas Luciferi excelsi!"

Anne heard Father Rosetti mutter the words as she finally reached him on the sun-blinding back lawns.

The Vatican priest had clearly said something about the demon. *Assassins,* Anne thought that she had recognized another of the Latin words. *Devils . . . and assassins.*

The other thing Anne noticed was that tears were streaming from Father Rosetti's dark brown eyes.

"What is happening?" Anne pleaded with the Vatican priest, actually grabbing a handful of cassock and shaking him.

"Tell us what is happening, Father. You must tell us now."

COLLEEN

The palest white and red wildflowers, the fluffiest reeds were everywhere her eyes looked up and down the rolling hillsides.

There was heather meadow, saffron, and Queen Anne's lace mostly. Leaves were turning free in the air like loose wandering flowers.

Colleen gathered buds and switches quickly and efficiently, paying no mind to her swelling stomach and dull constant pain. It made her remember picking vegetables in Maam Cross the previous spring—almost nine months before when she had worked on Mr. Jimmie Dowd's prosperous wheelbarrow farm.

This day, Colleen wore a dark green smock which matched the striking color of her eyes. Her long black hair was tied with a shamrock-green ribbon, the exact shade of a distant foothill way off toward the sea.

The young girl was singing in a sweet, lilting voice that seemed just right for a favorite song of hers.

A beautiful love song the virgin Colleen had first heard back in the winter . . . *on the night of January twenty-third.*

KATHLEEN

On direct and mysterious orders from Rome, and with the full permission of her family, Kathleen Beavier was moved out of Newport that afternoon.

At one-thirty, two silver-blue Lincolns skirted inside the elegant, porte cochere at Sun Cottage. The front door of the house was opened on signal; seven people scurried into the cars and they were off immediately.

As the cars streamed off the estate with a heavy police escort, the press was told only that Kathleen would be traveling to New York City, that there might be the opportunity for a news conference once she was safe.

For the first time in nearly two weeks, the Beavier house was quiet . . . and sane.

Around two-thirty that afternoon, with the grounds finally cleared of reporters and the curious, three nondescript sedans slid up in front of Sun Cottage.

More luggage was brought out of the house with

great speed and urgency. Kathleen and the others were hurried into the cars, which then sped north to Logan Airport in Boston.

Kathleen was on board Flight 342 before the limousine carrying maids and kitchen help arrived in New York City, the ruse finally discovered during a raucous scene outside the Park Avenue entrance to the Waldorf hotel.

At ten forty-five P.M. three more cars met the Beavier party arriving at Orly airport.

A baggage loader who observed the curious scene guessed that the shadowy figures—including men in flowing gowns—were Arabs come to France for secret oil talks.

He immediately got on a telephone and passed the tip to a news reporter who hounded the airport in search of visiting celebrities.

Anne slumped into the deep leather back seat of one of the chauffeur-driven sedans, the cushions almost seeming to be breathing under her.

She was beginning to experience an almost nonstop tension now. A tight fist was screwing into the small of her back. There were constant headaches. And a nervous stomach that never seemed to stop turning over. Growling. Complaining about the slightest bump or turn.

The virgin birth—the birth—could take place at any moment now. Off in Ireland Colleen Galaher might be having her baby. Kathleen could be going into labor in one of the two cars trailing behind.

Then what would follow?

What were the mysterious aftereffects which kept threatening to follow the divine birth?

As the car flashed through the dark, silent countryside—*Europe . . . France, for heaven's sake!*—Anne had a shocking flash of the falling, tumbling body of Mrs. Ida Walsh. She could hear the poor lost woman's final inhuman screams. Anne nearly cried out herself in the back of the speeding car.

Father Rosetti had told her that the devil was irresistibly drawn around Kathleen. *Satanas Luciferi excelsi.*

What did he mean by that? The devil will be exalted? Where? When?

How did he know as much as he seemed to know?

When was he going to tell the rest of them . . . and stop playing the investigator all by himself?

Anne took her eyes from the hypnotic smoky-gray highway. She watched the car's driver, a silent, thick-necked man in a traditional peaked black hat. She noticed mashed crayons and a dog-eared coloring book on the floor. Evidence of happier times in the family car.

"Intellectually, I know what happened today." Justin finally spoke across the back seat. "Emotionally, though, everything feels like action in a dream. I'm not sure of the rules. I'm not even sure if it's in color or black and white."

"Everything feels as if it shouldn't be happening now," Anne said finally. "It seems bizarre and medieval. I think that I have that exact thought fifty times a day now."

"What's happening reminds me of the way it was when we were children. When I was, anyway," Justin said. "In Cork, no one really told us the answers to our questions. We always felt out of control and completely in the dark."

"As if life was so very magical . . . and scary," Anne said.

"Life *is*," Justin looked across the back seat at her. "Life is both of those things."

As their gray Citroen bore down a blurred tunnel, a long tube filled with glowing modern sodium lights, Father Eduardo Rosetti was trying to communicate an important point to Kathleen.

"Kathleen, please allow me to tell you one more strange theory of mine," Rosetti said. "It's something I personally believe, something the Church in Rome believes, something which I will ask you to try and accept on faith, also. *Faith,* because this is the sort of spiritual matter to which our very empirical-minded world is not currently attuned."

"What is it, Father?"

"I believe, the Church believes, that evil is a powerful and tangible force on earth. It is believed that evil
flourishes and multiplies in demonic mimicry of Nature!
... The devil is a brilliant imitator, Kathleen. A master of
perverse mimicry!

"Those who would deny the existence of evil—
supposedly on a rational basis—are actually denying
what they see in the world, what they hear about, what
they themselves think and feel almost every day of their
lives. Please believe me, Kathleen; evil is all around you
right now."

Kathleen stared into the Vatican priest's sad, dark
eyes. She believed him, of course. She had seen hideous
evil marked across the face of Mrs. Walsh just hours
before at Sun Cottage.

"Father, what am I to do?" she asked.

Very late that evening, a dark caravan of cars arrived in the village of Chantilly, twenty-three miles north
of Paris.

The cars were separated from one another in a thick,
gray fog that had begun just outside of Orly Airport.

Here in Chantilly, Charles Beavier's younger brother
lived on a gentleman's farm with his wife and five children. The French countryside location seemed an excellent choice for Kathleen's hideaway until the child was
born. . . .

As the shadowy cars slid through the deserted streets
of Chantilly, everyone breathed a sigh of relief.

The villa of Henri Beavier and his family was a
lonely looking place surrounded by a heavy black iron
gate and high, dark hedges. It seemed secure and secluded enough, though a little forbidding at that hour of
night.

As the cars approached the gates, however, both
Anne and Justin saw something that completely shocked
and unnerved them.

A waiting abomination at the Beavier house in
Chantilly.

First, Anne and Justin saw a white van with colored lettering that read GDZ-TV.

Then they saw a squad of cameramen with minipaks strapped to their backs.

Then a huddle of reporters waiting beneath a copse of shadowy evergreens.

"They are here! They are here!" someone began calling out in French.

A middle-aged man tried to push his shaggy, bearded face inside the back window of Anne and Justin's car.

"Why have you come to France? *No, no, you aren't Kathleen!*"

It wasn't until the cars had hurried inside the front gates, not until they had stopped in front of the house itself, that they began to notice that something else had gone wrong. . . . Something that made all of their insides shrivel, and Anne scream out in the dark, purring Citroen.

There were two instead of three cars in the Beavier driveway.

Two pairs of glowing white headlamps.

Two Citroens with their badly confused passengers stepping outside now, whispering to one another, looking back in terror toward the crowded entryway to the estate. Being photographed again and again.

The *third* car had somehow vanished on the trip north from the airport.

The car which carried Father Eduardo Rosetti and Kathleen Beavier had simply disappeared.

TEN

THE SIGNS

Forty-five minutes before dawn, the white clay foothills of the Madre Oriental mountains just northeast of San Luis Potosí, Mexico, appeared to be peacefully, luxuriously asleep.

A red fox noiselessly parted brazilwood tree leaves and eyed a feeding, brightly feathered parrot.

Palm trees waved their heavy fronds in the slight mountain breeze. . . .

Suddenly everything went supernaturally quiet.

Then there was a sound.

A sound like no other ever heard in the Madre Orientals.

A sound like an army of men rapidly crawling on their stomachs over rocky terrain . . .

Coasting down the dark-shadowed mountain road in his ancient pick-up truck, Rosario Sanza's faded-yellow field boot crunched down on the truck's brake pedal.

Sanza's foot struck the brake so hard that the truck's suspension buckled. The farmer's straw hat flew off and out the open window. His knee cracked on the steering column.

Ignoring the pain, the fifty-four-year-old farmer flicked on his high beams; then Sanza just stared down the unwinding band of deep-purple road.

The farmer began to pray out loud in the cab of his truck.

The road, the whole side of the mountain, was crawling with shiny, slithering bodies.

A thousand beady eyes were frozen in a stare at the truck's intruding headlights. Sanza gasped in disbelief.

There were black snakes, milk snakes, rattlesnakes —perhaps thirty different types of snakes, ranging in size from less than a foot to a giant five-and-a-half-foot-long boa constrictor.

The snakes were coming off the mountain as if there had to be a flood or a forest fire raging farther up. . . . There were only snakes, though; no other animals were coming off the mountain. There was *no* fire on the mountain, *no* flood.

A blinding-fast black ribbon flashed across the red hood of Rosario Sanza's truck.

Sharp fangs struck suddenly at the farmer's face, right at his eyes.

The snake's jaw hit hard against the unseen windshield glass. Sanza immediately slammed the truck gears into reverse. He was getting the hell out of there— backward. Any damn way that he could. Alive.

The army of snakes watched the retreating truck, and they were well satisfied.

Something was so very wrong.

In Mexico's Madre Oriental mountains.

Everywhere.

COLLEEN

"Say now, chaps and ladies this is God's country, ya know. Sure 'tis. God's very home."

The publican in Conor's dutifully proclaimed this local gospel to every wide-eyed stranger who happened to wander in for a Guinness or Bushmill's.

So did the all-purpose store owner in Maam Cross; and Father McGurk, the parish priest; and old Eddie Mahoney, still mixing patent medicines in the 130-year-old chemist's shop.

This is God's country, ya know. 'Tis the truth.

That morning, the glorious hills surrounding the Irish village were shining through a misty curtain of gentle rain.

On a stone-wall–bordered path twisting down out of the hills the virgin and the black-cloaked nun slowly walked toward town. They were two bobbing heads in a sea of lush green with intrusions of purple sumac.

Colleen and Sister Katherine finally reached the spare, rocky crossroads into the village. There, five druids, gross products of the arduous life in the region, waited for the city milk-truck from Costelloe.

"Is the father among us, Colleen?" One of the village men perked up and called in his cruel odd-bird's voice.

"Won't ya at least tell us that, dearie? Who's the da for this kiddo?" asked a blond adult face under a checkered Donegal cap.

"I'd say she's ready for the Abbey Theatre with her fine actin' performance there."

"I'd say she's Anti-God!" a huge, scary one shouted in a voice like a human bullhorn. "Anti-God I say!"

As Colleen and the Mother Superior got a few paces down the cobbled road, a heavy stone thudded and kicked up a volley of dirt right at their feet.

Sister Katherine Dominica whirled about to face the gang of men. She cast a fierce, damning look back at them. *If they only knew who this was,* Sister Katherine thought. *If they only knew.*

"Just practicin' our road bowlin'," the Donegal cap

shouted. Road bowling was the popular sport all through the area. A pound and a half cast-iron ball was thrown around an arbitrary course that could run for miles; over streams and across bridges, through thick woods.

"No harm intended," one of the men called and laughed.

"Yeh, little whore, yeh!" another shrieked. "Colleen hussy!"

The Church of St. Joseph was a dignified stone edifice enclosed by a neat fieldstone fence. It sat at the village center, its immaculate tidiness contrasting sharply with most of the other buildings in town.

A large portrait of St. Patrick announced the church's highly polished wooden vestibule. So did plaster statues of Joseph, St. Columba, and the Sacred Heart. Perhaps eighty villagers had gathered for the early morning Mass inside.

At seven o'clock the village priest and a flaming-red-haired altar boy finally appeared in the heavy stone archway leading out from the sacristy.

"The Lord loves all of you for coming," Father Dennis McGurk blessed the parishioners.

There was the familiar sound of rustling skirts, chronic hacking coughs, St. Joseph's loose-bound prayerbooks being opened to the proper feast day.

The tiny young Irish virgin felt a terrible chill spreading through her pained, bloated body.

Colleen Deirdre Galaher knelt and began to pray for her holy child, now due any day—perhaps any hour, for all she knew about having a wee babe.

Colleen also began to pray for a young girl she didn't know at all: she prayed for Kathleen Grace Beavier.

She prayed that Kathleen was faring better now than she was.

ANNE AND JUSTIN

"I'm not just afraid for Kathleen today," Anne admitted to Justin the morning after the disappearance. "I'm also missing Kathleen terribly. I keep having these terrible flashes that she's been harmed."

Anne and Justin were picking at a light breakfast in the dining hall of Henri Beavier's country home in Chantilly.

It was an amazing situation—the elegant, bustling breakfast scene.

Anne and Justin were sipping coffee alongside special SDEC detectives and officials from the Paris police. Outside the dining-room windows all varieties of new trucks and police vehicles were parked around the circular courtyard.

After the meal, Sister Anne and Father Justin were offered one of the family automobiles. They were asked by Father Milsap to go into the city of Paris. Once there, they were to assist the police in any way that they could: information about Kathleen, identification, ideas they might have about Father Rosetti.

The short drive into Paris along Route A-1 seemed eerie and other-dimensional to both Anne and Justin. Some of the pastel-colored houses, olive trees, passing trucks, and French autos were especially real and distinct. Others were curiously vague and fuzzed at the edges.

It was one of those drizzly gray days when Anne thought she could readily subscribe to the notion that she might just be dreaming up her entire life.

Poor Kathleen, Anne was thinking. Where was she right at that moment? She truly had become a friend for Anne; someone Anne could talk to. Anne had even confided in Kathleen about Justin, about the possibility that she might leave the Dominican order, about self-doubts she had never been able to reveal to anyone else. . . . *What had happened to Kathleen last night?*

"I keep drifting back to Rosetti's paranoia," Justin said as he piloted their Citroen along the busy autoroute. "I don't believe that I've ever seen anyone as tense and obviously frightened as he was the day he went to Ireland. . . . He seemed frightened by nothing we could see or feel ourselves. By invisible ghosts."

"And that story he told about the bats attacking him," Anne turned in her seat. "I don't think he believes himself that it was some kind of hallucination. I think Father Rosetti actually believes that the Devil is following him. . . . I feel it too, though, Justin. More and more I can feel the strong presence of something so terribly evil in all of this. *Satanis Luciferi excelsi*. I'm certain that's what I heard Rosetti say back at Sun Cottage."

"Anne, all the time we were in Ireland I felt there was one important secret Rosetti was keeping from us. Maybe something revealed to him by Pius XIII. One incredible key to our understanding everything that he couldn't tell . . . if we could only figure out that one secret. What is the terrible secret of Father Eduardo Rosetti?"

THE FRENCH SAILOR

The Rue de la Huchette–Rue St. Severin quarter was a restless maze of twisting lanes in one of the oldest and shabbiest parts of Paris. . . . The ancient quarter was completely closed to auto traffic. It was nevertheless thickly crowded with students from the Sorbonne, strollers, failed musicians, cadres of sinister-looking Algerians in their dusty black overcoats.

The apartment buildings themselves were ponderous and depressing; drab, iron-gray affairs usually three stories or less. It was difficult to believe that anyone lived in the section by choice.

Near the Seine at the far end of Rue de la Huchette was an alleyway with the unforgettable name Rue du Chat-qui-Pêche.

The Street of the Fishing Cat.

A burly old man in a beret and navy greatcoat slowly walked down the greasy cobbled alley.

He stopped in front of one of the gray buildings, his eyes roaming up the soot-covered windows. He noticed a bent television antenna on the roof, a peeking view of the swirling river, a faded billboard for Dubonnet from around 1950 by the look of the costumes.

The old man stiffly climbed the crumbling front steps and rang a dangling bell.

A small middle-aged woman with a dragging limp finally came to the door. She was Madame Duvas, she said.

"Excusez-moi—I saw the sign. Do you still have a room available, madame?"

Madame Duvas quickly took in the whole of the large, poorly dressed man. He was in his late fifties, she guessed. Still very strong-looking, though. A husky workman type. Not likely to die during the winter at least, thought the Frenchwoman. . . . A broken-down sailor by the looks of him. Still some spirit left in his dark eyes, though not much spirit.

"I have a room—I must have one month in advance." Madame Duvas crossed her arms to show her intransigence on that point.

"I only wish to stay a week or two, madame. I don't have much money."

"One month in advance. That is my rule. There are other rooms in Paris, no?"

An hour or so later, Madame Duvas saw him climbing the front stairs with a young girl by his side. The girl wore old clothes, but she seemed very pretty at a quick glance. She didn't seem to be resisting the sailor, Madame Duvas noticed and smiled. The phrase *child bride* tumbled through the woman's mind.

Upstairs in the old building, Father Eduardo Rosetti thought that he had found an acceptable hideaway for Kathleen Beavier. Together they began to make the final preparations.

THE VIRGIN OF FORDHAM HILL

At 8:00 A.M. on Rue St. Honoré, on the Champs Élysées, at the Place de la Concorde, Parisians and tourists alike began to pick up their morning editions of the Paris *Monde, Le Figaro,* the international *Herald Tribune.*

They walked away from the news kiosks reading the front pages and shaking their heads. Some of them smiled, others frowned, some of them whispered prayers on the thickly crowded street.

VIRGIN DISAPPEARS IN FRANCE! *announced Le Monde.*
The *Monde* story and others just beginning to appear around the world were excellent fuel for the fires of curiosity, perversity, blind faith, and other conflicting reactions to the story of a possible divine birth in modern times.

Stories about Kathleen Beavier's "secret lover" Jaime Jordan were right then being circulated around America. A movie by a successful science-fiction director was already being considered.

A European news story revealed another "divine" birth about to occur in the Israeli village of Eilat.

In the New York City borough of the Bronx, meanwhile, a woman named Moira Flanagan, the Virgin of Fordham Hill, had been receiving regular vistations from Our Lady of the Flowers as well as Jesus since 1968.

Late on the afternoon of October tenth, Mrs. Flanagan suddenly found herself leading a cheering procession of over five thousand people to a hillside shrine on the grounds of Fordham University. Surrounded by bodyguards from her Fordham neighborhood, Mrs. Flanagan knelt in a makeshift grotto before a life-sized statue of Mary.

Several moments after she began to pray, Moira Flanagan turned to the swelling crowd and told them that both Jesus and Mary were now speaking to her.

"I can see Our Lord . . . Our Lady is with him. . . . They are both very beautiful. Oh, they're so beautiful. . . .

"Jesus is telling me that a divine child will be born soon," Mrs. Flanagan whispered in a voice that was so genuine it was difficult not to believe her.

"The child will be born on October thirteenth . . . on the feast of Our Lady of the Rosary in Fatima. Jesus says to believe," cried the Virgin of Fordham Hill.

"There was something else," the woman held up her hand for quiet. "Our Blessed Lady is coming forward now! Oh, there is a grand circle of light upon the dark skies. She is so beautiful!

"Our Lady says to beware. She says the Beast is strong now too. The Beast is everywhere! All across the earth there will be a battle . . . the Final Judgment is upon us . . . a final war between the hideous devils and the angels of God. Just as it has been promised in St. Mark, in Revelation. . . . Oh dear Lord, pray for the young Virgin! Pray for the Child!"

FRENCH DETECTIVES

"*A city of churches.* You know that saying about Paris, René? Consider. Notre Dame, Ste. Chapelle, St. Étienne, St. Eustache, St. Germain-des-Près . . . uh, St. Louis, Sacre Coeur . . . who goes to all of these churches? No one that I know!"

Two French detectives, Bernard Serret and René Devereaux, were riding across the Pont Alexandre III in a dirty-white Renault.

"What do you think of this Blessed Virgin Mary crap, René?" Bernard Serret lit up a filterless cigarette and sucked in deeply. The Paris detective was thirty-one years old, a very tough-looking man with a long knife scar on his cheek; a man who insisted on wearing a leather trench coat at least three seasons out of four during the year.

His partner, René Devereaux, sat silently, merely shrugging his shoulders in response.

"Myself, René, I stopped believing in Blessed Virgins as soon as I graduated from St. Martin's in the Quarter. That's where I made this enlightening discovery. . . . That the girls like to get it as much as the boys like to give it. So much for Virgin Marys, Virgin Jeannes, Nicolles, all the rest."

Bernard Serret glanced over at his silent partner, also his best friend in spite of their age difference.

"What's the matter, René? No sense of humor this morning? . . . Eh, who could blame you? The Superintendent calls you up at four A.M.! *Allo? René? . . . Please go spend the day searching for the Blessed Virgin. Yes, and start the day right now . . . !*"

Bernard glanced over at René Devereaux one more time.

Still no smile from the older man.

"I believe in this birth," René Devereaux finally shrugged. "I think that a son of God, someone like Jesus, is going to be born. Maybe even in France," René Devereaux said. "On Sundays I go to Mass at Notre Dame. Marie and I."

Bernard Serret shook his head.

"I'm sorry for making bad jokes. I didn't know you were . . . you know, you never said anything. . . . Actually, René, I don't *dis*believe. I'm somewhere in the middle."

"Ah . . . agnostic. I have a prayer for you, then." René Devereaux finally smiled. "The agnostic's Our Father. Here it is: 'Oh God, if there is a God, save my soul, if I have a soul.' "

Both of the detectives laughed. That was better. That was more like it.

"Last night I had a dream, Bernard. I had the dream before I knew the Beavier girl was even in France. . . . In my dream, we found her dead. You and I found her in some horrible Quartier Latin alleyway. This battered and violated pregnant girl—a young and pretty one, like so many others that we've found. What does that mean? My dream? I don't want to find this young virgin. I don't want to find any more dead young girls in alleyways."

"But you think we will, René?"

"I fear it in my heart. Jesus, Mary, and Joseph! Poor Joseph. No one mentions that poor bastard any more."

The detectives rode in silence for the next few minutes. They went past the complex of the Hôtel des Invalides, alongside the eye-filling École Militaire.

"When I was a young boy, Bernard, I used to serve the eight-o'clock Mass at St. Louis Church. Every morning for three hundred straight days one year. I loved it. The incense, the music, Mary and the child Jesus. Sometimes I think those were the best times in my entire life."

René Devereaux lit another cigarette. "I wanted this miracle to work out in some impossible way. I really did, Bernard. I think it would have been a good thing for everybody."

KATHLEEN

Three stories above the dark, steaming Street of the Fishing Cat, an amber square of light was shining brightly, like an oblong star over the derelict Paris district.

Behind the window, Kathleen sat hugging her throbbing stomach tenderly, imagining that she could feel and hear two living heartbeats racing inside her now.

Across the small room littered with newspapers and food containers from lunch and dinner, Father Rosetti knelt and prayed in a barely audible whisper. Italian? Latin? . . . Kathleen couldn't tell for certain.

On a blinking, gray and off-white television set, the lead story of the incredible hunt for her through France and other parts of Western Europe had just come on the evening news. A grainy clip of the September news conference at Sun Cottage was being shown. The camera was moving in on Kathleen's beautiful, innocent face. *"Who wouldn't believe looking into those sad, chaste eyes?"* asked a television commentator in softly flowing French.

"You said to tell you when I was ready, Father," Kathleen finally said in a trembling voice.

Suddenly she was so full of doubt and fear. Things completely unknown to anyone else were present in this small, shabby flat. Secrets about life; secrets about death; secrets about the frightening distinction between goodness and evil.

Above all else *the child* was present there.

The second tiny heartbeat.

The second life to be considered in all of Kathleen's decisions from now on.

"I think that I'm ready," Kathleen whispered, not certain whether she believed her own words. "You're going to pray for me? For my baby? . . . That's mostly what it will be?"

Father Rosetti rose and slowly walked over to a cracked, rusted sink in the room. He snapped open his black duffel bag and took out several darkly shadowed items.

"I'll tell you exactly what's going to happen, Kathleen. First I will read a number of pages from this holy book." Father Rosetti showed Kathleen a cloth book with a blood-red cross on its cover. "This is the Roman Ritual. There are nothing but the most sacred prayers inside, Kathleen."

The Vatican priest solemnly kissed a violet stole, then dropped it over the slope of his broad shoulders.

"The Evil One is called Moloch sometimes. Or Mormo—which means King of the Ghouls. He is called Coyote by cults which still exist among American Indians, or Beelzebub—which means Lord of the Flies. In much of Africa they call him Damballa, the Beast. His power there is much more in evidence. Much bolder there. The people believe in Damballa because they see his handiwork every day."

Father Rosetti blessed himself with lovely sweeping motions that reminded Kathleen of High Masses back at Salve Regina. Then the broad-shouldered, black-cassocked priest began to sweep across the room toward her. His dark eyes had never been darker.

"Lord God my Father," the trembling young girl prayed out loud. "Protect the child inside of me!"

Father Eduardo Rosetti moaned loudly—almost as if he didn't want to begin. The priest threw out tentative sprinkles of holy water at Kathleen Beavier.

He waited to feel the dreaded, all-pervasive Presence. Then the chilling, unforgettable Voice. Then perhaps an Appearance.

The exorcism of Kathleen Beavier and her unborn child had begun.

By the holy order of Pope Pius XIII.

"Dear Lord, please give us a clear sign . . ." Father Eduardo Rosetti said the most important prayer of his life. He felt the abominable hopelessness. The first step into eternal hell.

"Which virgin mother has come to bear the Savior? . . . Which will bear the hateful Beast?"

Almost at once, Father Rosetti and Kathleen could feel the dreaded Presence.

Then the deep, unforgettable Voice. . . . Laughing.

ANNE AND JUSTIN

Midnight struck, tower bells gently pealed across the city of Churches, and Thursday, October twelfth finally began.

Only hours now remained before the births.

Only hours remained before the feast of the mysterious Gentlewoman of Fatima.

Sister Anne Feeney and Father Justin O'Carroll had spread newspapers all over the carpets and period furniture in Henri Beavier's Paris townhouse. The two of them had spent most of the anxious day there, making themselves available to the Paris police.

"We're making a wreck of this lovely house, you know. It looks like a training camp for a litter of puppies," Anne said and began to gather up some of the papers.

So far the police had only visited them briefly at the townhouse. Nothing about Kathleen's whereabouts had been reported anywhere. The word *kidnap* was beginning to be used on television; Communist "terrorists" were now being mentioned as well; the Vatican had issued no official statement as yet.

Justin snatched up the international *Herald Tribune* and stared at the day's news one more time.

"It's awful, just awful, Anne," he said. "I'm feeling so damn helpless. Do they expect us to sit in here and *pray?* . . . Annie, was there *anything* that Rosetti might have said? Anything Kathleen said at any time?"

Anne looked up from the pile of collected papers and shook her head. They had been over that particular area so many times it seemed like a wrinkled road map in her mind.

Besides the bizarre story of Kathleen's disappearance, almost all the newspaper front pages contained particularly bad news, Anne and Justin had been noticing. *Signs,* she had once heard Father Rosetti call them.

There was the wildly contagious Polio-Venice epidemic covered in the day-old *Los Angeles Times* and the *San Francisco Examiner* and *Chronicle*.

There was a *catastrophic fire in a crowded circus tent just outside of Munich in West Germany.*

There were reports of a *burgeoning plague beginning to claim great numbers of lives in northern Ireland and parts of England.*

There was the *horrifying drought and famine in India.*

Did these horror-story events in the newspapers have anything to do with the virgins? With the births of the so-called divine children? Was the whole word suddenly going mad?

A little past midnight Anne and Justin ventured out for some air before bed.

They walked quietly together under a big black umbrella. They traversed the Boulevard Maillot which borders on the lovely Bois de Boulogne.

As they turned onto the busier Avenue Charles de Gaulle, the evening rain began to taper off and finally stopped.

A fresh clean smell swept into the night air. The Paris streets and all the speeding cars glistened quite beautifully in the wet darkness. The cars made a sound like sticky tape being stripped off the ruler-straight avenue. Through bare tree branches, a distant stoplight alternately turned emerald green, chrome yellow, deep crimson red.

I'm going to lose Anne after this week, Justin O'Carroll couldn't help thinking. *She'll be back in the White Mountains of New Hampshire with the orphanage girls. It will be as if none of this had ever happened.*

In a way he was angry at her for her final decision. In another way, Justin understood and he loved Anne even more for her courage, for her faith.

Basically he just didn't know very much about love, the young priest thought to himself as he continued down the Avenue Charles de Gaulle. It was curious and rather sad the way one person could love another person so much without the other person feeling nearly so strongly.

Somehow Justin knew that this was an important

time for the two of them. He understood that he and
Anne were getting very close once again. The way things
had been back in Boston. *Lord, if you still listen to
me . . . help me to do the right thing. Give me courage. I
love Anne very much.*

As they walked along, Anne was watching Justin
closely out of the corner of her eye.

The last few days had been both a blessing and a
terrible burden for her. Ever since Justin had come to
Newport her life had been a nervous blur, a series of
strained moments. One after another after another.

*In a few days we'll be back in America. In a week at
most, I'll be seeing Reggie, Gwinnie, Laura. All of this
terrible confusion—Kathleen and Colleen, Justin and me
—somehow it has to come to some clear and logical
conclusion.*

In the middle of the long shady gray-and-green Paris
block, Anne suddenly stopped walking. Justin saw her,
and stopped as well. It wasn't raining any more, but
heavy drops from overhanging poplars were splashing
down on both their heads.

I have to do this, Anne was thinking as her heart
clutched.

"Justin . . . I . . ." Anne started to say something but
found she couldn't finish.

Her entire body began to tremble uncontrollably.
Very unsure of herself, of both her actions and her
thoughts, she reached out one badly shaking hand.

Anne put her hand behind Justin's neck, lightly
touching his long, soft curls.

Anne's face was inches away from Justin's.

He was so close she could feel his breath on her
cheek. After all the months of preventing this from happening, there was suddenly no way to stop it.

"Oh Justin, Justin," Anne whispered and felt the
most glorious relief flow through her body.

They began to kiss softly, as tenderly and uncer-
tainly as children, under the gleaming street lamp.

Anne partly resisted at first, her mouth a little hard
with bone and teeth.

Then the twenty-nine-year-old woman finally accepted the kiss; she gave freely of herself; Anne kissed Justin with an honest passion that left them both a little shaken and breathless.

"Oh, I do love you, Justin O'Carroll," Anne finally spoke. "I do love you."

ANNE

As she lay in the still light and peacefulness of morning, almost afraid to breathe, listening to the vague early traffic murmurings outside on the Avenue Foch, Anne considered that she was no longer a virgin.

Anne was feeling little if any guilt, however. She was experiencing no sense of lost innocence as she had feared she would all these years.

There was just a kind of warmth, she thought; a simple glow inside her that came from being closer to another person than she had ever thought possible.

What had happened between her and Justin couldn't have been wrong, Anne thought. It had been too wonderful; there had been exquisite love and tenderness shared between the two of them. They did love one another. If she had any doubt about that before, it was gone now.

Anne sat up in their bed.

She stretched her long, slender arms high over her head. A smile brushed across her lips. A private smile that blossomed out from the center of whoever Anne Feeney really was.

Across the elegant bedroom she could see herself in an antique mirror slanting over the bureau.

She had healthy breasts, Anne considered with a slight smile in her eyes. Not too large, pleasantly upturned; nice in her opinion, anyway. . . . Her stomach was tight and fit. . . . Her longer hair complemented the sharp bones in her cheeks.

As Justin had tried to tell her many times, she *was* pretty. Why hadn't she been able to accept that before? Why had she acted as if the way she looked was a terrible curse?

Anne glanced down at Justin's bare back, at his rear, and she felt herself beginning to blush.

"Justin," she whispered so low he couldn't have possibly heard. "I love you so much, it's a little scary right now."

She felt like waking him up. She felt like a young girl, a very young schoolgirl, and it was quite nice to be that way for a while.

Suddenly Anne wanted to share all her new thoughts and feelings with Justin. She wanted to know how their night together had been for him. Was he feeling any guilt? Had he enjoyed her?

As Anne was considering the best way to wake him, the bedroom phone suddenly began to ring.

It was a shrill, petulant noise—something like a fire alarm going off in the quiet little room.

Anne looked down at her wristwatch. It wasn't quite seven o'clock. . . . Who could it be? The Police? The Beaviers out in Chantilly? Perhaps Kathleen had been found?

Anne maneuvered across the bed and reached for the phone receiver. "Hello? . . . Hello?"

A small, muffled sob finally came over the phone. Then a startling burst of eight clear words:

"Sister Anne . . . will you please . . . come get me?"

The bottom fell out of Anne's stomach, her chest began to pound insanely.

"Kathleen . . . are you all right, Kathleen? Oh, sweetheart, where are you?"

Kathleen sounded incredibly weary as she spoke again. The young girl almost sounded drugged.

"Father Rosetti called Chantilly already. I talked to my mother and my father. . . . Can you meet us? I'm not very far from my uncle's townhouse . . . you and Father Justin please come," Kathleen said. She gave Anne the exact address.

Justin's eyes had come open by now. His bright green eyes were questioning Anne: *Who was on the phone?*

"We'll come right now," Anne whispered. "As soon as we can get a cab. Are you all right, Kathleen?"

As he heard the girl's name, Justin sat up in the rumpled bed. An incredible look of astonishment crossed his face.

"Please come right now, Anne. We have so many things to talk about and not much time. I'm almost ready to have the baby."

KATHLEEN

Riding incredibly fast—yet not fast enough, it seemed—the white Peugeot cab slipped along the rain-slicked Avenue de la Bourdonnais; it raced beneath the heavy girders of the Eiffel Tower, then weaved through double lanes of traffic bordering the Parc du Champ de Mars.

Finally the impatient, horn-honking cab driver plunged the car in among the ancient buildings of the Sorbonne and the Pantheon; the seedy district of Rue de la Huchette–St. Severin.

During the past twenty-four hours, the police had knocked on selected doors all through the ethnic neighborhood dominated by wine bars, épiceries, triperies, exotic cooking, and asphixiating fuel smells. Not a soupçon had been stirred up in the close-mouthed district, however. No Kathleen Beavier; no dark, mysterious Catholic priest; no cooperation whatsoever from the locals.

Anne and Justin held one another as they climbed the steep front stairs of a crumbling building just off the Rue de la Huchette.

The dismal building's front door was unlocked and unlatched. Inside lurked another flight of dark winding stairs. Anne and Justin quickly climbed three splintering flights to a top-floor hallway that featured three paint-scabbing doors and a wired-over skylight full of soot.

Father Eduardo Rosetti suddenly threw open one of the three hallway doors.

White light flooded the hall.

"Sister. Father O'Carroll. Please, come in." Father Rosetti attempted a smile, but his face remained haggard.

Drained. Rosetti had lost nearly twenty pounds in less than a week. The skin on his face appeared sallow; it was sagging on his cheeks and around his eyes.

Across the small, bare room behind him, Kathleen sat on a ruined two-seat sofa. She must have seen the hurt and worry on their faces because she pushed herself up and came to them.

Kathleen hugged both Anne and Justin, resting her head on Anne's shoulder, beginning to cry now.

"I'm sorry for just leaving like that," Kathleen said to Anne. "I'm so afraid now," she whispered.

"We simply don't have time to explain everything to you!" Father Rosetti was suddenly pacing the width of the empty flat.

"Please believe me when I tell you that Kathleen was *unsafe* at Henri Beavier's château. We have contacted the family, by the way, and they'll meet us at Orly. . . . We have to move Kathleen one final time. To Rome. To the holy sanctuary of the Vatican itself. To St. Pietro's itself if need be."

"Please trust Father Rosetti," Kathleen said. "The baby must be born in the Holy City."

Anne and Justin asked Kathleen questions for as long as Father Rosetti would allow. Then the nervous Chief Investigator took the two of them aside.

"There is great danger for both virgin girls right now. Please trust me," Father Rosetti said. "You must trust me. My investigation is nearly complete. I believe that Our Lady has led me to the truth."

Justin found himself growing angry suddenly. For a moment, he was close to striking the Vatican priest.

"Why won't you *tell us something* so that we *can* trust you? So that we *can* believe you?"

"We want to help Kathleen, Father," Anne said. "You need help, you say . . . Father Rosetti, *trust us!*"

The weary Vatican priest seemed affected by their concern. He mumbled a prayer in Latin.

"Please trust us!" Anne repeated, staring into the dark tunnels that were Father Rosetti's eyes.

"I do, Sister Anne . . . I trust both of you. It is a

very difficult thing for me, but I do. I know how you care
for Kathleen," Father Eduardo Rosetti finally whispered.

He then began to tell Anne and Justin everything
that he possibly could about the papal investigation. He
spoke of an intensely frightened and very old Holy Father
who believed he knew a great and terrifying secret—but
who was under pressure from his own advisers, the Council of Six, to remain silent. Father Rosetti told them every
detail of his trip to the Apostolic Palace during the past
summer; his meeting with Pope Pius XIII. . . .

"I accepted a sacred mission from the Holy Father.
Before then, I had been an ordinary priest in the Congregation of Rites. My only qualifications for the job were
that I was a very thorough investigator . . . and that I am
a scholar . . . of the Apocalypse."

A scholar of the Apocalypse.

An expert on prophecies concerning the end of the
world.

Both Anne and Justin tried to get Rosetti to tell
them more. Father Rosetti said there was nothing more to
say. Not until tomorrow, the feast day of Our Lady of
Fatima.

"You said that you wanted to give me your help?
That is how we began this conversation, I believe. Did
you both mean that?"

"Yes, we'll help," Anne said. "Of course we'll help.
In any way that we can. But what else is happening,
Father? What are the rest of your secrets, Father? You
have to be open and honest with us."

"If you help me now," Father Rosetti said to them,
"you will be able to *see* the rest of it for yourselves. You
may not want to, you may wish that you didn't, but you
will know everything. Every last twist and infernal turn!
Every last trick of the abominable Beast!"

It *is* all happening again, Anne couldn't help thinking to herself. It's like the very primitive beginnings of
Christianity. . . .

A holy virgin.

Biblical signs.

Prophecies.

Finally, the birth of a divine child.

Do I believe that it can happen now? Am I truly a Christian? Anne thought to herself.

Do I believe that the Son of God became a man for my sins?

Is that what is really in question here? Is it all a question of our Faith?

Arm in arm, matching each other's steps, Anne and Justin walked down the narrow canyon of an ancient Left Bank alleyway.

They stopped at the lip of the Seine. They tried to let the sight of the smooth-flowing river partially calm their fears.

Standing together by an iron rail they listened to the nasal hoots of little stinkpots patrolling the water; they heard the gay shouts of French children at some inner-city playground hidden from their eyes.

It was odd about the children's laughter, Anne thought to herself. My mother died in Larchmont, and I heard the laughter of children somewhere nearby ... President Kennedy was killed—and children were laughing in the beautiful Westchester schoolyard where I heard the news. ... Everything was seeming dark and frightening now—yet the children were still laughing so innocently.

"We don't have to do what Father Rosetti has asked of us, Anne."

Justin was leaning all his weight against the old buckling railing. The river wind was pushing all his black curls way back on his head. "I'm not even sure if I believe Father Rosetti—"

"Oh, I do." Anne smiled. "I don't believe anyone could tell lies or stories like that. Justin, he looks so bad now. Father Rosetti looks as if he's *dying* right before our eyes. I feel so sorry for him."

Anne and Justin both stared across the swirling river.

They were to be separated in just a few minutes now, one to Rome, one to Ireland.

They were both afraid, and they didn't even know what to be afraid of ... *We will never see one another again,* both Anne and Justin couldn't help thinking.

"We'll be all right, Annie," Justin whispered finally. "Everything will be."

Anne suddenly reached out for him. She pressed her face into Justin's sweater; she felt his arms come around her. Tears began to flow down both her cheeks.

Once she had finally allowed herself to feel, Anne found that she suddenly couldn't stop her emotions; everything was coming, rushing, in such great, dizzying waves. She had a scary feeling that she was completely out of control now.

"I love you so much. Why couldn't I have told you that simple thing long before?"

Justin held her as tightly as he could. They pressed hard against one another, desperately trying to find the strength to do what they knew they had to do.

They were both beginning to feel alone once again. Just the beginnings of loneliness.

"Father! ... Father! Sister Anne!" They heard shouts coming from up the narrow cul-de-sac.

Father Rosetti and Kathleen were outside, all packed and standing in the shadow of the dismal gray building where they had spent twenty-four mysterious hours.

It was time to go.

Just before she and Kathleen left for Rome, Father Rosetti took Sister Anne aside in the secured Air France lounge at Orly Airport. The two of them talked alone for several moments.

"Sister Anne, I must ask you one more time to forgive me my habit of secrecy. It is the only way I know. It is the way I have pledged to our Holy Father."

Anne nodded. She listened as the Vatican priest continued.

"Sister, I hope and I pray that I know the final truth about the two young virgin girls now. I think that I do. The message of Our Lady of Fatima has provided a trail for me to follow; clues, if you will. The Bible had provid-

ed answers. The apocalyptic writings. But, Sister . . ."
Father Rosetti's eyes grew darker. "I am not certain. Not
completely so. Ultimately this must all be a matter of
faith. *It has to be faith,* Sister Anne.

"In Rome, at the moment of the birth, you must all
watch for a sign. Just as Our Lady did on October
thirteenth at Fatima, she has promised a sign at the
moment of the birth. The two virgins . . . the two infants.
. . . We will know which is the Beast, which is our Savior.
. . . Sister Anne, the Beast must be killed. *The child of the
Devil must be killed.* . . . So too, the child of God must be
protected at any cost to us."

Anne started to speak. Father Rosetti grasped one of
her hands in both of his.

"You will know what to do," he whispered. "It has
all been promised. Have faith, Sister. You must have
faith."

ROME

Swooping down low over the Borghese Gardens, the
Tiber, the vast Piazza di San Pietro, the Air France flight
eventually landed on schedule at Leonardo da Vinci airport.

It was 5:30 P.M. Rome time, October twelfth.

The Roman police, the carabinieri, soldiers from the
Italian Army had quite masterfully succeeded in diverting
news reporters, the paparazzi, and well-wishers away
from the correct landing gate.

Two solemnly black-suited emissaries from the Vatican were there to greet *la bella signorina* Kathleen, *la
bella signorina*'s mother and father, the others in her
important party.

The entire group was then led back out onto the
airport's runway where a Vatican state limousine was
waiting. The car was a specially made Fiat with the
gold-and-black SCV license plate assigned to all official
Vatican vehicles.

A police detective confided to Charles Beavier that
the impressive automobile was equipped with bulletproof

windows. . . . *Threats had been made. Nothing to worry about. Threats were always made in Italy these days.*

More than thirty thousand pushing, screaming, adoring people were massed on the airport access roads trying to get a look at the young American virgin; making a scene like a grand Italian opera.

The people were packed on both sides of the narrow concrete road; they were hanging off the heavy stone overpasses; they were crushed into all available window space in the different airline buildings.

Men, women, and little schoolchildren, they were all screaming—"Long live the Virgin!"

The black limousine finally approached the gates of the Vatican around sunset.

Pressed tightly together in the back seat, Anne and Kathleen nervously watched the great shrouded towers, the stucco palaces, and gold crosses outlined in the Roman skies.

Then they witnessed a miracle.

Against the backdrop of small shops and trattorias on the Via Merulana, a great column of worshipers nearly two miles long had come out to greet the holy virgin. . . . Two hundred thousand of the faithful had turned out with almost no warning of Kathleen's arrival.

The people wanted to believe.

The people desperately wanted to believe.

It was impossible for anyone riding in the limousine to comprehend fully the majestic, awe-inspiring scene of love spread before them.

It was impossible not to be moved by the magnitude, the devotion, the honest love in the eyes of the people. Beautiful flowers were being thrown onto the car, as if it were the Spanish Steps.

Anne thought of the great crowd that had somehow traveled to the village of Fatima during the war in 1917. She thought about the effect a miracle might have in this supposedly rational but oddly susceptible age.

Anne's body was tingling and she was feeling incredibly lightheaded. Suddenly, and for no reason she could specify, she felt that she believed.

Suddenly Anne believed in the holy virgin birth.

There was a strange feeling spreading all through her body, an old familiar feeling.

She believed.

On account of the clogged, nearly hysterical crowds it took three-quarters of an hour to inch along the final mile.

As Anne tensely pushed herself up out of the back seat ahead of Kathleen, she couldn't even begin to comprehend the solid brawl of smiling, screaming, happy-sobbing faces.

There was a colorful wall of Swiss Guards, two men thick, which drew a ragged circle around the limousine. Then came the hordes of emotional men, women, and children: waving simple peasant caps, cotton handkerchiefs, pictures of *the Bambino,* jumping, bobbing left or right to get a glimpse of the virgin girl. There was the sweet smell of burning incense over everything. Rows of priests in white surplices and flowing black cassocks. A burgeoning roar that gave Anne shivers.

Best of all, coming through the clearest, Anne could feel the love present in the streets outside the Roman hospital where Kathleen would bear her child. The people loved the Virgin Kathleen. They were all trying to communicate this desperate, overwhelming love to her. In that way, it was the most beautiful and touching moment so far. Anne could feel herself beginning to be overwhelmed with strong emotions. The powerful, matchless moment was so incredibly beautiful. Unbelievable.

Kathleen finally began to climb out of the Vatican state car. An even louder, thunderous roar swept up the Roman avenue. The hair on Anne's neck was standing. Her body was intensely sensitive and alive. Tears slipped down both cheeks, and she realized she was feeling tremendous love not only for Kathleen but for these Italian people as well.

Anne was letting her eyes drift back over the surging brightly colored mass when she saw a crack in the wall of Vatican guards and police. Her heart jumped.

"Over there!" Anne called, pointed, but she was drowned under the deafening crowd noise.

A thickset man in a dark suit coat and open-necked white shirt was pushing through the opening. The man was suddenly through. Rushing toward the limousine and Kathleen.

"Oh my God!" Anne screamed but couldn't even hear herself.

The man was bent down low. Coming even faster now. Running.

Sister Anne Feeney stiffened her back and legs. At the last second, she hurled herself between the onrushing man and Kathleen. She and the hulking figure collided.

Anne's neck was twisted sharply to the right. Her chest received a terrific jolting blow. Her right leg wrenched, then crushed under the falling bodies.

There was a bright, white explosion at the center of the thick ball of people. Police and soldiers suddenly fell on the man as well as the body of Sister Anne Feeney.

The badly frightened Roman policemen were screaming wildly at one another. A billy club lashed out and struck arms, legs. Kathleen was rushed off in the opposite direction—with no thought for what might be waiting in that part of the unruly crowd.

Anne's blurred, spinning eyes cleared enough for her to make out two uniformed officers. They were helping her up. "Paparazzi," the youngest of the two said. "Photo-grapher. Bad fellow. Are you all right? You did a brave thing. Very brave."

"I think I'm all right," Anne managed.

She looked out at all the faces crowding closer. They were beginning to cheer. The people were cheering for her now, Anne understood.

"Oh, don't do that," she whispered. Anne then smiled gratefully. The police hurried her into the hospital to be with the Virgin Kathleen.

At nine that evening it was reported on Italian television that Kathleen Beavier had entered Salvator Mundi Clinic, an expensive private hospital where high-ranking cardinals went for their operations; where the movie star Elizabeth Taylor had once been hospitalized during the filming of *Cleopatra;* where a team of six Italian and

American doctors would be supervising the virgin birth.

The first report out of Salvator Mundi came from the Italian chief surgeon himself.

An elegant dark-haired man in his early forties, his face rich with character lines, he met with reporters in a pristine-white conference room used mainly for staff meetings at the hospital.

"Kathleen Grace Beavier is in excellent condition." The *dottore* spoke with the most gracious smile and manner. "The birth of the child can be anticipated in the next twelve to twenty-four hours. We are expecting no complications whatsoever."

COLLEEN

She was actually going to be a mother soon; *a tiny baby was going to come out of her,* Colleen Galaher thought and was quietly astonished.

The young peasant girl continued to make herb tea for herself and for Sister Katherine Dominica. She cut into a dark loaf of soda bread marked with the traditional cross.

The simple act of tea-making kept her mind off the other things that were happening now, things that didn't make complete sense to young Colleen.

Tea she knew how to make very well. She made excellent herb tea, the parish priest Father McGurk had told her.

How could she possibly be having a baby? Colleen thought as a wisp of white steam finally appeared from the spout of her pot.

How would she be able to take care of the baby once it was born?

Where would the necessary money come from?

Would she ever be allowed to go back to Holy Trinity school?

"I'm only fourteen years old," the young girl finally whispered out loud. Tears ran down her cheeks. Her small, freckled hands began to tremble.

"I'm only fourteen," Colleen Galaher sobbed into her apron. "God in heaven, please help me. Please, please, please."

Colleen finally brought the tea and steaming bread out into the living room. She looked all over for Sister Katherine. Colleen called inside the house, then outside from the porch.

Sister Katherine Dominica was nowhere around the cottage.

The pain was suddenly unbearable, and Colleen Galaher was alone.

POPE PIUS XIII

From a distance, from the viewing perspective of the stone archway opening onto the vast room, Leo Corrado Lombardi appeared most austere and commanding in his pure-white robes and brocaded shawls.

Closer up, however, it could be seen that the Holy Leader of over seven hundred million Catholics was trembling violently as he sat in the hermetically sealed marble-and-granite vault inside the East Wing of the Court of the Belvedere.

Constructed in the early nineteenth century as a sempiternal companion for the Vatican Library, the Court of the Belvedere was now the Vatican's second greatest building. Only St. Peter's Basilica was larger, more impressive to look at and walk through.

Guarded by Gendarmeria Pontifica policemen, some of whom carried submachine guns on the premises, the top floor East Wing was the safekeeping place for essential documents elaborately detailing the secret life of the Church during the twentieth century.

Among these sacred, sometimes sacrilegious papers was the only copy of the message left with three Portuguese children by Our Lady at Fatima, the most important divination of the modern Church.

The one great miracle of this age.

Pope Pius XIII's gray eyes slowly took in the high-walled room which held the most important records from the Rota (the ecclesiastical Court) as well as papers detailing Church agreements both with and against the Fascists and the Nazis.

To help preserve the good and bad evidence alike, the room had been equipped with its own very expensive humidifier plus an expensive museum fire-alarm system that sprinkled dry powder rather than water.

For several moments Pius XIII sat without moving, the amazing document about Fatima resting stiffly on his white-cassocked knees.

The large room's subtle back lighting reflected off his small, bald pate.

One red-slippered foot tapped against the beautiful Carrara-marble floor.

Pius wished to read each of the letters about Fatima one final time before making his ultimate decision on the virgins.

The Holy Father was trying to judge the seventy-year-old messages and warnings against related events, *predicted events,* which had occurred during the past few days.

At that moment, Pope Pius was aching to talk with someone who might understand the way he felt about Jesus Christ, about God the Father, about the Church itself . . . someone with simple and direct faith to comprehend the wondrous miracles, perhaps the unholy destruction that was now so imminent.

If the faithful could only be told the truth about the virgins. . . . If the people themselves could only be told everything . . . about the Last Judgment . . . about the Child.

If my own advisers would only listen. If our eminent cardinals would only believe the sacred truths upon which their Church was built.

Pope Pius began to recall prophetic words from St. Matthew, beloved Levi:

> For as the lightning cometh out of the East
> and shineth unto the West, so shall the coming

of the Son of man be. . . . Immediately after the
tribulation of those days shall the sun be darkened.
And the moon shall not give her light. And the stars
shall fall from heaven.

His eyes stinging with sadness for the world, with
stubborn hope and determination, Pius XIII gazed down
on the sacred message from Our Lady of Fatima.

*There will be two Virgins who will appear across the
face of the earth* the Gentlewoman had told the Portuguese children in October, 1917.

*Seventy years from now there will be signs so that all
will know the time has truly come. Beware of the Devil's
guile.*

The time of the Last Judgment will be at hand.

LUCIA DOS SANTOS

Sister Maria das Dores (Mary of the Sorrows)
wasn't even certain of the year, but she believed that the
long-ago-promised day was finally here.

For weeks now, Sister Maria—formerly Lucia dos
Santos, the last survivor of the three children of Fatima—
had felt a strange new energy in the briny sea air at the
Convent of St. Dorothy.

Sometimes Sister Maria would pass hours remembering the day back in 1917. The breathtaking crowd
which had swept up over the hills in the Cova da Iria.
The feeling like electrical current that had surged through
her body. The brilliant, whirling light; the light and the
miraculous vision like no other before or after, which
nearly a hundred thousand people had seen with her that
day.

From her solitary half-moon window Sister Maria
das Dores watched a beautiful sunset that evening. The
ancient woman felt a strange oneness with the gold- and
purple-stained sky, the white-capped Mediterranean, the
red poppies quietly breathing on her ledge.

Sister Maria silently prayed that since October, 1917
the world had taken the beautiful Virgin's warning to

heart: "man has taken great evil onto himself, and this evil will destroy man."

FATHER ROSETTI

No one has the right to ask this of you. . . .
Not to damn yourself to an eternity in hell.

He struggled into the Dublin hotel room, noisily dropping his bag, but Father Eduardo Rosetti never bothered to switch on the overhead lights.

Instead, he walked over beside a water-streaked window. He stood there observing the cool, silent Irish cityscape.

He was certain now that he knew the truth about the two virgins.

He alone knew, and that perhaps was unwise.

The Beast had made brilliant use of artifice, illusion, imitation. But Father Rosetti had followed the clear signs in the message of Fatima. He was certain he had. His faith had never been stronger.

In his briefcase there were stacks of documents revealing everything. Before he left with Father O'Carroll in the morning, the papers would go into the hotel safe. The truth about the virgin birth would all be made available for the world. The truth about both births.

One final time, he heard the whispered command of Pius XIII:

You must find the true Virgin, my Investigator! The Church must find the mother of the divine child.

Father Eduardo Rosetti had found her.

ANNE AND KATHLEEN

It was an unforgettable last few hours between Kathleen Beavier and Anne Feeney.

For long periods they were both silent in the Salvator Mundi hospital suite.

The two young women sat peacefully beside the room's single casement window, looking out over the winking lights of Rome.

Just holding hands.

Waiting for Kathleen's labor to begin.

Kathleen badly wanted to be with someone she was close to right then. Anne was such a beautiful person, Kathleen thought. She understood now why Cardinal Rooney had chosen Anne from among all the other Sisters in the Archdiocese of Boston.

As she stared out over the Eternal City, the teenage girl felt a stitch deep in her stomach.

"Unh . . . Oh, dear . . . Okay now."

At every twinge, every pain, she wondered *is this it?*

Is it all going to start now?

Holding her breath, slowly massaging her lower abdomen, Kathleen waited for a clear, physical sign.

Her water finally breaking.

The mucus plug coming out.

No sign came. Not yet.

Kathleen grasped Anne's hand tighter than before.

"It's so very strange and scary for me right now." Kathleen hunched her shoulders and softly rocked in her chair. "I wonder if anyone has ever felt exactly like this before? Every fear I've ever shut in the back of my mind is coming right to the front. All my worst fears. Full-blown and so incredibly vivid.

"I keep thinking . . . will my baby be all right? Will I be? . . . Is it going to hurt much? . . . The questions won't stop coming now, Anne."

Kathleen became quiet again; they were both silent and afraid in the hospital room.

The simple act of hand-holding was enough.

In the meantime, the full blackness of night had slipped over the Roman hospital building like a Vatican monk's cowl. Outside Kathleen's door there were four Swiss Guards.

It was finally October the thirteenth—the day of the Virgin.

BOOK III

Most Blessed Virgin Mary, your life of faith and love and perfect unity with Christ was planned by God to show us clearly what our lives should be.... You are the outstanding model of motherhood and virginity.

—THE SECOND VATICAN COUNCIL OF 1964

ELEVEN

THE CHILD

The infant was standing upside down like a circus acrobat in its mother's small womb. The little baby was lightly holding the umbilical cord with one hand, a study in peacefulness.

The tiny head was wedged against the cervical mucus plug. The crabbed feet kicked out playfully into the mother's tender stomach webs.

The limbs, fingers, and toes; the child's nails, eyebrows, and eyelashes were all fully developed. The sex couldn't be distinguished. The heartbeat was steady and fine. The senses of sight, hearing, and touch were undeveloped but ready to blossom quickly once stimuli were provided.

The child was nearly twenty inches long, a little over six and a half pounds—quite average in that way.

The skin was rose-petal pink, but covered by fine black hair and wrinkled like a very old person's. The body was completely covered with a thin gauze like cheese skin.

In each tiny brain cell of the baby there was all the love and goodness, the unmatched capacity for both happiness and sadness, the genius, the wit and sense of irony, all the love of beauty and will for survival within the human race.

In all those ways, it was a child like any other.

ANNE

Everything was moving so fast and in such dangerously uncharted skies, Anne thought to herself and couldn't control a shiver.

What made logical sense to her? What didn't? Who could really sit back and coldly judge anything in these last few emotional hours?

Two virgins, Anne considered as she slowly walked down a deserted hospital hallway reeking with the strong vapors of rubbing alcohol.

Poor Kathleen. Anne unconsciously clenched her hands; she tensed and untensed her back muscles as she walked.

She couldn't imagine how a seventeen-year-old girl could survive all of this. Kathleen's life could never be the same, Anne thought with added sadness. No matter which way things turned out after today. . . .

Anne turned a corner into an identical marble-and-stone hallway. Standing in a staggered line of religious statues, a young Italian policeman with a rifle watched her coming.

"Signorina." The policeman tipped his visored hat, knowing that Sister Anne was the virgin's companion.

Justin and Father Rosetti would probably be at Colleen Galaher's by now, Anne was thinking. . . . Col-

leen was a very lovely young girl too. She was even
younger—more innocent?—than Kathleen. Anne remembered making tea with Colleen, calmly talking with the
girl about a soda-bread recipe. Anne recalled how she
had liked Colleen the moment she'd met her . . . why was
that? What was the Irish virgin if not another innocent
and confused young girl? *Both girls seemed so good. So
right. . . .*

Why had God clearly selected her and Justin for
these important tasks? Anne wondered.

Why was she here with Kathleen in Rome now?

Why was he off in western Ireland?

*What was going to happen to all of them in just a
few hours?*

Turning another dark stone corner, Anne found that
she had reached the far end of the hospital building. She
turned and headed back to the private room where Kathleen was still sleeping.

Millions of people around the world were wondering
about the young virgin now . . . about the mysterious holy
child. But Anne was actually there. It was difficult to
believe. It was a challenge to get her mind to supply the
hard edges of reality to the events that were happening.

As she passed through the stone portal into Kathleen's room, passed the somber quartet of guards, Anne
found that she was becoming uncontrollably nervous and
anxious. *It was so close now.* Her heart was racing.

Anne tried to make herself not hope too much.

She tried not to think of the wonderful possibilities
for this birth in Rome.

Out through the small window in Kathleen's room,
Sister Anne Feeney watched a burnt-orange and crimson
sun just floating up above the Trastevere.

A beautiful sunrise, Anne thought to herself. *A
sign.*

THE SIGNS

In the inner circles of his mind, Colonel Reese Monash tried to absorb the full glory of the magnificently

ordered chaos, the miraculous peacefulness, the incredible
beauty he was allowed to witness.

There were billions of stars, like a display of matchless jewels against an infinite blue-black backdrop. There
were whirling pools of soft-colored gas. Marbled white
and black meteors. An iridescent faraway planet with
Chinese-red rings coming into view.

Colonel Monash stared out on the heavens from his
seat at the controls of U.S. Skylab VI.

Reese Monash and Captain Mickey Kane had been
up for seventeen days now; a routine space probe. Just
four more days, then it would be back to terra firma:
Houston, Texas; Reese's twenty-nine-year-old wife Janie,
his boy Willie Mac. . . .

Speaking of which, earth, Colonel Monash could see
the pretty, twinkling lights of cities down across North
America now. Reese could see deserts. And the big
black stains that were the Atlantic and Pacific oceans, he
knew.

Sometimes Reese felt like a being from another planet himself when he was up in one of the space labs. The
astronaut felt that he was part of some great, other intelli-
gence; that he was supernatural, an infinite being.

Mick Kane said that he felt the same thing sometimes. In his way of thinking, Skylab VI was like a
church: a really jazzed-up interplanetary chapel where
you could go to think big thoughts. God knows, you
couldn't think on earth any more.

The senior astronaut's eyes suddenly shot over toward the far right side of the cockpit window.

Colonel Reese Monash saw a fast-moving colored
streak of light.

Colonel Monash saw it all right, but he wasn't ready
to admit it to himself until he stared for a good thirty
seconds or more.

Then he had to admit the reality of what he was
looking at.

Coming from directly behind the moon there was a
very large comet encapsulated in a grainy cloud of purple
and gray fog. Primordial matter that was flying at a

tremendous speed, throwing off small meteors like cold sweat. Matter which had been traveling in this form since the creation of the Universe: matter that had seen God, so to speak.

The nucleus was maybe a hundred miles long, Reese quickly calculated. Very goddam big. Bigger than Kahoutek, probably.

"Hey, Mickey, c'mon up front... Mick, there's a damn enormous comet coming our way. Coming right toward earth. I just spotted a huge goddam comet."

"You better call Houston." The other astronaut stared out into space. Suddenly Mick Kane saw it—*the comet*. "Jesus Christ, call Houston!"

JUSTIN

As the English Ford hummed along the gently undulating country roads, Father Justin O'Carroll sat and stared at the heavy, metallic sky towering overhead.

First Justin prayed.

Then he considered that there was no end to this miraculous day that he could even begin to imagine.

Finally, Justin had the frightening thought: *I shouldn't be here. I'm not strong enough, I can feel it. My faith isn't strong enough. I am exactly the wrong choice to be here.*

The Galaher house outside Maam Cross wasn't as it had been before, it seemed to Justin.

Suddenly an unfamiliar stucco bungalow and barn appeared in the Cortina's windshield.

There was an unremembered television antenna like a snarled branch on the thatched roof. The grass seemed loden-green. Too dark. The cottage itself seemed to be listing to one side.

Something was wrong. Justin was almost certain. *Something was different now... or was it his imagination? His fears?*

As they were climbing out of the car, Father Rosetti turned to Justin.

"Sister Katherine left the young girl yesterday. She wasn't strong enough. We have to be strong. The two of us. Yesterday you asked me to trust you. I trust you, Father O'Carroll. I trust no one but you and myself."

There were five Jesuit priests in the musty, fire-warmed living room of the cottage. The priests were all strong-looking men; all were in their thirties and forties.

The living room seemed different and new also, Justin thought. A big mahogany grandfather clock was ticking like the sober room's heartbeat.

"The Beavier child should have been born quietly too. Out of the public eye, just like this one," Father Rosetti whispered. "Under the holy care of priests."

Bending low to avoid heavy ceiling beams, Father Rosetti and Father Justin O'Carroll began to climb the creaking stairs to Colleen's bedroom.

"Will you please get me my stole, Father O'Carroll? Also the Manual."

As they entered the small, close bedroom, Jutin saw the young Irish girl in obvious discomfort. Colleen was undergoing severe spasms and labor pains. Her small, freckled face seemed especially wan, almost anemic.

"Where in God's name is the doctor?" Justin asked. "Why isn't the doctor here yet? Where are the anesthetics? The girl is in labor."

Father Rosetti seemed surprised by Justin's reaction. His brown eyes narrowed into slits.

"I will perform the doctor's or midwife's function," Father Rosetti whispered. "Father O'Carroll, you will assist me during the delivery. No one else will be permitted in this room, under powers vested in me by Pope Pius XIII and Our Lord Jesus Christ."

Father Rosetti shut the heavy pinewood door with a shove. Colleen's soft green eyes opened wide and looked at the two priests.

There had been no moment to match this one in nearly two thousand years.

"Are you sure about this child?" Justin whispered one final time. "Father, are you absolutely certain?"

KATHLEEN

No modern-day pope has been surgically treated outside the Vatican. Both John XXIII and Paul VI had prostate operations in a specially equipped operating room inside the papal apartment. Several cardinals, however, have been treated at San Camillo or at Salvator Mundi, where Kathleen Beavier was now staying on the fourth floor.

Salvator Mundi was staffed by Salvatorian Sisters as well as lay nuns. Many of the doctors there were American, and even the Italian doctors spoke some English because of the high incidence of wealthy American patients.

The hospital building was four stories, plain straw-colored brick with large churchlike windows. Both the hospital and the nearby Salvatorian convent house were enclosed by a high brick wall, shaded by tall umbrella pines.

That morning over sixty thousand people had gathered outside the hospital gates. Hundreds of thousands more were said to be collecting in the piazza of St. Peter's.

Inside the clinic itself, everything was quite luxurious. The marble and carved-stone corridors were wider than many streets in Rome. The floors were highly polished so that they mirrored movements and flickering lights from the brass wall sconces.

In suite 401–401A, Kathleen Beavier and Sister Anne Feeney waited and tried their best to prepare physically and emotionally for the childbirth.

"Push now, Kathleen," Anne encouraged, almost feeling as if she were bearing the child herself—feeling the same intense anxiety anyway. "Push. Push, Kathy."

"It's very hard work," Kathleen grunted. The young girl's long blonde hair was soaked dark and stringy already. Her mouth was dry.

Kathleen suddenly looked up and stopped the straining pushing exercise. Kathleen saw that she and Anne

were no longer alone in the Salvator Mundi hospital
room.

A man was now standing in the solitary stone archway leading into the hospital room. A solemn elderly man
she and Anne recognized immediately.

Pope Pius XIII had come to see the virgin himself.

VATICAN CITY—UPI REPORT

Italian police this morning mobilized an army
of two thousand antiterrorist agents and sharpshoot-
ers to guard young Kathleen Beavier as well as visiting dignitaries against possible assassination attempts
here in Rome.

Authorities ordered extra surveillance for
Argentine President Jorge Videla, described by left-
ist groups as a hangman; for Catholic Vice-President
Hugh Middleton of the United States; for President
Eleas Sankis of Lebanon; King Juan Carlos of
Spain; Princess Marie of Belgium; for the former
King of Greece; for President Bauer of the Federal
Republic of Germany.

Italian police experts joined the Vatican's own
security force in drawing up massive antiterrorist
measures, checking the vast square in front of St.
Peter's Basilica for possible snipers' nests and other
danger spots. Both Pope Pius XIII and Kathleen
Beavier are under heavy around-the-clock protective security.

THE FAITHFUL

All over the world the hope, expectation, and excitement was infectious; it built upon itself like nothing
seen for hundreds, maybe thousands of years.

A young, blond-haired priest stood on the grand
stone terrazzo of the Apostolic Palace.

Over four hundred thousand people were spread
before him, completely blanketing the majestic piazza of
St. Peter's, stretching nearly as far as his eye could see.

A feeling of overwhelming power flowed through the

young priest's body; he had an irresistible vision of one day being a great Church leader.

The young priest prayed quite beautifuly into a hand-held microphone. His rich baritone voice was like an archangel's booming out over the great sea of heads in St. Peter's Square.

The crowd answered the prayer in the most thunderous roar *imaginable.* They began to sing *Veni Creator Spiritu:* Come, Holy Spirit.

In Mexico City, nearly a million of the faithful attended an emotional Mass in and around the Basilica of Guadalupe, the site where the Virgin had first appeared to a local Indian in the sixteenth century.

All through Spain and Holland, throughout France, in Poland and Belgium, in West Germany, Ireland, parts of England, the great cathedrals were beginning to fill to capacity once again.

At the beginning of the workday, long lines flowed out of the most important churches in Amsterdam, Paris, Brussels, London, Madrid, Warsaw, and Berlin. The strains of *Ave Maria* swelled majestically into the crisp autumn air.

In the United States, the television satellite Telstar provided instant participation from New York, across the Midwest, to California. Record numbers of people tuned in to observe the birth on early-morning television.

In Boston, schoolchildren from all over the huge archdiocese were bused to a special open-air Mass held at Fenway Park where the Red Sox play baseball. The glorious sound of the children's Mass rose up toward the Massachusetts Turnpike, causing morning traffic to snarl all the way back to Route 128 going west, to the Callaghan Tunnel going east.

In Los Angeles, perhaps the single most emotional gathering of all was held in Frank Lloyd Wright's Hollywood Bowl amphitheater.

Sprawling out over fifty acres, the amphitheater easily accommodated over seventy thousand people. Natural acoustics were supplied by the surrounding hills, making

microphones unnecessary for the various celebrity and
religious hosts. At other times, the amphitheater had been
the site for the city's spectacular Easter dawn service. . . .
This morning it was the setting for an immense gathering of families and friends of those stricken by Polio-
Venice.

Together they all prayed for a great miracle. They
prayed for the Virgin mercifully to cure their loved ones.

In the last hours before the birth, a news magazine
calculated that over five million photographs were taken,
that nearly half a million recordings were made. For a
short, hopeful time, the people of the world came together
and offered a prayer for young Kathleen Beavier and her
unborn child.

"Holy Mary, Mother of God!" At St. Peter's Basilica, the young priest's voice continued to ring out against
the grand collonnades and towering, ancient columns.
"Pray for us sinners, now and at the hour of our death.
Amen."

"We trust in the will of God!" The people prayed
together in a deafening, chilling chorus.

"We believe in God Almighty!"

All over the world, people still wanted to believe.
After all the years of difficulty, the years of diminishing
spirituality, the people still wanted to believe.

KATHLEEN

The delivery room inside Salvator Mundi hospital
was very large and sparkling white; it was frightening in
the antiseptic way operating rooms sometimes can be.

A nervous group of Salvatorian Sisters in immaculate white uniforms with starched, veil-like headdresses,
was busily at work there, doing everything possible to
assist the special team of doctors.

As two of the Salvatorians effortlessly transferred
her from the gurney to the sterile white delivery table,
Kathleen let her eyes close. . . . She felt them take cloth
straps and begin to tie her down. They gently placed her

feet in cool metal obstetric stirrups. They swiveled down a polished-chrome mirror so that she could watch herself. They sponged her forehead with a tingling alcohol mixture.

Very much in pain, but also beginning to feel warm and dreamy, Kathleen let herself drift back to her earlier meeting with Pope Pius. The teenage girl could almost hear the Holy Father speaking. She remembered precisely what he had said—his inflections; everything:

"The message of Fatima, Kathleen. . . . All across the earth there may be a battle between the kingdom of God and the realm of evil. This could be the Last Judgment promised in St. Matthew, in St. Mark, in Revelation . . . There are two virgins. One will bear the Savior . . . one will bear the Anti-Christ."

"No! Please!" Kathleen suddenly spoke out loud in the bustling delivery room

"It's all right, Kathleen. Everything is perfect so far." The young girl heard a calming voice.

Kathleen's eyes blinked open in the overly bright and busy hospital room.

A very good-looking man in a loose-fitting white scrub suit, a doctor with beautiful dark-brown eyes was looking down at her. There was a slightly amused expression on this tall man's face. One of the hospital-room lights was glinting. It almost seemed to be winking out of the surgeon's right eye.

"I am Doctor Bonnano, you remember. We met last night in your room . . . I would like to give you something to help with the delivery, Kathleen. What we call an epidural local."

Kathleen nodded but also softly moaned in pain.

"Believe it or not, everything is absolutely perfect so far. You are in glowing health, wonderful condition to have a beautiful baby today."

"Thank you," Kathleen mumbled, beginning to feel that she was losing control for some reason. She wondered if this happened to all mothers just before they gave birth.

A second doctor pierced a long, sharp needle into her. It hurt terribly.

The chief doctor continued to speak to her. So effortlessly, Kathleen thought.

Anne was looking on from behind a white gauze mask. Her eyes seemed very much afraid. Kathleen wanted to talk to her for just a few more minutes. She wanted to get off this hospital table. Only she was strapped in so tightly.

"You're going to have a beautiful baby, Kathleen," Doctor Bonnano said. "This is my four-thousand-three-hundred-sixty-fourth baby. Did you know that? Absolutely true. Nothing to it," the handsome *dottore* whispered. "Watch me closely now."

COLLEEN

Justin kept hearing a single obsessive idea, repeated over and over in his mind:

If you can't believe there can be a blessed miracle now, a second divine birth . . . how can you say that you ever believed?

Did you ever believe in Jesus Christ, Father O'Carroll? Did you ever truly believe?

Colleen, meanwhile, was watching one of the priest's shiny black cassock sleeves flapping and fluttering around her face. The younger priest, the handsome one, was gently sponging off her forehead. He seemed so very nice and concerned for her.

Colleen was fully dilated now and was pushing very hard to deliver the child. The fourteen-year-old Irish girl had never been asked to work this hard, she thought. Nothing in her experience had prepared her for this intense pain.

Bent over now, just inches from the girl's face, Justin understood that he had never before known what it was for a woman to have a baby. Suddenly he felt humbled; he felt tender and loving toward the poor, suffering young woman.

If you can't believe there can be a miracle now, Justin heard, *how can you say that you ever believed?*

Once or twice, his mind completely left the close

cottage room in Maam Cross. Justin would find himself lost in the middle of a thought about Kathleen or Anne.

He wondered what was happening right then in Rome. He was afraid for both Kathleen and Anne. Terribly afraid for them. If anything happened . . .

He was beginning to believe that this might be the true virgin, this the true child.

If that was so, what would happen in Rome? What would happen? What were the final secrets of the Virgin?

Colleen suddenly began to moan and sob. She cried out in a voice that was so young and innocent it shocked both priests.

"Please don't hurt me any more," she begged them.

A tiny head appeared.

An incredibly small head began to slide from between Colleen's thin legs.

A child.

With a shiny-wet umbilical cord wrapped around its throat like a great king's necklace.

KATHLEEN

I must have the greatest faith, Kathleen cautioned herself as she began to feel the inevitable loss of concentration, hope, caring.

I must have the strongest faith now. All the rest of this is a test of faith.

It was unimaginably brighter and more vivid behind her eyelids than in the hospital delivery room.

Why was that?

What was happening to her now?

Wasn't it enough for her just to be having the baby?

Kathleen suddenly felt as if she were being lifted and carried far away from Salvator Mundi, that her baby was so insignificant in the sweep of the Universe and infinite time.

Kathleen felt a sameness between herself and all of creation. She felt an overwhelming *oneness.*

What was happening?

Oh my God, am I dying now?

Just then, the young girl began to experience an intricate, detailed vision.

Kathleen Beavier saw the young girl Mary. She saw a plain clay house high over the busy marketplace in Nazareth. She looked deeply into Mary's eyes, and Kathleen saw a truth about all women there; a truth about herself.

Then the scenes before her eyes began to change rapidly. They came and went in fractions of split-seconds. Somehow, though, Kathleen found that she could take in all the detail. It was almost as if she had known it before, that she was only being reminded now.

Kathleen Beavier saw Jesus, she thought.

Jesus was hanging pathetically on a grotesque wooden cross. Jesus was a lovely, dark-faced man with the saddest yet the strongest eyes she had ever seen. His body was scourged and wounded in so many unimaginable places. The flesh around the wounds was purple and yellow. Never before had she understood the heinous idea: Crucifixion.

Kathleen then saw the recognizable faces of famous people all through history. She felt related to them; she felt a oneness with them too. They had all believed in the sacredness and the dignity of man.

Am I just a pathetic mad girl? Kathleen thought.

No, I believe. I believe in a Creator of all this.

I believe in you and I love you . . . am I mad?

Suddenly the tone of the fast-flying images seemed to change.

Kathleen missed a few of the early ones.

Then something like a shattering earthquake appeared before her eyes. Unspeakable tragedy with many people dying senselessly.

I believe in God . . . I reject Evil with all my strength, the young girl prayed.

A tidal wave rushed like a flooding river down the crowded streets of a major American city. Famous buildings were crushed. Hundreds of thousands were drowned in an instant of horror and evil. It was a disaster predicted by nearly every major psychic of the age. Kathleen felt the all-powerful Presence of the Beast. The deep Voice.

The young girl's eyes suddenly opened.

Her body felt a rude shock, a jolting sensation like a punch. Her pelvis tightened. She was exhausted, helpless; no strength left.

She saw blazing kettledrum lights whirling over her head. She saw the swarming doctors and nurses. She heard distant cathedral bells pealing through Rome.

The child was coming now.

THE CHILD

Fourteen-year-old Colleen Galaher shrieked and sobbed loudly as she saw the snipping sewing-scissors floating over her quivering stomach.

The umbilical cord was carefully cut by Father O'Carroll—then the exhausted, dripping priest knotted the cord like a piece of wrapping twine.

Her baby, meanwhile, was being held up high like a beautiful little lamb, like a chalice at the consecration part of Mass.

She couldn't see the face yet.

Colleen had the thought that the light slanting in the bedroom window was making a golden robe around the child's shoulders. Tears were in her eyes. *I am a mother. . . .*

Father Rosetti began to rub the baby's throat in an upward motion with his thumb.

He then wiped away mucus with a swab of disinfected linen.

He gently flicked the sole of the baby's foot to ensure it was breathing.

Father Rosetti then carried the child out of the bedroom. He never let the young mother touch the infant.

He never once allowed Colleen Galaher to see her little son's face. He left Colleen crying, not understanding any of this.

Justin and Father Eduardo Rosetti hurried from the

lonely cottage, nearly running to their car. . . . They must have looked like kidnapers, Justin thought.

The car finally began to roll down the rocky dirt road twisting away from the forlorn cottage.

It carried away Father Justin O'Carroll; it carried away the Chief Investigator for the Congregation of Rites, who was gently cradling the infant in the back seat.

The question now, Justin thought—what were they to do with the child? What plan did Father Rosetti have in mind? What was the final truth about Colleen Galaher's baby?

Justin drove the car in magnificent electric silence.

It was as if fine copper turbines, thousands of them, were spinning furiously behind the tense gray land-mist.

They rode past eerie, broken-down farms on the road toward Costelloe; past vast stubbled fields of barley and potatoes; past a clique of frowning redheaded men in a crippled donkey cart, a young woman in a mackintosh and plastic bonnet—a girl who reminded Justin of Colleen Galaher.

They rose up, up a curving road onto a wild moor that was both mystic and cruel.

Smoking fog began to curl and crawl around the swift-moving car.

Terrible fear crowded in on Father Justin O'Carroll. He kept seeing the agonized face of poor Colleen Galaher. Over and over.

"Doesn't the baby need special care right after the birth?" Justin asked, turning and trying to peek inside the blanket at the same time.

"Where exactly is this Woodbine Seminary that we're headed to?" Justin asked.

Just then, the road turned in toward the Irish Sea, past a small wooden sign. The sign said WOODBINE 11 KM.

As Justin nervously steered the sedan along limestone cliffs over the sea, he heard Father Rosetti beginning to pray in the back seat.

Justin tried to listen above the car's loudly puttering engine. Above the gravel crunching under the tires.

It was Latin.

Corpus something . . . *Ad Deum qui* . . .

Ad Deum qui what?

Then Father Justin O'Carroll made out just enough of the whispered Latin words and phrases. His hands locked tightly onto the steering wheel.

Requiem aeternam dona eis he heard. His entire body froze.

The holy prayers of Extreme Unction, Justin knew. The Roman Catholic prayers for the mortally ill or recently deceased. Prayers for the dead.

Father O'Carroll stepped down hard on the brakes.

The small gray car fishtailed to the left with grand plowing slowness. The front grille effortlessly sheared away a row of baby scrub pines.

The tires and the undercarriage screamed.

The car continued its full three-hundred-sixty-degree turn, rolling over bushes and rocks, finally smacking hard into a full-grown fir tree.

Justin's forehead jumped on and off the front windshield.

His head rolled pathetically to one side, then back to the other; his head slumped down onto his chest.

Out of the corner of a bloodied eye, Justin then saw a quick, bounding movement. Father Rosetti was plunging out of the car's back door. A small bundle of pink blanket was clutched in one of his arms.

Justin reeled from the car himself. He staggered after Father Rosetti and the baby. He felt the jolting cold sea air, and at the same time saw fireworks shooting off around his optic nerve.

"Father! Father, please stop. Father Rosetti!" Justin screamed and ran forward, all the time feeling like sitting, throwing up on the mountainside.

The Irish Sea came into view as he made it to the top of a bare promontory carved into the black rocks and boulders. Justin's breath was taken away by the height and the sheerness of the dark cliff.

It was three hundred feet straight down . . . down to where great rollers were boiling over jagged black rocks that looked like broken tombstones.

Justin tottered across a foot-wide ledge to the next plateau of rock, spotted with slick-looking heather. He then carefully, painfully hoisted himself over a loose molar of shale slanted into the cliffs at a sixty-degree angle. He could feel a sheen of cold sweat across his forehead and neck. His lungs were empty, nearly ready to burst.

Maybe thirty feet above he saw the black-clad figure of Father Rosetti on another weathered rock face.

He saw flashes of the light pink blanket. The child.

"Father, *please stop and talk* . . . Please, Father! Just talk to me!"

Father Rosetti's cassock was billowing out like a madwoman's dress. His black hair was all blown forward on his face. It was hard to imagine how he could see through all the matted hair.

"You don't believe any more," Rosetti's powerful voice rolled down the steep cliffside.

"None of you believe! Not in Satan! Not in Our Lord! Not in anything that truly matters!"

Father Eduardo Rosetti was holding the child loosely in one powerful arm. They were both hanging out slightly over the edge of the rocks.

Then Rosetti suddenly held the child up in the air with both huge hands. The priest's eyes were like empty black holes as he stared down on Justin. All over the cliff, giant birds were arriving. Thousands of birds.

Justin's heart clutched. He couldn't breathe at all.

"This *is* the Beast, Father O'Carroll. All the signs in the prediction of Fatima have been met. The Virgin has guided me well. The holy investigation. *This is the Beast.* Satan is so wise, the girl herself never knew. Do you, a priest, find that so difficult to believe? Is it not possible for you to believe anything on faith? *Do you believe in your own God, Father?"*

Justin couldn't take his eyes away from the priest and the poor helpless child.

Above the two of them, the mountainside only rose another hundred feet or so. Up at the top, the rocks seemed to be piercing every passing gray cloud. More black birds were slowly circling. Screeching angrily. Screaming.

"How can you be so sure, Father Rosetti? How do you know that you aren't holding an innocent baby, Father?"

"How can you be sure that Jesus Christ became man?" Rosetti's voice rang out. "How can you be sure that Jesus has redeemed our souls from the eternal fires of hell?"

Justin couldn't catch his breath. He was feeling dizzy, impossibly unsure of himself on the high, slippery rocks.

A terrifying sensation like vertigo came and went. So did great rolling waves of nausea. *Control yourself. Somehow.*

Justin knew he couldn't look down, that if he looked down there the sea would be a spinning vortex tempting him, pulling him off the cliffs. Once again, Justin hollered above the crashing sea, above the piercing cries of gulls and crows and gannets combing over the cliffside.

"We can still go to the Woodbine Seminary! We can still perform an exorcism if that's what is called for, Father! We can talk about your findings . . . you know what I'm saying is best!"

As Justin gazed skyward, he saw Father Rosetti's broad shoulders sag forward. The Vatican priest carefully moved a step back away from the edge of the rocks. Bile was dripping from both corners of his mouth.

"Come up here," he said in a low voice. "Please come up here, Father."

Finally Justin was able to catch his breath. He took a single step forward on the loose, shifting rocks.

The sea winds meanwhile were flogging his face. Pushing him down, pushing him back. Something was warning him not to go up there; not to go any farther. No closer to Rosetti and the tiny child.

He took step after careful step on the rocks . . . Justin O'Carroll was twenty yards away . . . then twelve yards . . . only a few steps more.

His arms felt like blocks of stone. He was afraid he

wouldn't be able to hold the baby once he reached Father Rosetti.

Father Justin O'Carroll was afraid that he was about to die and that he would never even know why. That seemed the worst thing. Not ever knowing the truth.

A muffled cry finally rose out of the fluffed pink blanket. It startled Justin. A baby's cry. The sea wind quickly swallowed the tiny scream with its own howl and whoop.

Justin heard a hoarse tortured whisper from only a few feet above him.

"Pray for me, Father O'Carroll," he heard. "Father, please look."

The trembling Vatican priest slowly opened the woolen blanket and showed Justin the child's face. The sea birds everywhere screamed as one.

A second later, Father Eduardo Rosetti hugged the child to his chest.

They fell together; they seemed to hang by invisible wires for a few seconds. Finally they clapped the cold, choppy gray water and disappeared beneath the waves.

Father Justin O'Carroll dropped down hard on the rocks of the high cliffside. He began to sob uncontrollably, to pray for the eternal soul of poor Father Rosetti.

Justin had seen the face of a beautiful baby boy inside the unfolded blanket. . . . The boy had the glowing red eyes of a bat.

THE CHILD

At 3:04 P.M. on October 13, the immense crowd collected in the piazza of St. Peter's looked up into the sky as one person might look.

Mountainous thunderheads which had cloaked the sky since early morning suddenly began to shred and break up.

A golden glow appeared at the cloud edges and the sun finally came out.

The sun then began to quiver and oscillate dramatically high over the glimmering rooftops of the city of Rome.

The sun was like a gold-colored children's balloon suddenly losing air, diving into the spectacular oohing-and-aahing, gasping crowd at St. Peter's.

The sun appeared to be rotating on its axis, spinning at a dizzying, terrifying speed. It cast forth knife-blade splinters of bright red and violet light.

At its zenith, the sun looked like a dull, silvery plaque. Like no sun anyone had ever seen before that day. Hundreds of thousands of people knelt in the piazza of St. Peter's and began to pray.

In nearby Salvator Mundi Hospital, a child had just been born.

At 3:04 Rome time.

"My baby's all right? Please? . . . Is my baby all right?"

The words came in the softest, barely audible whisper.

It was the voice of a frightened seventeen-year-old girl.

The voice of a new mother.

Kathleen Beavier felt so confused—she wasn't even sure whether she had said the words or not.

All she could do for certain was stare up at the strangely dark and shriveled child. She strained to see the baby's face, to see her baby's eyes.

"Your baby is perfect," Doctor Bonanno said to her. "What else? Didn't I promise you that?"

The other doctors from Salvator Mundi meanwhile —the sister-nurses, her parents—were watching the mother and child in awed, reverent silence. The Swiss Guards were watching. Waiting.

Kathleen saw Anne smile first. A private smile just between the two of them. She had done it! The baby was born. The prophesied virgin birth.

Then the others in the room began to laugh and smile as well. They were hugging and congratulating one

another. A few of the Salvatorians were beginning to
cry. . . . The baby was born

*At 3:04 Rome time, the low sky over the Rajasthan
district grew ominously, frighteningly black.*

*Towering cloud columns hid the blazing sunset of
the so-called Great Indian desert. Jagged spears of light-
ning finally slashed down and struck the flaked, brittle
ground.*

*It began to rain again. It began to pour rain and the
Indian people rushed from their houses to offer loud
prayers of thanksgiving to their God.*

Something beautiful was happening.

A miracle. Chamaltkar.

The Italian chief surgeon lightly slapped the baby's
bottom. The tiny infant obligingly began to scream, an
unmistakable anguished and perturbed human sound.

Dr. Bonanno smiled wonderfully. The roomful of
medical and Church people smiled at the naturalness of
the child's response.

The baby was like them. The baby was human. The
baby was beautiful and good they were all sure.

*In the Jay Selznick Clinic in Los Angeles, Dr. Kim
May Chu watched closely, curiously, as one of the viral
organisms under her microscope suddenly seemed to stop
its slithering, writhing motion. Dr. Chu stared and stared at
the organism: afraid to blink, afraid to look away.*

*Other of the Polio-Venice microorganisms began to
stop; to die. "We have a vaccine," Kim May suddenly
cried out in the bunker of the Selznick Clinic. "We have a
vaccine! Oh my God, we have a vaccine!"*

At 3:04 Rome time.

Both Anne and Kathleen had noticed one particularly strange thing about the child. Something incredibly
surprising and unexpected.

Neither of them said anything.

Not yet.

Quiet fell over the room. Slowly. Dramatically.

The doctors, the Salvator Mundi nurses and techni-
cians stood still, staring with silent, awed faces as they
watched the tiny infant's first awkward moves. All of
them sensed that they were experiencing the most impor-

tant and beautiful moment of their lives. Some of them broke into sobs.

No one could have been affected any more than Anne.

She trembled and couldn't make herself stop. She whispered soft prayers.

Over and over, Anne kept hearing the words of Father Rosetti, the final time they'd spoken in Paris, at the airport.

Sister Anne, I hope and pray that I know the truth about the two young virgins now. . . .

Sister, the Beast must be killed. . . .

Just as she did on October thirteenth at Fatima, Our Lady has promised a clear sign at the moment of the birth.

Anne watched Kathleen and the child; she listened; she waited.

She continued to pray as she never had before. *A clear sign.*

In the midst of her thoughts, Anne heard her name spoken in a deep voice.

She looked up at a doctor nearby. His attention was occupied by the child and mother. He hadn't spoken her name, Anne thought. He hadn't heard the voice.

She turned toward a dark-haired technician monitoring the EKG machine. The voice wasn't his either. *Oh my God . . .*

Now the voice came again. Louder. Surer. Nearer.

"Sister Anne Feeney" it called to her.

"It must die, Sister . . . or we will. An eternity of suffering for mankind.

"Kill the child of evil!

"Kill the Beast, Sister!"

Anne found herself moving forward in the hospital room. Closer to Kathleen. Closer to the child . . . the voice . . .

"In the name of the Father, kill this child of evil!"

The baby's cry was the first room noise Anne had heard since the voice began . . . a thin, trembling cry.

Our Lady has promised a clear sign at the moment of the birth, Father Rosetti had said.

It is a matter of faith, Anne whispered to herself.

Did she believe in the Lord God become man for our sins?

Did she believe that a holy Savior could truly come to earth?

Anne bowed her head and screamed in silent prayer. She pleaded for guidance from God Almighty, from the Blessed Mother.

She recited simple prayers from her childhood. The Hail Mary. A Glory Be to The Father.

What am I to do now? Why have you put me here from the beginning, dear Lord? Oh please, please, please.

"In the name of the Father, and the Son, and the Holy Spirit, kill the child! Kill the child!"

Anne looked down on the infant, and in a clear instant of faith and recognition she finally knew the truth.

Over the tiny head she beheld the sign promised by Our Lady of Fatima.

A thin, glowing white nimbus. The two-thousand-year-old symbol of hope and salvation for all mankind.

Anne Feeney fell to her knees and wept. "Blessed is the fruit of thy womb, Jesus!"

The long-tailed comet actually struck the earth! Colonel Reese Monash and Captain Mickey Kane were certain that it did.

And yet there seemed to be no visible effect. No visible fiery explosion . . .

Then there was loud cheering from the NASA Space Center in Houston. Houston was yelling that the strange comet had missed earth. . . . But it hadn't missed earth at all, Colonel Monash and Captain Kane thought. . . . They had seen the comet fall somewhere in Western Europe. At 3:04.

Dr. Bonanno had observed something about Kathleen that none of the others realized yet. Something important. Perhaps the missing key to this baroque mystery, he was thinking.

Bonanno whispered the secret to his assistant, Dr. Francesco Galetta. "The American girl is no longer intact, Francesco. Kathleen Beavier *is not* a virgin any more," Doctor Bonanno said with regret obvious in his voice.

Finally, Kathleen was presented with her baby. She was allowed to hold the tiny child in her thin, trembling arms.

The young girl's soft blue eyes immediately filled up with tears.

Kathleen Beavier looked into the little baby's sweet face and the mother's love she felt was completely overwhelming to her.

At precisely 3:04 P.M. new cures were reported in the grotto of Lourdes where Bernadette Soubirous had seen the Virgin eighteen times during the spring and summer of 1858.

Other miracles were reported in Castalnaud-en-Guers, France—where the face of Jesus suddenly appeared to a congregation of three hundred; in Mexico's Sierra Oriental; in Turzovka, Czechoslovakia; Liverpool, England; Gerpinnes, Belgium; Carabandal, Spain; Denver, Colorado—all sites where the Virgin had previously appeared to people during the past thirty years.

At 3:15 P.M. a portly, florid-faced priest was attempting to walk in a most dignified and proper way down the boulevard-wide stone corridors of Salvator Mundi hospital.

His shining black brogans were clacking like stones against the marble floor, echoing in the empty hall like tap-dancing shoes. His soutane was shaking like a ruffled bead curtain.

Bishop Antoine Riconne had been chosen by Pope Pius XIII to make the formal announcement about the birth.

It had already been decided at a late-night meeting of the Council of Six that neither Pius nor any high-ranking cardinal should make the dramatic statement. Bishop Riconne had been chosen because Pius personally liked Antoine—but mostly because no one on the Council was afraid of the holy and unassuming bishop.

Nearing the front lobby, the fifty-three-year-old bishop, the Vatican's Substitute Secretary of State, finally broke into an undecorous run.

His long red cassock billowed out around his ample hips. The gold cross around his neck bounced rudely against his breastbone.

Bishop Riconne was running like an excited schoolboy, he suddenly realized. Just like the happy boy back in Florence who once upon a time had taken such passion and pride in his beloved Church, in his city's famous paintings of the Madonna and Child by Giotto and Cimabue. Not since the streets of Florence, in fact, had Antoine Riconne felt such joy, such complete love for his God.

Only as he was about to enter the elegant klieg-lit hospital lobby—filled to its doors with important reporters from all over the world—did the bishop slow down to a walk. Only then did Bishop Riconne attempt to regain what would be considered the proper decorum.

"I bring news and joy for the world this afternoon of October thirteenth. . . . The Beavier child is born, and the child is healthy," the red-faced bishop said simply and joyfully to the press.

Then, just as simply, Bishop Antoine Riconne announced the most unexpected news of all.

"The child of Kathleen Beavier is a very beautiful baby girl!"

THE COUNCIL OF SIX

With the long day's glowing red twilight bright at their backs, they came alone and in uneasy pairs, slowly walking from humble monks' barracks in the Domus Mariae to the golden domed Apostolic Palace.

There were three eminent cardinals from Italy, one from the United States, one from the Netherlands, one from Asia. Next to Pius himself, they were the most powerful and widely respected men in the Church.

That night of the virgin birth, they secretly convened on the third floor of the Apostolic Palace. Their mood was one of great raging confusion; there were even hints of sullen bitterness.

Had they not warned Pius of the potential dangers in

connecting the Church too closely with this explosive, perhaps even blasphemous event?

Hadn't they told Pius again and again that unforeseen problems could arise? Problems such as the danger of unauthorized cultus: the worship of Kathleen Beavier and her child . . . problems such as a female savior?

Cardinal Marchetti, the Archbishop of Milan, a moderate Christian Marxist, finally raised his voice to address the select group, which included Pius himself.

A rangy, cadaverous-faced man whose bald, domed head made him look like a practicing ascetic, Cardinal Marchetti now stood with surprising power and might, tightly gripping the rosewood conference table under high Apostolic Palace ceilings.

"Eminent Cardinals, Your Holiness. I am convinced that *time* is the most important factor for us now. I believe we must act with dispatch, or this 'divine birth' could easily bloom out into the areas of heresy and schism."

A cardinal with an elegant, oval face politely interrupted Marchetti. This was Cardinal Johan Weiss from the Netherlands.

"I have one addendum to what you say, Cardinal Marchetti. I believe we should *decide* quickly. Then, if our decision is a wise one, we can *act* at a more deliberate and cautious pace."

"Spoken like a true traditionalist," Cardinal Marchetti smiled through thin, purplish lips.

"The child is a girl," contributed Cardinal Antonelli, the withered seventy-two-year-old patriarch of the archdiocese of Rome. "Nowhere that I know does it speak of a woman Messiah in the Scriptures."

"That doesn't signify much of anything," Pius XIII spoke to his old friend Antonelli. "We are all aware of the unfortunate bias of the writers back in those days. The idea of a woman as Messiah would have been unthinkable."

"The mother is not intact. It was not a virgin birth anyway," the American cardinal, Blanchard of New York, spoke out.

Suddenly Pope Pius could see where this important,

historic meeting was heading. Cardinal Marchetti was leading the others, as he always did: the Secret Pope, Pius knew Marchetti was sometimes called in the Curia.

"What of the birth in Maam Cross?" Pius asked the assembled cardinals. "There were clear signs of evil present. There was the terrible tragedy that followed. We have been in constant contact with the priests who were at the Irish cottage. We have spoken with poor Father O'Carroll."

"Holiness, the *presence of evil on earth* is something that none of us dispute," said Cardinal Marchetti.

"What of the warning of Our Lady of Fatima, then?" Seldom if ever before had Pius been so dominating at a Council meeting. "What of the striking occurrences today in India? At Lourdes? All through Spain? . . . I personally don't believe that all these happenings could be mere coincidences. . . . I don't believe any of you can dispute that the message of Fatima has been disturbingly accurate on many points here."

"Holy Father," Cardinal Marchetti began to speak in a warm and conciliatory voice.

"We understand your special involvement with the virgin of Fatima. We understand why you have pursued the complete truth in this delicate matter. We have also taken note of the aberrations in nature which have occurred near the time of the birth of the Beavier child . . . near the time of the Galaher birth, for that matter.

"We are not six unjust or ungodly men," Cardinal Marchetti said. "We are trying to come to a fair decision about what is best for our Church at this time. Even what is best for the Beavier girl and her child. Do you believe that much, Holy Father?"

Pius XIII nodded his head. If nothing else, he believed that the intentions of these holy men were good, that they wanted to do what was best for the Church.

"There are disturbing facts that countermand much of the positive evidence you have suggested, Papa. First of all, the child *is* a girl. Nothing in the Scriptures prepares us to accept a woman Messiah. Secondly, since

Kathleen Beavier did not remain intact, it was not a virgin birth, as there was when Christ was born."

"There are uninvestigated facts of the case which we must carefully consider," Cardinal Tiu from Southeast Asia nodded agreement.

Pope Pius very slowly and succinctly whispered his next few words.

"My most eminent cardinals," he said. "Do you believe in your hearts, are you certain, that Our Lady delivered the Lord Jesus and remained a virgin?"

"I do believe it," Cardinal Marchetti said without hesitation.

"This is a sacred article of our faith," said Cardinal Antonelli.

"My cardinals and my friends." Pius now rose and stood above the ornate conference table. "Do you not believe that women have immortal souls just as we do? Do you not see that the ancient men who wrote the Scriptures down might have had a biased view of women? . . . Do you not see that all through the history of our Church this problem has existed?"

There was an uncomfortable silence in the formal meeting room. For once, Pope Pius XIII was speaking as the clear leader of the Church. Pius was being forceful; he had obviously touched some of the holy men already.

"Perhaps I have a solution that could be acceptable to us all," Cardinal Marchetti said. Very slowly he walked around the table until he stood beside Pius.

"Shouldn't we give this important matter over to the Congregation of Rites?" Cardinal Marchetti asked. "Surely this would be a prudent and appropriate next step. A step of both immediate action and wise caution.

"Until the Council's investigation is concluded, Holy Mother Church could not recognize or encourage special treatment of Kathleen Beavier or her child. Doesn't that seem like the right course of action? Doesn't it seem fair and just to you, Holiness?"

The Holy Father could feel his strength and inner resolve weakening. The Congregation of Rites was one of the most rigid and conservative of Church bodies. The

Congregation's final decision might take twenty years, thirty years . . . and yet in his heart Pius couldn't deny that those who sat on the Congregation were very good and capable scholars, that they were holy and truth-seeking.

Dear Father, please have mercy on all of us gathered in this room. Pope Pius XIII lowered his head and silently prayed. *You have given us clear signs, I believe, but we are weak. Above all, I am weak . . . please give us another chance, Father. Give us another chance.*

The Church would *never* recognize the Beavier child as divine. Pope Pius knew right then in his heart. *Never.*

The Church would *never* encourage the appropriate joy and thanksgiving to God for the birth of the holy child.

The Church, Pope Pius finally understood, *no longer believed in miracles itself.*

TWELVE

THE VIRGIN

On a still and crystalline night many years later, the winter resort of Tyler Falls, Vermont, seemed almost frozen in time, the only movement a shower of silver-white moonlight raining across the Green Mountain National Forest.

A dark army of scrub pines and taller evergreens resolutely climbed high in the snow up the ski mountains. The crackling black ice of the village skating pond was partly cleared, and that night was lit up by a half-circle of gleaming car headlights. Tattered ribbons of smoke trailed the shadowy roofs of nearly all the ski houses and country inns.

Anne's eyes slowly drifted down from her snow-streaked bedroom window.

She looked at Justin, rebellious young Andrew . . . then the soft white faces of her daughters—Mary Ellen, Theresa, and Carole Anne.

"What a tremendously handsome family you are." Anne stared up at them from the fluffed pillows propped for her head. "How fabulous a mother I must be."

"I've been telling you that for years," Justin smiled. "For years and years, Annie."

Looking at all of them gathered together, Anne suddenly remembered that she was going to miss Mary Ellen's big wedding in the spring.

It was odd how that bothered her. It almost seemed petty and uncharitable on God's part: *Why not at least let me stay on here through the spring? Let me see Mary Ellen's wedding. Then you can permit this pathetic disease to do its dirty work.*

The brief interior conversation reminded Anne of a book she'd read recently: *The Whimsical Christian* by Dorothy Sayers. Both she and Dorothy Sayers apparently believed that the Lord appreciated a decent sense of humor, plus candor, in all communications.

Anne was startled by Justin's eyes, suddenly down very close to her face.

"Do you need anything, Annie?"

Anne whispered "No . . . thank you . . ." then she let her own eyes close for just a moment.

"I love you more than anything else in this world," she heard Justin whisper.

"I love you more than that," Anne whispered back to him, then smiled.

Lying there with her eyes closed, her mind extremely active and excited, Anne suddenly remembered the face of Kathleen Beavier very clearly; she remembered exactly what Kathleen had looked like as a teenage girl. Ann remembered Colleen Galaher as well. The Irish girl was now a nun, she'd heard. Cloistered in the convent at the Holy Trinity School for Girls.

Apparently she'd never been able to explain the

things that had happened to her. So the Church in Rome claimed.

One particular scene now passed before Anne's eyes —only it was a scene that she had trouble placing immediately in her memory . . .

Kathleen's long blonde hair was all set in magnificently ringed curls and waves. She was wearing some sort of a gown; she had on a fancy cloth wrap.

Suddenly Anne understood.

She was able to make complete sense of the mysterious scene before her eyes.

Anne was somehow observing Kathleen on the night of January twenty-third.

She was about to find out the great secret of the virgin.

Kathleen was riding alongside Jaime Jordan, whose every physically imposing feature Anne remembered now.

They were in a fine sports car with a dark shiny interior. There was a gleaming instrument panel; the radio was blaring loud popular music.

Jaime suddenly began yelling at Kathleen over the rhythm-heavy rock music. He was cursing so badly that Kathleen finally held both her ears. They were speeding back into gloomy, pitch-black Sachuest Park late at night.

"I told you *no!*" Kathleen was insisting.

"Please, Jaime? Please listen to what I'm saying."

She felt a rough hand mauling her chest. Suddenly she was very afraid of him. So helpless and afraid in the dark, deserted park.

She bit down hard into the back of Jaime Jordan's hand.

"That does it, bitch," he yelled out in pain.

The MG door was thrust open and he pushed her roughly. Jaime was screaming at her; his face was incredibly red.

Then Kathleen was stumbling out on the crunching, frozen roadside. The raw smell of freezing cold ocean filled her nose. The top of her head tingled from the cold.

The wind swirled powdery snow up into her face and the young girl began to cry.

She had never seen anyone so angry in her entire life. So insane about not getting what he wanted. Did Jaime think that her body *belonged* to him? What was he thinking? What was he doing?

The MG accelerated, shooting up a spray of gravel, white smoke, and dirt. Jaime Jordan was heading back to Newport without her.

Oh my God, it's freezing, Kathleen thought and began to panic. Oh God, oh God.

He can't just leave me out here . . . how can he be so mad? I don't belong to him. He has no right . . .

Tears were stinging Kathleen's eyes. The harsh wind coming off the ocean blew right through her cloth coat. Dervishes of powdery snow were swirling around her shoes.

He has to come back for me. I'll freeze out here. . . .

Kathleen's face began to burn as if the skin was being flayed off. Shooting pains from the cold traveled up her legs.

Finally she began to walk on the crusty, dirt road. She walked toward the distant pocket of lights that was the city of Newport.

She tried walking backward, her face buried down in the collar of her coat. She was even more frightened now. Her mind raced in desperate circles.

Everywhere she looked there was a faint, eerie ground glow. All around her the ocean was roaring like a squadron of low-flying airplanes.

One of her half-heels struck a sharp, protruding rock.

The young girl toppled over, striking the ground hard. She wrenched her leg; her hand was scraped and bleeding. Finally Kathleen Beavier curled herself into a small, safe ball on the ground. . . . *That felt better . . . much, much better than facing the freezing cold.*

Kathleen wondered if she could sleep right there. *Be all right in the morning . . . just sleep.*

Then Kathleen saw Jaime's car speeding back down the black stretch of park road.

"Damn you anyway," Kathleen whispered out loud. "Now you get to be the big hero. Well, I won't let it happen."

The bright lights were flying through the bare-limbed trees. Gold and reddish lights were flashing up the deserted, pitch-black road. Afterimages danced before Kathleen Beavier's eyes. There were looping red and violet rings. Waving streaks of silver like a dreamy dance hall.

Kathleen pushed herself up off the ground. Sharp stones were sticking into her hands. She began to brush off her coat, her crushed, stained gown. She tried to catch her breath. She tried to stop the tears still streaming down her cheeks.

Suddenly Kathleen stopped brushing at her coat. Her hands flew up to her mouth. A scream was ready to burst out.

It wasn't the red MG that was coming up the winding dirt road.

It wasn't anything that was possible.

Kathleen stood her ground and stared at a beautiful woman, bathed in lights, walking straight toward her. The most amazing sight she had ever seen in her life.

"Kathleen," the woman finally spoke in a soft, strangely familiar voice.

"Try not to be afraid. Don't be afraid. You are filled with wonderful grace and with divine love."

At that extraordinary moment, as the woman continued to speak to her, Kathleen suddenly understood the vision.

Kathleen knew, as if by intuition, who the woman was. It was almost as if she had always known it.

Kathleen knew why the lady had come to her.

Then she began to feel something else, something curiously powerful and moving. It was a stirring recognition of an ancient truth; it was a sacred truth that had always been a part of her, Kathleen now saw.

Kathleen trembled and shuddered. The young girl knew that somehow, in some miraculous way, she was staring at an image that was herself. . . . Kathleen realized that she was the Blessed Virgin. She was the beautiful Gentlewoman.

She had come to earth specifically to bear a holy child for this unholy age. The child would be a girl; a girl with all the divine attributes and special powers of Jesus.

"Don't be afraid. There is nothing to be afraid of now" Kathleen heard as she continued to shake and shiver, as she began to cry out loud.

"You are going to have a child. The child is the hope for the world, if the world can still believe."

The child is the hope for the world . . .

Anne was spellbound as she listened to the final words. Not understanding what had happened. But feeling it. Sensing the truth of what she had just seen.

The past scene at Sachuest Point was so real before her eyes; it was so beautiful.

The striking vision was serene; it was moving in the way of great cathedrals and the most beautiful Gregorian hymns. Anne had never been more in touch with the faith she had held for nearly sixty years.

The child is the hope for the world, if the world can still believe.

Anne's soft blue eyes suddenly opened wide in the Vermont bedroom. . . . Her beautiful vision was ended.

Justin stared down at Anne and tears began to come into his eyes.

He felt for Anne's life-signs, but there was nothing.

For one of the very few times in his life, Justin was completely confused, not knowing at all what to do next. He gently kissed Anne's forehead. He brushed away loose strands of her long hair. He said something to the children and they came and hugged him and began to cry over their mother.

Justin very badly wanted to be with Annie for just a minute or two longer. . . . *Just a few seconds, please. Please . . .*

He needed to hear Anne's voice just one more time.

He wanted to tell her how much he loved her one final time.

With trembling fingers, feeling hollow and achingly empty inside, Justin closed Anne's eyes; he tried desperately to accept the idea that she was dead.

For the first time in many years, he prayed the words of the sacrament once known as Extreme Unction, now called Anointing the Sick. Justin prayed over Anne as an ordained priest, something he would always be according to his Holy Orders and his vows.

"By the grace of the Holy Spirit, may Our Lord save you and in his goodness raise you up," he spoke in a trembling, choking whisper.

"Mary our Mother . . . love this good woman Anne . . . who loves you, I know."

Anne meanwhile could hear the Virgin speaking to her. Softly, so softly. *"Don't be afraid, Annie. Don't be afraid."*

EPILOGUE

*And there appeared a great wonder in heaven; a
woman clothed with the sun, and the moon under
her feet, and upon her head a crown of twelve stars.*

—THE REVELATION OF ST. JOHN

NOELLE

Noelle Beavier was just nineteen years old at the
time of the accident. She was living more or less anony-
mously with her mother in a small farming town in the
grain belt of midwestern America.

In her entire life, she had never seen anything like this

automobile crash at the Vandemeer Avenue intersection.

It shocked and saddened Noelle, forcing tears into her soft, blue eyes; it brought on an overwhelming feeling of nauseousness.

Why was the terrible accident on Vandemeer Avenue allowed to happen?

How could a truly just and loving Father permit this to happen?

For the first time in her life, Noelle felt tremendous doubt about the crosspurposes of God. Her eyes slowly went back to the impossibly twisted wreckage.

The bright yellow station wagon had struck a solid chestnut tree at a dangerously high speed. The unyielding tree had easily split open the poorly built car, passing through the engine block, through the front and second seats, finally coming to rest in the third seat or trunk space. Almost seeming to be growing there now.

The driver and his young wife were dead in the front. Three small children were dead. A fourth little girl in slipper-feet pajamas had been thrown free of the car. She was lying on someone's lawn, softly crying, being attended to by men and women from the neighborhood who had rushed to the tragic accident scene.

Finally, Noelle could stand the naked horror and suffering no longer.

She turned and walked away from the devastation, the unbearable sadness, the wails of approaching police sirens.

Then, when Noelle Beavier was far enough away so that no one in the crowd could possibly know—she prayed and made the lost family whole again. Noelle brought the family back to life, just as Jesus had once done with Lazarus.

It was the first of her miracles.

As the lovely, lonely young woman walked farther and farther away, Noelle had no way of knowing that she was being watched in spite of her care to avoid detection and the problems of notoriety.

A single pair of curious eyes followed Noelle Beavier all the way up the pretty oak-lined street. All the way to her home.

Gleaming red eyes.

ABOUT THE AUTHOR

JAMES PATTERSON is the author of four previous novels, including *The Thomas Berryman Number*, which won the Edgar Award in 1977. He is a creative director at the J. Walter Thompson advertising agency and lives in New York City.

DON'T MISS
THESE CURRENT
Bantam Bestsellers

☐ 14431	**THE THIRD WAVE** Alvin Toffler	$3.95
☐ 13545	**SOPHIE'S CHOICE** William Styron	$3.50
☐ 13101	**THE BOOK OF LISTS #2** Wallechinsky & Wallaces	$3.50
☐ 20025	**THE FAR PAVILIONS** M. M. Kaye	$4.50
☐ 13752	**SHADOW OF THE MOON** M. M. Kaye	$3.95
☐ 13028	**OVERLOAD** Arthur Hailey	$2.95
☐ 13828	**THE RIGHT STUFF** Tom Wolfe	$3.50
☐ 14140	**SMILEY'S PEOPLE** John LeCarre	$3.50
☐ 13743	**MADE IN AMERICA** Peter Maas	$2.50
☐ 14396	**TRINITY** Leon Uris	$3.95
☐ 14611	**HOW TO SPEAK SOUTHERN** Steve Mitchell	$1.95
☐ 13624	**NAME YOUR BABY** Lareina Rule	$2.25
☐ 01203	**WHEN LOVERS ARE FRIENDS** Merle Shain	$3.95
☐ 20134	**THE PRITIKIN PROGRAM FOR DIET AND EXERCISE** Nathan Pritikin w/ Patrick McGrady, Jr.	$3.95
☐ 14174	**LONELY ON THE MOUNTAIN** Louis L'Amour	$2.25
☐ 20138	**PASSAGES** Gail Sheehy	$3.95
☐ 14500	**THE GUINNESS BOOK OF WORLD RECORDS 19th ed.** The McWhirters	$3.50
☐ 14686	**LINDA GOODMAN'S SUN SIGNS**	$3.50
☐ 14852	**ZEN AND THE ART OF MOTORCYCLE MAINTENANCE** Robert Pirsig	$3.50
☐ 14736	**DR. ATKINS' DIET REVOLUTION**	$3.50

Buy them at your local bookstore or use this handy coupon for ordering:

Bantam Books, Inc., Dept. FB, 414 East Golf Road, Des Plaines, Ill. 60016

Please send me the books I have checked above. I am enclosing $_____
(please add $1.00 to cover postage and handling). Send check or money order
—no cash or C.O.D.'s please.

Mr/Mrs/Miss_____

Address_____

City_____ State/Zip_____

FB—7/81

Please allow four to six weeks for delivery. This offer expires 1/82.